★

Since the second victim appeared to be an adult male, who must have occupied more space in the world than the four square feet he was crammed into now, I did not want to think about what it must have taken to get him in there, or how he was going to look when we got him out.

I found a tree pruner with long wooden handles and three-inch forged steel jaws. We left the container lying on its side, and I attacked the top right-hand corner, confidently at first, then doggedly, and finally in a humiliated rage. I was dripping sweat by the time the slit in the barrel opened wide enough to let us pry out the second victim.

His rigor mortis was so far advanced he could not be uncoiled. Trudy, Pokey and Ted began circling his tormented doughnut shape, muttering in frustration at the impossibility of examining, testing, or photographing a body so curled up on itself.

"I don't know where to start," Trudy said.

"Or how to continue," Ted added.

"...the best yet in an outstanding series."

—*Booklist*

"...a superior series."

—*Publishers Weekly*

Previously published Worldwide Mystery titles by
ELIZABETH GUNN

FIVE CARD STUD
SIX-POUND WALLEYE

ELIZABETH GUNN

SEVENTH-INNING *STRETCH*

W☉RLDWIDE.

TORONTO • NEW YORK • LONDON
AMSTERDAM • PARIS • SYDNEY • HAMBURG
STOCKHOLM • ATHENS • TOKYO • MILAN
MADRID • WARSAW • BUDAPEST • AUCKLAND

SEVENTH-INNING STRETCH

A Worldwide Mystery/June 2003

Published by arrangement with Walker Publishing Company, Inc.

ISBN 0-373-26458-5

Printed in U.S.A.

Acknowledgments

Many people contributed to the credibility of this book; any mistakes that occurred in translating their expertise to fiction are mine, not theirs. Sergeant Mike Walsh, of the Rochester, Minnesota, police department, helped with several pieces of policemen's lore and found me an unused house number in Joliet, Wisconsin. Rhonda Fay, a technician on the Rochester PD support staff, helped me follow the development of electronic record keeping. John Sibley, retired deputy chief of the Rochester PD, dredged up useful details about pre-electronic fingerprinting techniques.

At the Bureau of Criminal Apprehension in St. Paul, I am indebted to Superintendent Michael Campion and Laboratory Director Frank Dolejsi, who kindly gave an overview of operations and let me pick the formidable brains of several forensic scientists: Patricia Wojtowicz, supervisor of evidence check-in procedures and the awesome computer system called "The Beast"; Dennis Hughes, electronic fingerprinting wizard; and Ann Marie Gross, who understands DNA testing so well she can even explain it to me.

For other medical details in this book, I am indebted to Dr. Bruce Parks, chief medical examiner of Pima County, Arizona; Dr. Paul Belau, coroner of Olmsted County, Minnesota and L.P.N. Mary Anderson, of Rochester, Minnesota.

ONE

THE PAGES OF the Burke file were still warm from the printer when I stuffed them into the last folder. Humming, I put a fresh tape in my recorder, hurrying to off-load the whole pile of work onto my People Crimes crew while my luck held. In the year since I'd been chief of detectives at Rutherford PD, I'd been hustling just to stay even with rising crime rates in a fast-growing town. Till this month, I hadn't even thought about cold cases. Now suddenly, just as the funding came through so I could bring two new detectives on staff, the incidence of serious crimes against persons, ironically and inexplicably, had fallen to zero.

"Did somebody repeal the law of averages?" the chief asked me.

"Somehow I doubt it," I said, "but I intend to seize the moment."

The stack was too tall to pick up. I divided it in two, set my recorder on top, and took the whole slippery pile into my arms. I was in my doorway, carefully juggling my load, when the phone rang. "Oh, shit," I said. I thought about letting the machine answer, but phone tag wastes so much time. I sidled back to my desk and dumped everything, reached across the pile, and said, "Hines."

"Jake? Could you come in here a minute?" Kevin

Evjan sounded anxious. So soon? Two weeks ago, when he assumed command of Property Crimes, he had been somewhere beyond gung-ho, beaming like a lamp.

"Whaddya need?" I said.

"All my guys are in my office here, talking about an amazing string of oddly similar complaints. If you could sit in a minute—"

"Just about a minute," I said. "Not much over."

"Now?"

"Be right there." I walked three doors north to his odd-shaped office, newly jury-rigged out of his old cubicle and half a supply closet. Kevin didn't care what it looked like; he just grew incandescent every time he looked at the sign on the door that read, "Lt. Kevin Evjan, Property Crimes."

"Here, take this chair," Andy Pitman said, shifting to a stool by the wall. He had just earned his sergeant's shield and joined Kevin's section after an eventful couple of years as a POP cop turned him into something of a street legend. Assigned to a neighborhood that had been thoroughly cowed by a couple of thuggish gangs, Andy surprised his peers by keeping his ungainly body in one piece while making so many arrests they began calling him Andy Pit Bull. He was good with the hapless and helpless left behind after the cleanup, too, so he was having neighborhood babies named after him by the time we lured him indoors.

I wedged in between him and Clint Maddox, another new investigator and veteran of the Problem Oriented Policing program. Kevin and I had agreed he'd take new guys into the Property Crimes section and let them break in on bike heists and car theft before they tackled the tough stuff.

Darrell Betts, hugging the wall on Clint's right, was the

veteran detective of this crew, and slated for People Crimes eventually, but helping Kevin's section while they settled in. Behind his desk, Kevin flipped through a stack of report forms, counting under his breath. "Fifteen, sixteen, seventeen"—he looked up—"seventeen of these weird complaints since Monday." His last name rhymes with that bottled water from France, but Kevin Evjan's father is Norwegian to the tips of his four-buckle overshoes, and his mother was an O'Toole. The two northern European bloodlines battle for supremacy in his big handsome face. Usually he's as cheerful as a bird. Today he looked preoccupied.

"Andy, you go first," he said.

"Complaint came from Herbie Toller," Pitman said, "runs the 7-Eleven on Eleventh Avenue, there by the tire shop? A woman, maybe forty years old, medium build, brown hair, with a blond female child aged eight to ten, came in yesterday about the middle of the morning and bought two bags of groceries. One bag full of milk and juice and fruit and cereal, another one of beer and chewing tobacco and cigarettes."

"So, a funny combination."

"That's why he remembered it. The kid drove Herbie nuts all while the woman shopped, touching everything in the store, running to her mom all the time with things, saying, 'Can we buy this?' And then putting them back in the wrong place when the woman said no. Every so often the mother would say, 'Honey, stop touching things now,' and the kid would lay off till her mother wasn't looking and then go right back to feeling up the merchandise. Came time to pay, the bill came to sixty dollars and change, the woman put out three twenties and a ten, the kid was pulling at the bags on a candy rack by the counter. Herbie counted out change, and the woman looked in her wallet and said, 'Wait a minute, I think one of those bills I gave you must have been a fifty.'"

"Ah," I said.

"Yeah. He showed her the twenties and the ten he still had sitting on top of the register, and she said, 'Oh, wait, I see the fifty here now—' and just then her kid knocked over the candy rack and little candy sacks flew all over the store. The mother yelled at her, 'Can't you ever leave things alone?' and grabbed up her food and hustled the kid out the door while Herbie was still looking at the mess on the floor. When he looked back at the counter, all the money was gone."

"So she got the food for nothing?"

"Plus the change, nine dollars and something."

"Pretty standard hustle," I said, looking at Kevin. "Why—"

Kevin held up his hand. "Last night about eight-thirty," he said, turning Andy's complaint form facedown and picking another off the stack, "they pulled the same thing at the Circle K on North Broadway, same woman, same child. Clint, you investigated that one, right?"

Clint nodded and said, "Same MO, almost exactly." Clint is a smart, capable guy whose slightly comical appearance gives him an extra edge on the street. He's learned to make devastating use of that first five seconds after bad guys look at his jug ears and freckles and decide he's harmless.

"Monday afternoon"—Kevin picked up a third form— "the same complaint at the Rexall Drug near the fairgrounds, but the swindle out there seems to have been pulled by a different woman."

"A different woman but the same child?"

"As near as we can tell. All three complainants describe the little girl as pretty, blond, eight to ten years old.

But the druggist at the Rexall store says the mama was a flashy blond, wearing high heels and a low-cut blouse that showed a lotta''—he gestured—''va-va-voom. Lessee, you talked to that one also, Clint. Tell him—''

''Basically the same story as the other two. The woman was loading up on toilet articles and cosmetics, so the tab was higher, a little over a hundred, and she paid with two fifties and a ten, so the take was higher too. But what's interesting here''—Maddox grinned, showing the gap between his top front teeth—''is that this other woman, the blond one, seems to match the description of a woman Mickey Halloran called in about.''

''Mickey Halloran of Mickey's? That bar on East Center?''

''Yeah. He claims this sexy blond in a tight dress came in his place a couple days ago with a red-faced potbellied guy, and Mick was pretty sure he'd seen them work a Murphy game on one of his best customers.''

''Using the what, the old Hoffman Hotel across the street there?''

''Probably. The guy didn't complain to Mickey, but then they don't, you know, guys that get stung that way. They pay the man pimping for the flashy broad at the other end of the bar, and then she leaves and the mark goes to the hotel room with the key he's been given, and when she's not there—he might come back looking for the pimp, but if the pimp's gone—''

''Well, sure,'' Andy said, ''he feels like a dumb shit, he's not gonna tell the bartender.''

''But Mick's afraid he lost a good customer over it,'' Clint said. ''So he asked around and found two other bar owners who remembered the same couple, mostly because the flashy blond didn't seem to match her partner, but they never figured out what the pair was up to.''

I looked at my watch and said, "Listen, this is fun, but—"

"Hang on, the fat lady sings now," Kevin said. He picked up four or five report forms and pointed them at Darrell Betts. "Tell him about the coin caper."

"Wait," I said, reaching for his desk phone, "if this is gonna get any better, we ought to get Bo in here." Bo's worked vice detail, up and down the Mississippi, for over ten years. I thought he could speed up this soap opera.

He answered his phone, "Dooley," the way he always does, quick and flat, like talk is money and he's deep in debt. He came into Kevin's office without saying hello to anybody, refused a seat with one quick headshake, and stood just inside the door, scanning the room with his ice-blue eyes. Sometimes I long to ask Bo Dooley if he suspects the building is on fire. I said, "Kevin's crew is having an interesting week. So far they've got, what, three quick-change hustles?"—Kevin nodded—"and several Murphy games, all apparently executed by one man, two women and one child."

Bo looked from me to Kevin and said, "That's it?"

"No." Kevin pointed his fistful of reports at Darrell and said, "Go ahead."

"Five complaints Monday," Darrell said, "all involving a swarthy guy with a Hispanic accent. He approaches somebody, in a crowded hotel lobby or the atrium at Methodist Hospital, says he just found this envelope full of coins and he's a stranger here and needs help deciding what to do with it. He's very nervous because he's a foreigner and doesn't want to get in trouble. The coins are from three or four countries, like a small collection, a couple of them are fairly old. There's a name and phone number on the outside of the envelope—"

"Let me guess," Bo said. "The mark calls the number,

and a woman says, 'Oh, goody, you saw my ad in the paper, huh?' and tells him she's offering a big reward.''

Darrell looked up from his notebook and said, ''How's come you're answering property complaints? I thought—''

''It's one of the oldest scams in the world,'' Bo said. ''The woman asks them to bring the coins to her, right?''

''Well, right, yes, she can't come downtown because she can't leave her sick mother, but she'll pay a thousand dollars if they'll bring the envelope—''

''And the guy who supposedly found the coins says he's afraid, the police in his country trap people for ransom sometimes—''

''Something like that, yeah, so he says, I don't care about the big reward, just pay me a couple of hundred dollars, and you can keep whatever she pays you.''

''So the mark pays him two hundred and takes the coins to the address the woman gave him, and it's an empty lot.''

''Okay,'' Kevin said, breaking into this Frick and Frack routine, ''even in dear old Rutherford we see something like this every so often, but this one's got a fun wrinkle. A couple of times, when the mark got a little suspicious and started to walk away, a second guy turned up and joined the conversation.''

''Uh-huh,'' Bo said, ''and he says, Hey, a couple of those coins are really valuable, I'll give you two-fifty for the lot.''

''Jeez, you know the whole routine, don't you?'' Darrell said. ''When the helper shows up and gets a bidding war going, the Hispanic guy gets more. The top figure I've heard about so far''—he flipped through his notes— ''was three hundred and seventy-five dollars.''

"But the best part is the description of the helper," Kevin said. He held out a report form. "Read it."

Darrell's iron-pumper's shoulder muscles stretched the seams of his neat blue shirt as he reached across the desk. He resettled his glasses and read, "Second suspect is middle-aged, potbellied, talkative, with a large red nose."

"Mr. Murphy Game," Kevin said.

"Busy guy," Bo said.

"You know," I said, standing up, "I'm kind of busy too." I looked at Bo. "I'd say we've been invaded by an extended family of grifters, wouldn't you?"

"Yup. They often travel in a pack."

"You're saying they're gypsies?"

"Not necessarily. But they live like that, drifting around. Like—what's that thing Ali used to say?—'float like a butterfly, sting like a bee.' Usually by the time you figure out what they're up to, they're gone."

Kevin looked at me. "You ever catch any?"

"Once. I spotted a couple pulling pigeon drops. Got help from a would-be mark, set 'em up while they thought they were setting him up, caught 'em dead to rights passing a shoe box full of shredded newspaper that was supposed to be money. It was a lot of work. And when I had 'em safe in jail, I couldn't get the county attorney's office interested in prosecuting."

"So you what? Just let them go?"

"Had to. Ask Milo. I'll bet he'll tell you it takes more time to compile the evidence on a scammer than he can ever get a judge to give them in jail time."

"So you suggest we tell all these people to just forget it? Kiss the money good-bye?"

"Well, no, you can't say that, exactly. Try to throw 'em a bone. Shopkeepers, tell them to contact their trade associations and circulate a warning. Individuals, yes, best thing for them to do is file a complaint, I guess. Tell 'em we'll pick 'em up if we can, do our best to put some heat on 'em. But—cash money, no witnesses usually—it's pretty much caveat emptor. Bo, will you give 'em your thoughts on this? I gotta go.''

''Most people,'' I heard Bo telling Kevin as I went back to my office, ''think scams are kind of funny. Till they end up on the short end of one.''

Back in my office, willing the phone to silence, I grabbed the stack of case files and my tape recorder and hustled to the south end of the hall, clattering over bare concrete. We were tearing out walls to shoehorn our People Crimes team into an open semicircle of cubicles, facing a glass-walled executive office designed by and for Ray Bailey.

When I asked him to head People Crimes, his total response had been ''Okay.'' But then he quickly added, ''If you're doing some remodeling, can I tell you how I'd like my office?'' So I knew he had been thinking about it for a while.

His crew was humming like a hive poked with a stick.

''See, if we'd both back our desks up to the partition between us,'' Rosie Doyle was urging Lou French, ''we'd each have room for two chairs in front of the desk, and all our cords could run through one conduit to that outlet in the hall.''

''Which is only half big enough,'' Lou said, ''plus if all I got between me and you is this little thin partition, Rosie, how am I ever going to hear any of my phone conversations?''

''Bitch bitch bitch,'' Rosie said, absentmindedly. ''Hold the other end of this tape, will you?'' She'd been the only woman in the detective division for almost a year, and was well past letting anybody bully her. ''The outlet's no problem. We can get another surge control to plug our cords into, can't we, Ray?''

''I guess,'' Ray said, looking morosely at the tangle of power cords on Rosie's desk. ''How many extra ports you got hooked up to that thing, anyway?''

''One extra printer and a Zip drive and a scanner, is all,'' she said. ''Well, and an extra set of speakers, but—''

''You're probably gonna set the wall on fire,'' Bailey said, ''but hey, it's a brick building, I guess most of us will get out. Hi, Jake.''

''I brought you the cold cases we talked about,'' I said.

Ray looked around his chaotic section. ''Probably oughta work in the meeting room.''

''Work?'' Lou French said, sneezing into a big red farmer's kerchief. ''Now, there's a change of pace.'' He was grouchy because construction dust had aggravated his asthma. Inhalers and cough drops were strewn across his desk, and his red eyes wept. He was due to retire in three months, so he had minimal interest in his office setup, anyway. Basically, he was keeping his chair warm for Buzz Cooper, who had applied to come on board as soon as he had his sergeant's badge. The rest of us just wanted to get Lou to his retirement party alive.

The group squeaked across plastic bubble wrap and then clattered over bare floor to the meeting room. When they were seated around the oval table, I started on my stack, describing the contents of each folder as I handed it to Ray, who slid it along to the investigator of his choice. ''Let's start with the oldest one,'' I said, ''a murder-suicide ten years ago on Seventh Avenue Southeast—''

''Presumed murder-suicide,'' Lou corrected.

''You didn't agree with the coroner's conclusion?''

''Most of that statement, if you read it carefully, the

coroner was just covering his ass. And we sure as hell never proved anything.'' Lou sucked on a cough drop and ruminated. ''I worked that one with Frank,'' he remembered, ''and we were both unhappy about the positions of the bodies when they were found.''

''Why don't you have another look at it, Lou,'' Ray said, ''since you remember it so well.''

''I won't say it's a pleasure,'' Lou said, pulling the dog-eared file toward him, ''but—oh, hey, these are all the original records, aren't they?''

''Sure,'' I said. ''Conversion to electronic record-keeping is working backward from last year. They're in 1999 now, but it's turned out to be incredibly time-consuming. Frank's applying for a grant for more support staff, but—they may never get back as far as this one.''

''Even when they do, they told me,'' Ray said, ''they'll always keep all the original records and evidence on the big cases.''

''Who decides what's big?''

''Dunno,'' I said. ''Probably Frank and I go into a dusty room and hold one of those interminable arguments.''

''Go straight home after, will you?'' Rosie said. ''I don't want to see you.''

The truth is, the argument may never happen. Rutherford PD has put a small fortune into the concept of electronic record-keeping over the past couple of years, but working investigators still like print pages they can pore over and scribble on. And they trust the original piece of paper better than the replica. It won't surprise me if we never discard one scrap of paper.

''Jeez, think about it, Ray,'' Lou said, skimming the softening pages of his file, ''we didn't have DNA testing when we worked this case.''

"Or a national fingerprint database," Ray said. "That's the upside. The downside is all the witnesses you can't find anymore. What else you got there, Jake?"

"Three armed robberies over one weekend in the winter of '96. You worked on this case, didn't you, Ray?"

"You bet. My first year as a detective. Same MO on all of them, all liquor stores. One man alone, in a black rain jacket and a baseball cap, all in an empty store just before closing. And one shooting victim, I seem to remember."

"The liquor store owner on the third heist. Yeah. Ernie Brotzman. Who died in the hospital a couple of days later."

"That's right." Ray leafed through the smudged pages of the top file. "The chief got really hot over this one. Ernie was in his high school class, and Frank wanted his killer bad. He attended every shift briefing for two days, going over and over the eyewitness accounts from the other two owners. We even got an FBI hotshot to come down from the Cities to profile this guy's personality, his probable birth order, shit like that. And then the holdups stopped. The bad guy left town, I guess."

"Disappeared, anyway," I said.

"Or went into some other line of work. We never saw his baseball cap or that big Dirty Harry 44-mag Smith & Wesson again."

"Remember the Band-Aid he used to wear on his nose?"

"Oooh, yes. He was a real piece of work, that guy." He pushed the three folders across the table. "Here, Rosie, have some fun with these."

"Did anybody figure out what was wrong with his nose?" Rosie asked him.

"Probably nothing. Haven't you ever heard about that

trick? Typical smart-ass con trick, wear a Band-Aid or a bandage somewhere when you're pulling a job. They think it distracts attention from their face, makes identification less likely. Little do they know how inaccurate most eyewitness accounts are. If I remember correctly, you're gonna find the second victim never even noticed the Band-Aid.''

We worked up through the stack, Ray keeping a couple for himself and setting some aside for Darrell, who was still busy in Kevin's office. We reassigned, in quick order, a vehicular homicide in which all the important witnesses disappeared the day after the accident; an extortion complaint from a terrified old lady, almost certainly the work of her unctuous niece-caretaker; and a suspected domestic abuse case that had escalated into a horrifying brawl, sending a whole family to the hospital. When we got to the 1999 drowning death of a toddler named Ruth Ann Burke, Ray started to give it to Lou, then said, ''No, wait, you been over this enough times already,'' and handed it to Rosie.

''Jake and Lou and I, we all suspected this was done deliberately to cover up child abuse,'' he said. ''But the family had no regular doctor, and the emergency-room doctor said the evidence was inconclusive. Read through it, will you? I'd write you a letter of commendation if you could show me,'' he said with sudden passion, ''anything at all that we missed.'' I had not known till then that the Burke case still haunted Ray as much as it did me.

Bo came in and took a seat silently, and we gave him the four old drug busts we'd been saving for him, all cases that predated his move to Rutherford.

''Most of these are close to three years old,'' I said, ''so the statute of limitations is just about to run out on 'em.''

"But don't feel any pressure," Ray said, and everybody laughed. "Actually"—he went back to looking morose—"I guess you'll be reading 'em mostly for laughs, anyway." Bo looked at him quizzically. Ray said, "Drug busts that year were almost a joke. We scooped up the pushers, their lawyers bailed 'em out, and they disappeared. That little bit of bail that judges gave first-time offenders, the big dealers just wrote that off. It was a game with them."

"It's still a game," Bo said, "only now the small-timers all go to jail and we feed and clothe them at great expense, while their employers live better than ever." A muscle jumped in his jaw. "Don't get me started," he said.

"I won't," Ray said. "Why don't you also take this rape-murder that we worked on all during 1998? Be a little change for you."

"Fine." Bo's pale eyes met mine, and he said, "You might want to talk to Kevin again." I raised my eyebrows and waited, but he shrugged minimally and looked down at his files.

"Okay," I said, and got up. "Lemme know if you find any smoking guns, guys." By the time I was halfway to the door, Ray and Rosie were peppering my back with questions about equipment. I held up my hands without turning around and said, "I'm late for an appointment. Write me a memo, and I'll do what I can." I hurried back to my office, thinking that while some of my enlarged management chores still seemed difficult, I had just about mastered evasiveness.

Kevin bounded out of his office as I approached my door. "Oh, good, you're here," he said, following me in. "Lemme run something past you."

"Run it fast," I said, sliding my weapon onto my belt,

stuffing ammo and dark glasses and cell phone into my briefcase. "I'm already late for qualifying at the range."

"Okay. You remember I used to work at the *Times-Courier?*"

"Indeed." A couple of months ago, Kevin dug out some old department dirt I needed from the files of the local paper, and as soon as I didn't need it anymore, we reburied it together. That job showed me he was an imaginative investigator and fair computer geek and not an idle gossip, so despite some reservations about his youth, I pushed for his promotion.

"I'm still buds with Frannie up there. You know him? Writes the About Town column?"

"Francis Coughlin? Sure. So?"

"So I'm thinking, if there's not much use in arresting these swindlers, how about fixing it so their games don't work here anymore? Maybe if they got a little publicity, they'd think about taking their act to another town."

"Uh...we don't want to get sued over this caper, Kevin."

"I wouldn't name any names. Hell, I don't *know* any names. And nobody took their pictures, but if we quote a couple of the descriptions we've been given—Bo says most people think this kind of crime is amusing. So okay, what if I ask Frannie to play it that way? A funny story about stings that are being perpetrated right here in little old Rutherford, just like a movie with Redford and Newman. But once the stories are out, the scams won't work anymore."

"Or at least they might figure they won't. I see what you mean."

"So maybe they'll decide it's easier to leave town than get a whole new schtick."

"Protect us," I said. "Everything has to be alleged."

"Oh, *I* know *that*." He strode back into his office, grinning. As I went down the front steps, I heard him on the phone, smooth-talking his friend at the paper.

I hurried out to the firing range to be humbled by John Wiggerstaff, the department firearms training specialist. Four times a year, he lowers my self-esteem by glaring coldly at the holes where my Glock's bullets have pierced the target outside the kill zone and saying, "Better practice more." He's not impressed that my scores are above average. He reminds me that in tight situations, average gets you killed. I know it's his job to keep me sharpened up, but I can't ever seem to swallow his taunts without wanting to break his nose.

I was still pretty steamed when I started the forty-mile drive home that night, but when I turned left at the little town of Mirium and saw my girl's car sitting in the yard, happiness blew all my cares away. Trudy Hanson, the smart, pretty crime lab technician who turns me to pudding, agreed to share this house with me last October. Sometimes when I see her there, I still can't believe my luck. She handed me a beer when I walked in the door, and led me out in the dusk to the place on the south side of our ninety-year-old farmhouse where she'd found pink tips of peony shoots pushing up through the remains of last year's bushes. A major benefit of our first spring in this old yard was turning out to be these sweet surprises coming up out of the earth, like welcome notes left by all the people who've lived there before us.

At dark we went inside, talking about the garden we would plan after dinner. But when I got up to clear away the plates, I yielded to an impulse to kiss the back of her neck, and the dinner dishes ended up waiting till after breakfast. I was rushed but very cheery by the time I got to work Thursday morning, and found Kevin Evjan crowing over the morning paper.

Francis Coughlin had done an elegant job. The grifters were depicted as Runyanesque characters using greed and ingenuity to avoid working for a living. The victims' haplessness was softened by a shrewd quote here and there, and Fran had pointed up the versatility of the group, making the most of their ability to play different roles.

Handed this journalistic tour de force on a slow news day, the editors at the *Times-Courier* had moved his column to the front page and run it above the fold, the top column on the left-hand side. Kevin was extensively quoted. Never shy, by noon he had shown the story to everyone on the third floor and was enjoying jolly phone calls from friends. By late afternoon he got another phone call from an ecstatic Francis Coughlin, who had just had word that the story was being picked up by a news service for reproduction in major newspapers nationwide.

On Friday morning at ten, by previous appointment I went to Frank McCafferty's office, where we romanced two councilmen for half an hour. For me this is the steep downside of an advance in pay grade, but I managed my part without melting down, largely because Frank carried the ball on most of the conversation. As soon as they were out the door, I stood up, briefcase in hand.

"Sit a minute," Frank said. "Or is somebody waiting for you?"

"Only messages and report forms," I said, putting my briefcase back down. "It's almost frightening, Frank; you got me all this new help, and now I *never* seem to have enough time."

"Welcome to the wide world of executive privilege," McCafferty said. "Success means never having to say you're caught up." He leaned back and scratched his cheeks. "Is Kevin mature enough to ramrod Property Crimes?"

"If he isn't, he'll grow. Soon as he found out I was considering him for the job, he made it clear he wouldn't give it up without a fight."

"Uh-huh. Did you okay him planting this wild story in the paper?" He plucked the front page out of a pile and slapped it on his desk. I had already noticed that it looked a little loonier in print, on the front page of the paper, than it had seemed when Kevin suggested it.

"Well…yeah. The Property Crimes section had been running on a high lope all week investigating scam complaints, and they were getting hot to make some arrests when he called me. I told him how hard it is to put a grifter in jail. Before long he got this idea about planting a story with his friend the reporter. He thought maybe they could make Rutherford feel too hot for this merry band of pranksters."

"Hmm. Seems a little showboaty."

"Maybe. But I don't see any harm in it, and it might work."

"He's gotta go by the book, Jake. Don't let him get the idea police work can be cute."

"He's a hard worker, Frank. Bright and energetic. And I gave him Maddox and Pitman, both sensible, experienced street cops with years of experience."

"Yeah, they were both good choices. You know, it's really something"—he shook his head, looking bemused—"all this good work lately by old Andy Pitman."

"You're surprised?"

"I always knew he was smart, but—he walks funny, you know? And can't seem to control his weight. Kind of a guy my dad would say looks like a bed tick full of harrow teeth." He grinned. "But his record as a POP officer has been really outstanding.'' He sat back and switched gears. ''Tell me again, will you, why you picked Ray Bailey to boss People Crimes? I kind of thought you might go for Bo Dooley.''

''I talked to Bo about it, but he's got a lot on his plate at home, so I decided to leave him where he was. He handles vice well, and he can help out on either team when we need him.''

''His wife still in detox?''

''Home, but still pretty fragile.''

''Huh. Hard on his kid.''

''Right. So I want to give him a little slack for a while. He's worth it; he's got unique skills.'' I didn't tell Frank that Bo Dooley had not only turned down a promotion but said he might go back into uniform to get forty-hour weeks till Diane was stronger. To save him for the investigative section, I gave him three months of no weekends and told him to keep the arrangement to himself.

''Ray Bailey's quiet and careful,'' I said. ''He doesn't get excited. He's a planner.''

''Hell you say.'' He flipped a pencil, thoughtfully. ''Hard for me to judge from here, I guess. He always looks kind of discouraged.''

''He can't help that. He's a Bailey.''

''That's true.'' He laughed. ''His uncle Gus was in my grade in school. We called him Gloomy Gus, of course— they all look like that. I didn't dare look at Gus during a test; I knew I'd cry.''

''There you go.'' I added a clincher. ''Another thing, Ray's got no problems managing Rosie Doyle.''

''Rosie went to People Crimes? You don't think that might be a little rough for her?''

''I think she'd bust a gut if I didn't put her there. Rosie

likes action.'' I checked my watch. ''Are we just about done here, Frank?''

''I just want to say this one more time.'' He stared at me, twitching restlessly, deciding between his short delegation speech and his long one. ''You've got good people, Jake. Now, to make this bigger crew work, you need to delegate authority so you can supervise.''

''I know.''

''Maintain an overview,'' he said. ''Don't bog down in small stuff.''

''I'll *do* it, Frank.'' I got out before he could start the long speech.

I knew McCafferty was worried that my scruffy childhood and antiestablishment mind-set could trip me up now and make me blow my hard-won promotion to captain. I figured my ambition would help me handle all that, but I privately admitted to reservations about full-time administration. The unpredictability of police work, the grit and push and jangle of street life that's so hard to get used to when you join the force, exerts a powerful lure once you learn to handle it, and it's very hard to give it up when your pay grade changes.

I do have brains enough not to shoot myself in the foot, though, usually. So I didn't think I'd tell my boss that a big part of me still wanted to have it both ways.

TWO

"PUT IT HERE," Trudy said. "Right between my legs."

"I can't," I said. "I'll faint with pleasure."

"Come *on*, Jake."

"Okay," I said, "remember you asked for this." I slid my head between her knees and asked her, "Here?"

"Forward just a—there." She backed off a step and watched approvingly as I pounded down the stake. Black Minnesota mud, smelling like roots, decay, and a hundred years of manure, splattered away from the wooden marker and covered her boots.

Trudy had measured the outside corner of the eastern-most compost bin several times from both directions; she knew exactly where it should go. My lover dotes on precision; square corners turn her ticker up.

I like things tidy too, but working with Trudy in our own yard on the first warm Saturday in April was making me so happy, I couldn't resist fooling around a little. In fact, ever since the gray, blustery March day when we sat shivering in the cold marble austerity of the First National Bank, waiting to sign the mortgage on this funky old farm, a perverse bubble of joy had been percolating through my brain, threatening to loft me completely out of touch with reality.

I knew we'd just promised to pay large sums of money every month for thirty years, which is the same as forever.

Also, we had recklessly agreed that if some calamity prevented our paying for a couple of months, the bank could take everything back. And after the cold winter we'd just endured here, I certainly understood that the ancient house behind us would never outlast the contract in its present condition. The wiring was shot, the plumbing predated Prohibition, and the insulation compared unfavorably to an igloo. Only a fool would claim to know how much time and money we'd plow into this place before it was convenient.

I couldn't seem to stay worried about any of it, because sometime during the gritty, difficult winter just past, this place had started to feel like home to me. I grew up homeless, and I'd been trying to find a home all my life, without any firm idea what to look for. Now I had a pile of documents that said I was there and I owned it, jointly with this handsome woman who was standing over my head with a tape measure. Bank loans fade to inconsequence in the face of luck like that.

"Looks good, huh?" I reached for the spade. "Time to set the corner posts." I had the square frames of the sides and tops, braced and covered with chicken wire, stacked up in the barn. The four-by-fours that would anchor the back were already bolted to the barn wall. As soon as we set the three corner posts, I was going to bolt in the sides, and install the fronts and tops on hinges. We'd have three compost bins in a row, in which Hines/Hanson organic wastes could be dumped, turned, and eventually decomposed. In a few months I'd be producing the rich black biomass of a gardener's dreams.

Trudy watched me dig a few spadefuls, then handed me the posthole digger, took the spade, and said, "I'll start the other two holes." We worked a few minutes in silence, warming up as the sun got around to the south side of the barn. When she stopped to take off her jacket, she stretched her arms up to the sun and said, "Hoo-eee, babe, I tell you, it feels good to be home on a Saturday morning."

"Treat for me too." She'd been working six-day weeks since the first of March, going back in on Saturday to the Bureau of Criminal Apprehension to learn the technique of DNA testing. She was home today only because it was her week to be on call for the outreach van. If the state crime lab got called to assist at a crime scene anywhere in the state, she'd be off. "Let's hope there's no crime in faraway places, huh?"

"Yes, pray for peace." She stretched again and went back to digging.

"Has the Awesome Asian thanked you for all the extra hours you're putting in?" Her boss at BCA was a driven Hawaiian biologist named Jimmy Chang.

"You can't expect Jimmy to say anything like that." Chang's cold workaholic exterior covered, as far as I could tell, a cold workaholic interior.

"You ever think of telling Jimmy Chang to stuff it?"

"All the time. Ted and I are writing the exit speech. It gets better on every long trip."

"Just you and Ted? Megan won't help?"

"She used to. She seems kind of subdued lately."

"Well, I'm glad you're still venting. But I haven't heard you seriously talk about leaving BCA since... uh—" I fell silent suddenly, thinking, Don't go there, dumbhead.

"Since last year, when I was trying to flee from your fatal charms. Don't remind me. But to be fair to Jimmy, you know, there isn't much more he can do for me. The bureau's pay rates are inflexible. I couldn't get a raise before October if I was a certified genius."

"So is it worth all the time you're giving up?"

"To learn DNA testing for free? Sure." She shrugged, as much as she could with a spadeful of dirt in her hands. "It's a once-in-a-lifetime chance." The Minnesota legislature voted to extend DNA record-keeping to all felons, giving the crime lab a mountain of new work at the same time that improved methods required retesting the ten thousand samples already on hand. "Think of it as a savings account. I'll be worth more to us later on."

"Hey, if you want it, I'm for it. I miss you on Saturday, though."

"Sure." She smirked. "Except for the three out of four Saturdays you end up back in Rutherford working in your own office."

"That's gonna change. Soon as I'm done reorganizing my crews, you're gonna have a different housemate. Delegatin' Jake, they're gonna call me."

"Why do I find that hard to believe?"

"Trust me. I got in the habit of working all the time when I was living alone. But now I've got you, we've got this place, we're gonna have a life. The truth is"—I hoisted an extra-heavy load out of my posthole, grunting—"if I wasn't busy reorganizing the section right now, I could be sitting pretty right now with a clean desk. We've got a lot of screwy little complaints keeping the Property Crimes section busy, but capital crime has bottomed out in Rutherford this spring."

"Why, I wonder? It's flourishing all around you, believe me."

"A fluke, probably. But let's enjoy it while it lasts." I found the tape and measured my muddy hole. "One more scoop, and I'm ready to set this post, kid. You ready?"

"I'll get the gravel," she said, and then, "Is that the phone? Where is it?"

"In my tool kit." I dug it out, poked Send, and said, "Hines."

"I'm sorry to call you at home," Andy Pitman said, "but I thought I better."

I stood watching crumbles of dirt and pebbles drop back into my posthole while my watch scrolled from 9:45 to 9:46, 9:47, and finally 9:48. I said, "Uh-huh. Uh-huh," from time to time, while Andy Pitman ruined my day.

"What?" Trudy said, watching my face as I folded up the phone.

"It's my own fault for talking out loud about time off." I put the phone in my pocket and set the tool kit back in the barn. "My newest investigator's standing all alone downtown by a trash barrel that he says has a dead body in it."

I CLEANED UP and changed clothes in twelve minutes flat, not bad considering I was talking on the phone most of that time. I called BCA first, described the location of the body, and got their dispatcher's promise to send help. Trudy took the phone when I was done and told the crime lab dispatcher she'd be waiting for the van at the Mirium exit in forty-five minutes. We live halfway between our two jobs, a quarter of a mile off Highway 52, so the van would have to pass our house anyway.

As soon as Trudy was off the phone, I called the coroner and the county attorney and got them both headed downtown. Once in my red pickup, rolling south on the highway, I called Rutherford dispatch on the cell phone, to check on their search for the rest of my People Crimes crew.

"Ray Bailey's at a farm auction over by Mantorville," Schultzy said. "He's wearing his beeper, but he must be in a dead spot. I got the name of the farmer from the county extension office and called; the wife's sending somebody out to the pasture to bring Ray to the phone, but they must be riding a very slow mule. Rosie Doyle took a couple of nephews to a Little League game in Elgin; her beeper worked, and she's coming in now. Lou French was at a yard sale in Eyota; he's on his way too. Darrell Betts was working out in his own basement with his beeper upstairs on the dresser, can you beat that? He finally came up to take a shower and saw the light blinking; he should be downtown by now.''

''Nice work, Schultzy,'' I said, and punched Off. As I slid the phone into its holder, it rang, and Schultzy said, ''Hang on, the chief wants to talk to you.''

''Well, your system's not exactly perfect yet, is it?'' he said, peevishly, without saying hello. ''Here you are, headed into town, and your crew's scattered all over hell-and-gone. Wasn't this supposed to be the week when Ray Bailey started handling street details, and telling you all about it on Monday morning?''

''Gimme a break here, Frank. It's Saturday, and every-thing's been so quiet. Ray knew we had a detective on Saturday duty at the station, so he went out to a farm to help his dad with something; he'll be back in a few minutes. But Andy Pitman's only been a detective for two weeks, and now he's got a homicide dumped in his lap. He was afraid he might skip something important. I'd say that shows good judgment.''

''Well, granted. But now, don't bog yourself down with a shitload of details. I'm gonna need your help with the budget next week. You gotta put your foot down, Jake.''

''I will. I just want to make sure things get started off right.'' I asked him if he wanted me to call him later, and he said, Well, yes, sure, if I had time. The truth, unacknowledged between us, was that he could hardly keep from hopping in his own car and running downtown to see for himself what was going on.

As soon as I hung up, I opened the windows to let in the earthy breeze. It was one of those classic April mornings that in Minnesota can start you thinking maybe the universe just got a new deal. Pink buds pushed stickily out of tree branches; pussy willows blossomed fat and furry by the creeks. Red-winged blackbirds flashed in the ditches by the road, and once I heard a meadowlark in the field. I took a couple of deep breaths of the winey air and forgot for a few minutes that I was driving toward an apparent homicide.

Two squads and an unmarked department car were parked end-to-end in the alley back of the Lotus Flower, a Chinese restaurant on South Broadway. A two-wheeled Toter, the brown plastic household garbage model, stood near the back door of the restaurant, looking superfluous in front of a fifteen-foot-long blue metal Dumpster.

Andy Pitman was pacing nervously around the Toter. Two uniforms, Hanenburger and Casey, had finished stringing crime scene tape in a forty-foot circle around it and were securing the perimeter now, keeping people outside the circle and explaining to the occasional truck driver why they had to block the alley. Lou French was walking a careful grid pattern inside the tape, scanning the ground on either side of his feet as he walked. Rosie Doyle had already begun working the tape line, talking to the bystanders who had begun to cluster there, and I saw Darrell Betts a few yards south of the tape, knocking on back doors in the alley.

The coroner's ragtop Jeep pulled into the alley behind my pickup. We took the last two spaces along the west wall, behind the second squad. Milo Nilssen, the county attorney, pulled his shiny new silver Suburban past us without slowing.

The coroner banged his ill-fitting door shut and walked up to my side of the pickup, carrying his bag. "Hey, Pokey," I said.

His nickname is Minnesota copspeak for Adrian Andreyevich Pokornoskovic, which none of us can say. Hampstead County has no full-time medical examiner; Pokey fits coroner duties in around a dermatology practice. My impression is that he does the zits for a living, and puts his heart into his forensic work.

"Hoo, Milo got fancy new wheels," he said. "Guess he's the man now, hah?" Two weeks ago the county commissioners had finally removed "acting" from in front of Milo's title, where it had squatted as a sneaky slur for almost a year, ever since his former boss flamed out in scandal.

Pokey's foxy little face crinkled with amusement as Milo pulled up front beside the lead squad, his gleaming new bumper touching the yellow tape. Pokey survived Soviet work camps and an unsanctioned hike across much of Europe while he was still in his teens, so he's hard to impress.

Al Hanenburger strode across the tape circle and told Milo he'd have to move. Milo argued. Al explained; I saw him gesture about the need for access to the crime scene. Milo argued some more. Al pulled out his pad of traffic tickets. Milo sputtered outrage. Al entered the date on his pad with grave deliberation and then watched, stone-faced, as the CA put his car in reverse and roared backward down the alley. Pokey and I jumped sideways as he flashed by us. He backed into the street without pausing and barely escaped death at the hands of a Grainbelt beer truck with an earsplitting horn.

Pokey, watching the entire performance with undisguised delight, said, "Is so not cool, that Milo, huh? Honest to Johnson." Besides being critically short on articles, Pokey picks up slang from three generations of patients, and recombines it with carefree disregard for its era of origin.

We ducked under the yellow tape. I said, "Pokey, you know Andy Pitman?" They shook hands.

"So," Pokey said, looking around, "where's body?" Andy opened the lid of the brown plastic trash container. Pokey said, "Ah," and pulled on gloves. He touched the face and neck, put a thermometer in the ear, lifted an eyelid. "Kinda smashed down lookin', hah?"

"Wow," I said. "For sure."

Whoever put the body in the barrel must have taken out some of the garbage, crammed the dead man in feet first, and packed the bags back in around him. He looked as if he'd been compacted a little to make him fit; he seemed to be upright, but with his head canted sharply sideways, resting on his shoulders. The angle of his shoulders and elbows didn't look quite natural, and his right forearm wandered across the garbage sacks in a random way that argued for broken bones. The left side of his face was uppermost, and was terribly battered; the cheekbone looked smashed, and the ear was torn.

"What's he got in his mouth?" I said.

"Dunno." Pokey parted the swollen lips gently. "Looks like money."

I leaned to look under his hand. "Jeez, it is money. I see a one and a five." We stared at each other. "What the hell?" Pokey shrugged. "You gonna leave it there?"

"Uh…yah, better not mess around till we get him out of barrel, I can see better. Step back a little, huh?" Pokey slid his hand inside the open collar of the cheap blue cotton shirt the victim was wearing. He squinted, muttered something to himself, moved his hand a little. Moving a little aside, he said, ''Feel shoulder here.''

I pulled on gloves and slid my hand inside the collar. Beneath the rigid tissue, something moved, like pebbles. I jerked my hand back and said, ''Jesus.''

Pitman said, ''What?''

I looked at Pokey. ''He is dead, isn't he?''

''C'mon, Jake. How cold and stiff you want?''

''You got some gloves with you?'' I asked Pitman. ''Put them on and touch his shoulder, right here.''

Andy's reaction was the same as mine; he jerked back, as if he'd been burned. He asked Pokey, ''Why's he so...crumbly?''

''Bones all broken, I guess.'' Pokey lifted an eyelid again and shone a light into one flat, milky eye. He murmured, ''Maggots hatching,'' and I saw the whiteness moving there. ''Need to get him out of there, yah? Anybody got plastic sheet?''

''BCA will bring one,'' I said, ''just hang on a minute.''

Andy walked up to me and said, ''Jake, this is Sam Chow.'' I knew him by sight as the youngest and jolliest of several Chow brothers whose family had run the Lotus Flower as long as anyone in Rutherford could remember. Sam was followed by a smaller, less confident Chinese man in a smeared white apron.

''Sam called this in,'' Andy said. ''He came out to tell you about it.''

''This is my dishwasher, Louis Wang,'' Sam said. Louis bobbed and smiled nervously. Sam said something I couldn't understand, and the small man answered in the same language. ''Louis brought a sack of our garbage out here to the Dumpster this morning,'' Sam translated, indicating the big city trash container that stood head-high by his back wall. He asked a sharp question, got a nod and a couple of words from his employee, and went on. "This brown plastic trash barrel was in the way. Louis tried to move it, but it was very heavy, so he opened the lid to look inside. Then he came running to me"—Sam smothered a smile—"very fast." He turned to Andy. "I came out to look and called the station. They sent the two officers and then you."

"Is this barrel usually here?"

"I've never seen it before."

"So you have no idea when it got here or—"

"I came in the front door this morning, so I didn't see it then," Sam said. "I didn't work last night, but I've just spoken to two of my brothers who were here. Neither of them had any reason to come out in the alley last night. They're looking for the dishwasher who worked the shift with them, and when they find him, I'll let you know what he says."

"Hey, nice work, Sam," I said. "Wish we could put you on steady."

"Take my card," Sam said, grinning. "It might beat chopping veggies."

Milo walked stiffly up the alley from wherever he had parked outside. A few steps behind him, looking even sadder than usual, Ray Bailey hurried toward us.

I started toward the two of them, saying, "Hey, Milo," as our paths converged. He asked me angrily, "What's the name of that officer who made me move my car? I'm gonna change his attitude—"

"Milo, come on, he didn't mean anything personal. He's just doing his job; we asked him to keep the alley clear. Excuse me a minute, will you?" I said, and turned to catch Ray before he got to the tape.

"Stupid beeper didn't work," Ray said, mortified.

"Don't get all bent out of shape about it," I said. "We all know there are a few dead spots around, and there's nothing we can do about it. What you need to know, Ray, is that Andy Pitman handled this call exactly the way you'd have wanted him to. He knew he didn't know enough, so he told dispatch to find you right away, and when they couldn't, he called me." I filled him in on Andy's phone call, and told him about the broken bones and the money in the mouth. "We're waiting for BCA now," I said. "Rosie's talking to people on the tape line, and Lou is walking a grid around the trash barrel. Darrell's canvassing the stores along the alley."

"Any ID yet?"

"No. Maybe he'll have a wallet in his pocket. Why don't you come and have a look at the body? Soon as the lab crew gets here and takes pictures, we'll want to get him out of that trash can so Pokey can have a look. And then since your whole crew's here, I'd like to send Andy Pitman back to the station so there's somebody there to take calls."

"Sure, he can go anytime. Where's the—oh." We had arrived at the barrel. "Man, a mashed cat, huh?" He stared morosely into the barrel. Ray Bailey had exactly the right face for his job. "You said his mouth is full of—" He stooped and peered. "Oh, yeah, I see it now. Man"—his voice dropped almost to a whisper—"that is just really goddamn weird, isn't it?" He straightened and looked at me. "You ever see that before? Money in the mouth?"

"Can't say I have." My phone rang. I answered, and Trudy said, "We're in front of the Lotus Flower, and we can't see any of you."

"You need to come around in back," I said, "but it's

a tight fit in this alley. Hang on there till I make you some space.'' I asked Hanenberger to move his blue-and-white to the street and then run around to the front and guide them in. He was back in a few minutes, walking backward, making hand signals for Megan Duffy. She eased the big van into the alley, favoring the center as much as possible. When Hanenburger rolled his hands around each other, she cramped the wheel hard right and snubbed the nose up tight against the wall, with the rear end far enough out so they could get the doors open. As soon as she killed the motor, the whole BCA crew jumped out and began working like ants.

''I'll do the first set of pictures,'' Trudy said after we'd shown them the body, ''and you can start the blood samples, okay, Megan?'' Ted Zumwalt set up an easel and began measuring and sketching the crime scene.

I stepped to Trudy's side and muttered, ''Try to get me a couple of pictures of the money in his mouth, will you?''

''The money in his—''

I showed her. ''Think you could get a shot or two without, uh, making too big a deal about it?'' It was the kind of detail cops like to keep closely held till they find a suspect.

''How about that? His mouth is actually full of money,'' she said. ''Wow. I'll need a lot of light, but— yeah, I think I can get that.'' She walked over to Ted's easel to ask him to help. I heard him ask sharply, in the mock-magisterial manner he affects to cover his youth, ''What are you mumbling about, m'dear? Get pictures of money where?'' Trudy moved to his side and shushed him, but his voice had carried clearly across the alley, and I saw Milo's eyes turn toward him and then toward me.

In a few seconds he was close behind me, breathing on my ear.

"I just saw the KORN-TV truck pull past the end of the alley," he muttered, "so they'll be in here in a minute. Whaddya got for me so far?"

"Stand here," I said, giving him my precious space near the crowded barrel, "so you can see, and I'll tell you all I know."

"Hmmm. White male, is that what you're calling it?"

"Think so. Maybe forty, but give or take ten years."

"See what you mean," he said, "so beat up it's hard to tell. Any ID?"

"Not so far. We're hoping when we get him out of the barrel—"

"Which will be when?"

"When Pokey and the BCA crew tell us we can. They're running this part of the show."

"Okay. What were they saying just now about money?" Trudy looked over at me and shrugged apologetically.

"I'll show you," I said, "but unless the TV guy asks you, keep it to yourself, will you? It would be helpful to withhold it for now." I showed him where to look.

"How bizarre," he said. "Now, why would anybody do that?"

"I don't know. His bones are all broken, too," I said. "You wanna feel? I'll get you a glove."

"No, thanks," he said quickly. "Just tell me."

I told him. He asked a few more questions about how and when the call came in, making hurried notes in a tiny spiral notebook. He palmed it while the photographer posed him just outside the yellow tape line, and I stayed nearby, out of the camera's eye, in case he needed an information boost during the interview.

Milo's always been a workhorse lawyer who organizes cases painstakingly, but the public relations part of his job gave him fits when he first made acting county attorney. He used to go into anxiety spasms, grooming his hair, smoothing his tie, and tossing little glances off to the side that made him look sneaky. Watching him stand quietly now, only shooting his cuffs once while he answered the reporter's questions, I thought he had just about licked his fear of the camera. He never mentioned the money, and he came up with a polite way to say "broken all to hell." On the evening news later, looking grave and capable with a trace of spring breeze ruffling his hair, he came across as knowing somewhat more than he did, without actually saying anything he'd have to take back later.

As soon as I was done helping Milo, I sent Andy Pitman back to the station, saying, "Damn good job for your first time out."

"It was kind of awesome being the first investigator on the scene," he said, "but now that you're all here, I'm beginning to enjoy myself."

"Sorry to spoil your fun. But somebody's gotta look after the store."

Pokey made a couple of phone calls and then began following Trudy around the barrel, sweet-talking her with outrageous compliments. "Betcha wore that sweater just to make me feel better, hah?" I heard him say. If anybody but Pokey had pulled those cornball tactics on her at a crime scene, she'd have ordered him out of her space. But Trudy and the coroner have a mutual admiration thing going; she calls him "Pokorino" and "Dockydoodles," and she's told me, any number of times, how smart he is.

"Some people think it's just instinct that gets him those quick answers," she said once, "but Pokey notices *everything*."

Ray Bailey joined their strange minuet, following Pokey while Pokey followed Trudy, talking in his other ear. Ray was trying to get current with the case after his late start, and I was trying to stay out of his way till he worked his way into the flow and I could leave him. Trudy stopped shooting pictures to make a call, and then Pokey made another call and they all talked some more. When Ray beckoned to me, I walked over and joined the procession around the trash can.

"Pokey's anxious to get the body out of the barrel," Ray said, "and Trudy says that would be good for her crew, too."

"Yeah," she said. "Ted could take the rest of the pictures, and Megan and I can do fingerprints and trace evidence together."

"You're going to do fingerprints here? I thought you'd wait till you got him up to St. Paul."

"Oh…well, Pokey doesn't want us to take this body."

"Oh?" I looked at him. "You want to do the autopsy here in Rutherford?" Frank was on record as favoring state crime lab autopsies when we could get them.

"Victim's been in plastic barrel some time in warm weather," Pokey said, "gettin' kinda ripe. Bugs movin' in," he added matter-of-factly.

"And Jimmy Chang's out of town this weekend, and both lab docs are at a conference," Trudy said. "I called and checked with Inez and she said there were three autopsies scheduled ahead of this one Monday morning, so your victim would have to wait till late Monday or possibly even Tuesday morning."

"Long time in cooler," Pokey said. "Lotta changes happen. You want good autopsy, I found empty lab at Hampstead County, Doc Stuart says we can set up for tomorrow morning."

"You want to do it on a Sunday?"

"You got a thing about Sunday?"

"No, but—are you able to be there, Ray? Might take most of your day."

"No problem for me," Ray said.

"Let's do it, then," I said. If Ray attended the autopsy on Sunday, by Monday he'd be in charge of the case for sure.

Rosie appeared suddenly at Ray's side, her red curls bouncing in the breeze, and asked him, "Can I go with you?"

Ray hesitated for one uncomfortable heartbeat and then said firmly, "No. There's too much else to do, Rosie, we can't afford to double up on anything." Rosie turned toward me, getting ready to argue, but I walked away and began talking to Lou. I heard Ray say, behind me, "I'm glad to know you're willing to do it, though, Rosie, and I'll get you into one as soon as I can, okay?" Ray was going to be okay with Rosie.

Ray asked Pokey, "What time tomorrow?"

"Nine o'clock. Now—" Pokey looked at his watch. "You gonna get him out of barrel pretty soon?"

"Whenever you say. But let's clear the alley first." Ray went and found the two uniforms, who moved everybody but law enforcement personnel out of the alley and blocked both ends. Rosie and Megan spread a plastic sheet, using various tools to anchor the corners so they wouldn't blow away. Lou held the cover open while Hanenburger and Casey gradually lowered the two front corners, with Ray belaying the handle in back and Darrell and I each bracing a wheel with our foot.

Ray suggested we leave the filled garbage bags inside the Toter and hope they would keep the body from shifting. Having had no previous experience decanting bodies out of barrels, I didn't argue. What we couldn't see till too late was that the garbage wasn't all in plastic sacks. There were beer cartons and some loose newspapers and something soft we didn't discuss, and it all began sliding as we tilted past a hundred degrees. The dead man was heavier than we expected, and the Toter was greasy in spots and less rigid around the top than it looked, so while we all grunted and turned red and said things like "Watch it" and "Grab the—" and "Ouch," in the end we dropped him the last foot and a half, and a lot of coffee grounds and orange peels and some of that mysterious soft slop slid out onto our clean plastic sheet along with the dead man.

So we were all down on our knees, guiltily tidying up around the corpse, when Ray glanced inside the barrel and said softly, "Hang on a minute, guys." He slid a foot nearer the barrel, craned his neck, and said, "Godalmighty."

"S'matter?" Lou said.

"There's another body in there."

THREE

He was naked, curled on his right side and tightly wedged into the bottom of the barrel

"Gonna be a bitch gettin' him out of there," Ray said. "Maybe I could—"

"Lemme look first," Pokey said. "Push back a little, hah?" We pushed the Toter, still on its side, a few feet away from the plastic sheet, and Pokey crawled in, dragging his black bag. He stayed several minutes in the filthy brown container, grunting and swearing softly in several languages, while his legs, from the knees down, thrashed on the asphalt. Finally he backed out, stood up, brushing crud off himself, and said quietly, "Gonna hafta cut him out, I guess."

The coroner had lost his penchant for gallows humor; he was grim-faced and quiet now, like the rest of the crew. One dead body in a downtown alley, even one with money in his mouth, had seemed like a slightly offbeat street crime that could be handled in a routine way. But suddenly finding we had two dead men, packed one on top of the other like sardines, in a filthy trash can with garbage added for packing had added an ominous edge to our working day. The way the bodies had been compacted into the too-small space was so demeaning it made everybody jumpy. There was a feeling in the air now, a little vibe just below audible pitch that felt like somebody had been here, maybe was still close by, who got off on evil. I found myself wondering, Are we gonna be finding more barrels like this one? My chest felt tight.

The body that was already on the ground was badly damaged, too. Rigor mortis held him stiffly fixed in the odd-shaped heap in which he had slid out of the barrel, but when it passed, I thought, his original shape and size might be hard to ascertain. Both shoulders and at least one of his arms appeared to be broken, and he was covered with scrapes and cuts and puffy purple bruises. I didn't envy Pokey the job of deciding which injury killed him.

The blue cotton shirt we had seen in the barrel turned out to be all he was wearing. Below it, his pale naked shanks and shrunken privates suggested further abuses. I couldn't be sure, because his legs were folded up behind him at the knees. Rigor mortis held them there for now, but his knees were so large and purple that I thought his legs, when they came down, might swing both ways.

And since the second victim appeared to be an adult male, who must once have occupied considerably more space in the world than the four square feet he was crammed into now, I did not want to think about what it must have taken to get him in there, or how he was going to look when we got him out.

Ray said, "Jake, you got some tin snips, anything like that in your truck?"

"Lemme see." I carry a big weatherproof toolbox, a gift from Trudy last Christmas, bolted to my truck bed in back of the cab. Rummaging through it now, I found a tree pruner with long wooden handles and three-inch forged steel jaws. I bought it years ago at a garage sale, before I owned any trees or even a house. Garage sales succeed because human brains, confronted by bargains, turn to mush.

"Jesus," Hanenberger said when he saw it, "talk about overkill." He was wrong, though; the heavy plastic Toter turned out to be a lot tougher than a hedge, and in fact was just about all my pruner could handle. We left the container lying on its side, and I attacked the top right-hand corner, confidently at first, then doggedly, and finally in a humiliated rage. I was dripping sweat by the time the slit in the barrel opened wide enough to let us pry out the second victim.

His rigor mortis was so far advanced he could not be uncoiled. Trudy, Pokey, and Ted began circling his tormented doughnut shape, muttering in frustration at the impossibility of examining, testing, or photographing a body so curled up on itself. Trudy sent Megan over to take a swab of my sweat, in case I had dripped any on the victim. There was no way to tell by looking, she rightly pointed out. The body that came out of the bottom of the barrel, besides having bruises, contusions, scrapes, and cuts, was covered all over with coffee grounds, mud, blood spatters, and fecal matter.

"I don't know where to start," Trudy said.

"Or how to continue," Ted said.

"What are those dents on his back, I wonder?" Megan murmured, swabbing sweat off my upper lip.

I looked and said, "Guess he molded to the inside shape of the trash barrel," and she made a little hiccuping sound.

She sealed and stowed her sample, moving with that silken skill the state techies get from constant practice of their crafts. Megan had changed remarkably since last year, when she joined the outreach team as a cheery jock in athletic team T-shirts, wearing braces on her teeth. She

had discarded the baseball cap she used to wear, her po-
nytail was tamed now in a neat braid like Trudy's, and
her smile blazed with flawless white teeth. I had been too
preoccupied to notice her much this morning, and didn't
want to be distracted by her now, but seeing her blooming
appearance up close, I found myself speculating idly,
What's come over this kid?

Ray called dispatch to tell them we'd found another
body, and after some discussion accepted a new ICR number for the second victim.

"I think it's all the same case," I said.

"So do I," he said, "but I didn't want to waste time
arguing about it, and they said they'll cross-reference 'em
anyway."

"The hearse is here," Hanenburger announced, pointing to the south end of the alley, where a long coach with
a "Dowd's Funeral Home" logo on the side was idling
its motor. "You want me to let him in?"

"Gonna get crowded as hell in here," Ray said.

"Ask him to hold up a minute," I said, and to Ray, "I
just remembered. Sam Chow hasn't seen the bodies since
we got them out of the barrel, has he?"

"Not that I know of."

"Well, they were right outside his back door. I'm
gonna ask him to take a look."

While I was at it, I brought the dishwasher too, though
he nearly cried when I asked him, and he barely glanced
at the dead men before declaring he had never seen them
and scuttling back inside.

"He's had a lotta trouble in his life," Sam said. He
took a good long look and declared he didn't recognize
either victim.

"Anybody else in your place that was here last night?"

"Staff? No. Customers...I can ask." He went inside

for a few minutes, came back out, and said there was nobody. I checked with Darrell and Rosie, who declared they had not found anyone so far who would admit to having been in the area last night. "Well, then," I told Ray, "I guess we can let 'em go as soon as the crews are finished."

"Top guy can go, far as I'm concerned," Pokey said, "but ask BCA guys." Trudy polled her crew and said, "Yeah, we've got everything we need from the first one," so Ray sent Hanenburger to the end of the alley to parlay. He came back with the driver, a gurney, and an extra-large body bag, which together they managed to fit around the distorted body. They hoisted their awkward bundle onto the gurney, and the grumbling driver took a long time wheeling it back to the hearse over the pitted blacktop of the alley.

Megan and Trudy were already taking prints and blood smears from the second body, while Ted, who had been shooting photos at speed, put the camera away for a few minutes and made a second set of sketches showing the dimensions of the ruined barrel and the original positions of both bodies inside it.

Trudy and Pokey were chatting collegially about blood and tissue work, fingernail scrapings. "And we'll take hair and fiber, of course," she said. "What about the trash barrel, though?" She turned to Ray. "You want us to—"

"Kinda hard to get in the van, huh?" he said. "We can take care of that here, can't we, Jake? The prints and the…uh…trace evidence." He surveyed the stinking garbage spread around the crime scene.

"Sure. If we find anything that needs analyzing, we'll get it up to them later." In the first half hour after his late arrival, Ray had put the rocky start behind him and begun to establish his authority over the crime scene. But the second body had thrown him off stride, and now he was slipping back into the habit of asking me questions. I did not want to stand in front of Frank's desk and discuss delegation again on Monday. But I was not about to leave a crime scene as chaotic as this one, either, so I said, "Ray, whaddya think? Let's get our crew together for a minute and decide where we go from here."

We stood in a circle against the wall opposite the Lotus Flower, in front of Casey's blue-and-white. Ray said, "Well, one thing, Rosie, I guess you've got your autopsy if you still want it."

"You bet," she said. "When?"

"Pokey hasn't got a time yet," he said. "Might be tomorrow afternoon, can you handle that?"

"Any time. Just let me know."

"Okay, if that's settled," I said, "what's anybody got so far?"

"Rigor looks fully established in both bodies," Lou said. "I'd say they were killed about the same time."

"Agreed," I said. "Anybody want to guess when that was?"

"Well," Ray said, "full rigor, you don't get that before six to twelve hours, give or take two or three, and it lasts maybe twenty-four."

"Or forty-eight," Lou said. "I've seen—"

"Okay," I said hastily. "We could go on and on with the variables. But the flies have been here, and the worms are just hatching, that argues for closer to twelve. Right? So"—we all looked at our watches—"getting close to noon. Two or three hours either side of midnight last night?"

"Or the night before," Lou said, stubbornly.

Darrell nodded. "Sometime after dark, anyway, right?"

"Mess like this?" Ray said. "I'd sure think so."

"I've only found two people who'll admit to being around here after dark last night," Rosie said, "and one of those was waiting tables in the vfw. The other one was a customer in Louie's Bar, two doors south. They both say they never heard a thing." She turned to Darrell. "You knocked on some doors. You find anybody who heard a fight?"

"No. But South Broadway? On Friday night? Not too surprising."

"I found this over behind the Dumpster," Lou said, holding up a shoe in a bag. "It could be from one of our victims. Or not."

"Man's brown oxford," I said. "Guys don't wear them much, anymore."

"They go with suits," Lou said. "The man in the blue shirt could have been wearing a suit, I guess."

"Or the other one might have," Darrell said. "How do we know?"

"We don't. And that's the next thing to get started on, I've been thinking," Ray Bailey said, "a thorough search of the alley here, both sides, all the way to both ends. Looking for clothes, a wallet, weapons, all the stuff that should be here and isn't."

"And another thing, Ray," Darrell said. "Let's be careful with the garbage that came out of the barrel, huh?" His bland, boyish face took on a shrewd expression. "You can learn a lot from garbage sometimes."

Humor glinted briefly in the depths of Ray Bailey's dark eyes, but he nodded solemnly. "Absolutely. Garbage containers, too. So I'd like to put you in charge of that detail, Darrell. Get all the garbage bagged up, find a way to get the barrel down to the station and processed for prints, and then go through the garbage and see if you can figure out where it came from." He turned away from

Darrell's fading enthusiasm and said, "Lessee, that leaves four of us, right?" He met my eyes. "If you're gonna stick around?"

"Sure," I said. "And when you're ready, Darrell, I'll help you take your barrel to the station in the pickup."

"Jeez," Darrell said, "now it's *my* barrel."

I stepped over to where Trudy knelt, zipping samples into a bag, and said, "Will your crew be going back pretty soon?"

"Half an hour or so. If we can get all this stuff checked into the lab fast enough, and they don't have any other calls, I might get home for dinner."

"How, though?"

"Megan can drop me at the farm, and I'll drive my car in. You going home?"

"No…I think I'll stick with this for a while. Lot to do—"

"Take care."

"You too." I touched the back of her arm above the elbow and walked back to my crew.

We each took a side, starting from the back door of the Lotus Flower, walking the length of the alley to the street, and doubling back. We tested doors and peered into cracks, checked the covers of manholes for any signs they'd been tampered with, and squeezed carefully into the narrow interstices between buildings. We looked for anything—weapons, clothing, medication, a purse, or a wallet—hoping all the time to get lucky and find something that would make us say, "Ah, so."

We kept at it for a little over two hours. I had the easiest section, the side with the fewest doors, on the short south end of the alley on the west side. Even so, I was the last one back to the rendezvous point, because I broke off my search to help Darrell load the Toter into my pickup and take it to the station, and stopped there to put the two homicides in BOLOs, the Be On the LookOut notices that are passed on to every shift as they come on duty. "I've got two pairs of panties, a fanny pack, and three empty vodka bottles," Rosie said, holding up her evidence bag when we met back at the rear of the Lotus Flower. We all showed similar finds: condoms, odd bits of clothing, empty half pints, and some dope paraphernalia that looked too dirty to have been used recently. None of our hoards looked at all helpful, though we agreed to turn everything in as possible evidence and get it fumed for prints.

It was five past three. Trudy and her BCA crew were gone. Milo had left before Pokey, who followed the hearse to see the bodies safely to the morgue and check on tomorrow's arrangements. Casey and Hanenburger were still with us, keeping people out of the alley.

"Wanna try another canvass?" I asked Ray.

"Yeah," he said, "but this time let's go in pairs. One to ask questions and make notes, one to watch people. Don'tcha think?"

"Suits me." I followed Rosie, watching people's faces as they answered her questions, listening to their voices. I was hoping to spot a witness I somehow knew was lying about last night, then jump on the lie and ride it wherever it led. We took the south end of the alley, talking to everybody we found on both sides. Ray followed Lou on the north end. At five-thirty we met again at the Lotus Flower Dumpster to share what we had learned, which was, essentially, nothing.

"We could try the canvass again later tonight," Lou said. "We'd catch a different bunch of folks." His face had turned the color of old putty, but he was revved, after his office-bound winter, by being out on the street with his peers.

"Ray's got an autopsy to attend tomorrow, Rosie may have one too," I said, "and we're busting the budget with all this overtime as it is. Let's hang it up for now."

They were all tired and hungry; they should have been glad to go, but they headed for their cars reluctantly, still peering into cracks as they walked away. I could see they all felt the way I did, that we must have been looking right at something important and missed it. Nothing obvious like clothing or a wallet—we wouldn't have missed that—but maybe a stain, a spatter, a shred of cloth. Or witnesses. Somebody had to have heard something, we all kept saying; there must have been a lot of what Kevin, who had only recently abandoned comic books, liked to call oof-splat-boom. Even if seasoned murderers had done this crime, they weren't magicians; they had to make noise to end two lives with such violence.

Except I bet they didn't end here, I thought suddenly as I backed out into rampaging Saturday-afternoon traffic on Third Street.

I had pulled many a night shift in this part of town while I wore the blue uniform, and I well remember what a lively scene its back alleys could be, especially on weekends. Rutherford's bottom feeders used them to fight, borrow money, have sex, and score pot. Between Friday afternoon and Saturday morning, one of the least convenient places in town to kill a guy would be the alley in back of the Lotus Flower.

So the victims were killed somewhere else and brought here? In the Toter? Awkward damn thing to move, in anything smaller than a pickup. And as Darrell and I had shown ourselves this afternoon, hard as hell to load and unload, even when it was almost empty. For a Toter with two bodies inside, I could guarantee you'd need a ramp.

But unless the bodies were in the container when it

came into the alley, it must have come from somewhere pretty close. Because even surrounded by the happy lunacy of a Friday night on South Broadway, murderers would not want to go rumbling around pushing a stolen Toter, while their friends followed with the bodies in—what? Automobiles dripping blood? Forget it, I decided; somehow the bodies came to the alley in the Toter.

I called the station to tell Darrell to get a list of locations for household garbage Toters from Rutherford Waste Management. Dispatch said he had just checked out. I got the shift captain on duty and asked him to add a request in BOLOs for all shifts to be alert in their neighborhoods for missing garbage containers. If we could pin down the area of the killing… "Darrell already asked me to do that," Spencer said.

"Give them a chance to show you," McCafferty's voice said in my head as I hung up, "that they deserve the confidence you've placed in them."

So since he was harassing my brain anyway, I called the chief at home and told him as much as I knew about the two homicides.

Which was not much. "No ID on the victims, no cause of death yet. Beaten to a pulp is my best guess—is that a medical diagnosis? Hard to believe they were killed where we found 'em, but damn hard to see how they got there otherwise."

"Sounds like you like this case a lot."

"Oh, you bet." Then I told him about the money in the top victim's mouth.

"Boy, the reporters are gonna love that," he said.

"Well, I believe we succeeded in holding that back. For today, anyway."

"You believe, but you're not sure?"

"I got the word to Milo before he did the TV shot, but

if anybody heard Ted Zumwalt when he said it out loud, it won't be long before it's out there.''

"For sure.'' He was quiet a few seconds, and I could hear him doing that tapping thing with one finger that he does when he thinks. "Does it feel like a gang thing to you? Or anything somebody…organized?''

"Because of the money?''

"And the fact there's no ID?''

"Maybe. There's really very little to go on so far, Frank. The one on top was wearing a shirt.''

"That's all? Just a shirt?''

"Which is one more item than the victim underneath was wearing.''

"Huh. So is this likely to get gross before we're done?''

"You mean a sex crime? Possible, I guess.''

"Better and better for the newspaper and TV. Chamber of Commerce will hate it.'' He was already thinking about damage control. "Well…so you got your full crew to work, finally, did you?''

"Everybody from People Crimes, yeah.'' I skipped over Bo Dooley's absence. "And a crew of three from BCA, plus Pokey and Milo and the driver from Dowd's, and three or four uniforms, most of the time. Tight squeeze in that little alley.''

"Who decided to do the autopsies here?''

"It was kind of a group decision. The first victim's scheduled for tomorrow; Pokey was still working on a date for the second one, last I heard. It's the best thing, Frank, they're lined up waiting in St. Paul.''

"Uh-huh. I just think the forensic docs up there sometimes find things the medical mind doesn't usually look for. But okay, no use arguing if it's already decided. Anyway, once we found everybody, our new system handled this homicide the way it's supposed to, right?''

''Exactly. People Crimes detectives working the scene, BCA techs collecting physical evidence, the coroner there to certify death, and Milo collecting information to start building a case, and talking to the media. By the book.''

''Yeah. That statement he gave the TV station, though, that only mentioned the first victim, right?''

''Uh…yeah, come to think of it. We hadn't found the second one when he did the interview. I'll call him, Frank.''

''Yeah, guess you better. Because the radio station guys were there after he left, weren't they? And the print reporters?''

''You're right. I better make sure they all have the same information, or all hell will break loose, huh?''

''Better believe it. I hate it when we have to put out news like this on the weekend.'' Frank sighed. ''People have all day Sunday to think about it, and by Monday half of Saint Kate's parish will be calling me up, asking what's happening to our nice little town.''

''Which it hasn't been for a while. Little, I mean,'' I added quickly into his silence.

TRUDY DIDN'T GET HOME for dinner. She called a few minutes after six to say she was on her way to Elk River with Ted. ''Couple of heroes got in a bar fight up there. Over a *pool game,* for God's sake. Now one's in the hospital, and the other one's dead. What is it about testosterone, anyway?''

''Be reasonable, Trudy,'' I said. ''If a guy keeps taunting you when you're taking your shot, you can't just stand there and do nothing.''

She groaned. ''Sometimes when I think that I've actually moved in with a man," she said, "I wonder if maybe my brain's gone soft."

"I'm crazy about you too, kid. Why is only Ted with you? What happened to Megan?"

"Funniest thing," Trudy said. "Jimmy called shortly after we got back to the lab and said to put her on the phone. She listened to him a minute and said, 'Yes,' and listened a little more and started to cry. She hung up and cried some more, and then said she had to go home. That was two hours ago, and we haven't heard from her since."

"Son of a gun. What do you think?"

"I don't know. I can't believe he'd just fire her like that without even talking about it, but I don't see what else it could be."

"Well...will you and Ted be able to manage all the jobs?"

"From a bar fight that turned into a homicide? I should hope so. We're not gonna be looking for rare and unusual clues." Trudy's point of view skews alarmingly toward hard-boiled as she nears the end of a week in the van.

"Well, but if you get any more cases tonight—" Her week was up at seven in the morning.

"Then we'll call Jimmy Chang and tell him to get us some help or stuff it," she said, sounding as if she might prefer the latter.

I nodded off in front of a *Seinfeld* rerun, woke with a start when I started to fall off the chair, set the coffee for 6:00 a.m., and went to bed alone. When the sound of a car in the yard woke me, I ran downstairs in brilliant sunshine and found Trudy coming through the door, white with fatigue. I poured coffee right away and drank a cup while she showered and I scrambled eggs.

"This bacon tastes so good, it's making my eyes water," she said.

"More toast?" She spread jam on her third piece and ate it with little purrs of pleasure. Big strong Swedish girls need their nourishment, and then, if they've been up all night, they need to snore like hogs for at least six hours before they're safe to be near. Before she tucked in, though, I brought the clothes hampers from the bathroom and bedroom and said, "You got the strength to talk me through that whole light-dark thing one more time? I'll do laundry today." She started a brief protest about how I didn't really have to do that, but abandoned it quickly when I reminded her how fragile my good intentions are.

For the next five minutes, I flung clothing into piles at her direction. When the hampers were empty, I told her she was the sexiest boss I'd ever worked for and received, in return, her assurance that if I would really do all that washing today, this evening she would fold my socks and jump my bones, not necessarily in that order. As soon as she was in bed, I bagged the laundry, checked my supply of soap and quarters, and drove to the Laundromat, still basking in the glow of my mate's approval.

I had been trying harder than usual to please her lately, because a little storm cloud was troubling our horizon. Trudy Hanson, the cool technology wonk whose hobbies were body-wedging up rock faces and rafting white water, who had the chutzpah to take a mixed-race man like me as a lover and live with him in proud disregard of objections from her picky mother and sister and God knows what comments from her friends, turned out to be not just careful with a dollar but frugal to a fault. She clipped supermarket coupons and recycled leftovers, composed a thoughtful budget every month, and followed it rigidly. "I know I'm kind of looney-tunes about money," she said once. "It's because of Mama."

"Oh-ho, the Blame Mama defense," I said.

''No, no, I'm not blaming her, it wasn't her fault my father walked off like that.''

''What?''

''Went to the grocery store and never came back. Mama had a hard time putting food on the table for a long time after that, and ever since, she's made every dollar count. And preached to us, 'You girls have got to learn to be careful with money'—''

''Trudy, that was them. This is us.''

''Oh, I know. But I still need to know where I stand.''

We thought our big problem, when we started talking about living together, was that our jobs were eighty miles apart. We solved that by finding an affordable rental halfway between Rutherford and St. Paul. The owners needed to bail out fast when the husband's job took him to another state. Moving in, we were like kids playing house. The shortcomings of the house seemed unimportant, since the rent was so low.

But once the owners got settled in Texas, they decided to sell the place. Between us, with some stretching, we managed the down payment. As soon as it was ours, though, the old farmhouse began to look less like a funky lifestyle choice and more like a problem requiring solutions. That's when we began to learn that money does not come in fixed amounts, as we had always thought. Money is flexible, even fluid. A terrifyingly large loan at a bank, for instance, can morph into a ridiculously puny pile of chump change while it's being carried to a building contractor.

Faced with this anomaly, all spring Trudy and I, whenever we could stand the pain, had been trying to prioritize the coming summer's household repairs.

I would begin by saying that, at a minimum, we had to install some decent insulation if we were going to stay here another winter. Trudy would point out that new insulation would be wasted unless we reshingled the roof. But, I would say, if we're gonna tear up the top of the house like that, we'd be crazy not to replace the wiring at the same time. Then we would visit building contractors and collect estimates, and find that we had already spent more than we could possibly borrow, and had not yet talked about repairing the furnace.

At that point, I would usually say that I really ought to sell the boat, and Trudy would remind me I wanted the farm in the first place mostly because it had a barn for boat storage. I would reply that I could hardly enjoy sitting in a fishing boat knowing I was too dumb to figure out how to fix up the house we lived in, and she would say something like, "There, you see, this is what I was afraid of, this farm is ruining our relationship."

"Aw, jeez, Trudy, don't start with that relationship stuff," I would plead, and then there'd be that long cool silence to get through again. We reached flash point in this conversation faster every time we returned to it. Thursday night, we had skipped over construction details entirely and gone straight to the money.

"We both have wallets full of credit cards," I said. "Now's the time to use them."

"Oh, Jake," Trudy said, shocked. "Pay those bandits what they charge? That's usury!"

"Maybe so, but it's legal. Nobody's getting arrested for it."

"It would take years to pay off. We'd pay times over."

"And we'd be living in a comfortable house while we paid it."

"I think it's irresponsible to throw away money like that."

"I think a man's reach should exceed his grasp." I was

pretty sure I'd read that somewhere, but I pretended I thought it up myself, and Trudy was too busy challenging my logic to worry about plagiarism. At the end of that conversation we took two long walks, one for each of us, in two different directions.

To me, it felt like a needless conundrum. We had moved in together because we had great mutual affection and respect, plus we could not walk past each other without wanting to cop a feel. Why let some unscheduled house repairs get in the way of the fun? I have the standard American attitude toward debt, which is that anything that keeps me from delaying gratification can't be all bad. But it was plain that Trudy wasn't going to be comfortable under a new roof if she was anxious about paying for it, so while I drove to the Deer Creek Laundromat and started the soap-and-quarters ritual, I told myself, for the twentieth time in a month, "Smarten up, Jake Hines. Think of something."

Nothing brilliant struck me while I watched a couple of hours of whirling cottons, so while the towels and Levi's finished drying, I took a stroll. I was not really headed for Mac's Bar, which I knew wasn't open, but the sidewalk led me past the place, and I found Ozzie Sullivan there, unlocking the door.

"Aren't you confused?" I said. "This is Sunday."

"Mac got this great idea," he said, "to install a stovetop and a microwave in the storeroom and call it a kitchen. So now we can serve burgers and potato skins and egg rolls, and he can give blue laws the finger and open Sundays. You wanna come in?"

"It's only a few minutes after eleven."

"Set your watch ahead. I won't tell if you won't." Ozzie was wearing the cynical, pissed-off expression he gets when the weather's good enough to farm but he has to tend bar instead. "I should be out harrowing my corn-field," he bitched as he popped the top on my beer. "A good day like this? But instead I'm in here still trying to earn seed money."

"Oz, if you want to talk about money," I said, "you should save your breath till you get somebody in here who knows something about it."

"You too? Ain't it the pits?" He shook his head. "I damn near broke even last year," he mused, holding a glass up to the light. "But I never have quite enough land. Or I can't afford the help when I need it." He finished polishing the glass and hung it upside down in a rack over his head. "You and Trudy, though, you both have good jobs in town. What's keeping you broke?"

"We bought the farm."

"That place you were renting from the Andersons? No kidding? You *bought* that place?" He tried to hide his amusement.

"Yup. Just a couple of crazy kids from the city." I did not appreciate his attitude. I would finish this beer, I decided, and leave.

"Cammy and Jeff were the same way about that place," he said. "They were always talking about what a great bed-and-breakfast it was going to make, but they spent the whole time they lived there fixing up one room." He chuckled. "Listen, though," he said, suddenly serious, "did you get all the land too?"

I shrugged. "It wasn't so much. Ten acres across the road from the house—"

"And another ten or twelve in the pasture out in back," he said, "and that great big yard."

"What, Cammy offered it to you first?"

"People around here pay attention to land. Have you decided what you're going to do with it?"

"Oh, I want a garden. Not too much this year, though. Have to fix up the house first."

He stared at me. "You're just going to let it sit there?"

"We didn't come out here to farm," I said. "We need to live halfway between our two jobs, and we both like the country."

Ozzie Sullivan eyed me appraisingly for a few seconds, and then smiled. "Time this bar bought you a beer," he said, and popped a fresh one.

"Oh, no, listen, I've got towels in the dryer—"

"They won't go anyplace." He waved airily. "Tell me what all's wrong with your house."

"Old age, mostly." I described the rotten shingles, the nonexistent insulation, and the brittle wiring.

"And I suppose you went to some of them contractors in Rutherford, and they offered to fix it up for about what you paid for the whole place to begin with?"

"Something like that."

"People out here," Ozzie said, thoughtfully, "do a lot of swapping." He had begun to look at me with interest. "You gonna be home later this afternoon? Probably if I came over after I'm done here, I could make some suggestions."

"Uh—" I felt a little shiver of reluctance. Ozzie had always seemed absolutely straight to me, but now I thought we were moving a little fast. "I'll be there. Trudy might still be sleeping. She worked all night last night."

"That's no problem. You can call me—you want some pretzels?" He put a sack of them by my fresh beer and wiped the counter all around me. "You just call me when it's convenient," he said, "and I'll come over."

I went back and folded my clothes into bags, moving a little slower from the pleasant fuzziness of two midday beers. At home, I set the bags in the kitchen and went back outside, where I did the quietest job on my weekend list, which was weeding the asparagus bed. Shortly after two, Trudy got out of bed and began wandering around the house, bumping into things and grumbling. I called Ozzie Sullivan.

"She's up," I told him, "but we better give her a couple of hours to get over being ornery. Can you make it around four?"

"Okay if my brother Dan comes along? He works in construction, and we help each other out sometimes."

They drove into the yard at two minutes after four, in the '81 Chrysler Imperial I had seen parked in front of Mac's Bar. It had a trunk that looked like it would hold another whole car, and the leather upholstery was still in amazingly good shape. Trudy was sitting in the lawn chair under the maple tree by then, wearing clean jeans and a sweatshirt out of my laundry piles, and blinking hazily at a mug of hot coffee I had just handed her. I offered beers to the Sullivans, but Ozzie said, "Let's take our tour first."

"You want to come along?" I asked Trudy.

She waved vaguely and said, "Maybe I'll catch up to you later."

They wanted to see the house first. We walked the roofline, edging carefully over the rotten asphalt shingles. Then we crawled in through the attic window and crouched around the damp, cobwebby space between the joists, peering out of holes and assessing water damage. Dan Sullivan produced a metal tape and called dimensions to Ozzie, who wrote them in a small lined notebook.

"Now the cellar," Ozzie said. I walked them around the furnace, explaining my theories of why it didn't work. Then we followed the wiring from the fuse box to the kitchen, around the walls of the first floor and up the stairs, while Ozzie clucked and Dan shook his head.

"Okay," Ozzie said, "I guess we got a pretty fair grasp of the problems. Now show us the goodies." He seemed brighter and more engaged out here than he ever had at the bar. The brothers were physically similar, with straight sandy hair, clear blue eyes, and small mouths. The balance of power between them was interesting; Ozzie did most of the talking, but whenever Dan muttered or gestured, his brother turned to him with quick attention.

We walked the pasture first. Then I drove my pickup north on the main street of Mirium, did a U-turn, and came back and repeated the maneuver on the county road so they could see two sides of our ten acres of alfalfa and weeds.

"Whatcha got in the barn?" Dan asked suddenly, the first question he had not transmitted through Ozzie.

"Oh…just some tools and my boat. You wanna see?" The Sullivan brothers turned toward me like sunflowers toward the sun and nodded.

They climbed into the two haylofts, nimble as billygoats, came back down in a few minutes, and walked together, muttering, around the dusky space between. When they stopped by my aluminum Pro-V, I pulled the cover off and showed them the live well, the outboard, the little trolling motor and adjustable seats. They circled the boat, looking canny, asking the usual questions about age, horsepower, handling, and speed. Somehow I felt they already knew most of the answers.

They helped me put the cover back on, and we went out in the yard, where I showed them the asparagus bed and raspberry bushes. For the first time since the moment in the bar when I told him we bought the farm, Ozzie Sullivan looked at me with respect.

"Asparagus," Ozzie said. "Takes years to get started right. And these berries—you really got something here, Jake."

"Thanks," I said, "we're starting to like it a lot."

Dan muttered something, and Ozzie said, "What do you say we come back and see you in a couple of days? Me and Dan," he explained, "need to figure out a few things."

Who doesn't? "That'll be fine," I said. "We'll be right here." I only meant to remind them there was no commitment on either side, but they blinked at me as if I might have said something devious. They walked past the empty chair where Trudy had been sitting, to where Ozzie's faded blue car stood in the front yard. Dan got in and sat silently, facing forward, blinking thoughtfully. Ozzie shook hands, slid into the driver's seat, and then, with his hand on the ignition key, rolled down the window to say, "You pretty much got your materials estimates already, huh?"

"Oh, indeed," I said. "Several lists."

"Good," he said. "'Cause we'll just be talkin' about labor, of course."

"Understood," I said.

Watching them roll out of the yard, I halfway wished I had never let Ozzie talk me into getting involved with them. In the bar, I had thought he was just interested in trading labor for the use of my land. Now it was obvious he was after my boat as well, and I was beginning to wonder if he thought they could move my asparagus bed. We were neighbors in this small community. If we got into hard bargaining that left either side dissatisfied, we might not be friends anymore.

In the kitchen, Trudy looked up from slicing boiled potatoes into a bowl and said, "What was that all about?"

"I'm not entirely sure," I said, "but I think the Sullivan boys want to make us an offer on remodeling the house."

"Ah." She sliced another potato and said, "Let's not talk about it tonight, huh? I need to be a little better rested before I tackle that subject again."

"Agreed," I said. "You want me to grill some hamburgers to go with that potato salad?"

"That'd be good," she said.

"And then after supper"—I moved a little closer—"didn't we talk about folding socks and stuff?"

FOUR

MONDAY MORNING, four grunting teamsters carried crates
containing a high-gloss oak conference table and eight
chairs up the broad front stairway of the Government Center and down the hall to the People Crimes section of the
investigative wing. They set them up in the space between
Ray Bailey's almost-finished office and the cubicles of his
crew. I heard the nerve-jarring scrape of the heavy chairs
on the bare floor and braced myself for a lot of angry
questions about when the new carpet was coming. But
when I walked into the bright space under the skylight a
few minutes later, I found the whole People Crimes crew
seated around the table, already conferring, if that's what
you call making a mess with notebooks and coffee cups
while they jeered at Darrell Betts.

"Number eight," he read from a sheet of paper, "he
wants to transfer to the K-9 Unit because he's decided he
looks good in a collar—"

"What's going on?" I said.

"Stupid cop jokes Darrell just copied off the Internet,"
Rosie said. "It's called, 'Ten signs your partner needs a
vacation.'"

"Number seven, he wants you to call him Judge
Dredd—"

"I hate to interrupt the entertainment segment of your
morning," I said, "but could we take a few minutes to

talk about this murder that's all over the newspaper?'' The *Times-Courier* had given it front-page, above-the-fold coverage on Sunday, and had a follow-up, mostly a re-write of the same material, as the lead story this morning, under a tall headline that read, ''Murder Victim Had Mouthful of Cash.''

''So much for holding something back,'' I said. ''Who leaked?''

''Pitman, for one,'' Lou said. ''He feels awful. But you sent him back to the station before you got the word out to all of us that you weren't gonna release that information. A reporter at the TV station heard a rumor about the money, and the cameraman remembered seeing Andy there, so he called him at home.''

''Even so,'' I said, ''he should have known not to talk about a case we're working on.''

''They tricked him. Asked him how much money the dead man had in his mouth, and before he thought, he said nobody knows that yet. After that he clammed up, but they could tell they made a good guess, so they went after the hearse driver and the gurney guy at the lab.''

''Cute.'' I made a note to tell Kevin to finish Pitman's indoctrination, but really, I had known the crime scene was too big and porous to hold a secret for long.

''Jake, time out?'' Ray said. ''I gotta tell you, this new table's great. We're gonna use it all the time.''

''I can see that.'' I pulled a chair out, wincing at the noise. ''And the new carpet's due any minute. Now. I'd like to review the crime scene again. In retrospect, what stands out for each of you?''

''You mean besides two naked bodies in a barrel?'' Darrell said. ''Kinda hard to top that.''

''Well—'' Lou French said, and sneezed. ''There was my big find''—wheeze—''of one brown shoe.'' Searching dusty cracks in the alley hadn't done his asthma any good at all.

Dooley sat motionless, watching. I had briefed him on the new homicides as best I could before the meeting, but he was still playing catch-up. The rest of the crew were avoiding asking why he had not been with them Saturday by pretending he did not exist. The silence around him was almost palpable, like a presence.

"Is everybody satisfied with our search?" I looked around. "Have you thought of anything we ought to do over?"

"We went over everything twice," Ray said, "didn't we? Jiggled all the door handles, looked in all the cracks."

"Talked to all the store owners," Rosie said, "all the bystanders. Must have talked to two hundred people Saturday."

"And got?"

"Squat. I haven't typed up my tapes yet, but I know what's in 'em." She raised her hands, palms up. "Nobody heard anything, nobody saw anything."

"You doing any good with your garbage search, Darrell?"

"I haven't been through it all yet, but so far it looks like household garbage that coulda come from anyplace. Not much paperwork in it. The fingerprint guys are dusting the barrel this morning and fuming some lids and cans I found."

"How about finding out where the container belongs?" I asked him.

"I found a number on it and called Rutherford Solid Waste Management Saturday afternoon. Got a message tape that said they'd be back in the office Monday morning. Gonna call 'em as soon as we're outa here and ask 'em where that number belongs and follow on from there.''

"Good man. Okay, let's talk about the autopsies. Pokey did them both yesterday?"

"Yeah," Bailey said, "with that Dr. Stuart at the Hampstead County Lab. Aren't they a stitch together?"

"Yeah. Dr. Rambunctious and Dr. Sedate. So, you attended the first one—"

"John Doe number one. First guy out of the barrel. Rosie took number two."

"And you got what from that?"

"Both docs agree with us," Ray said, "from the temperature of the bodies, development of rigor mortis, and flies' eggs and so on, that the two men probably died at or close to the same time. But they're as cagey as usual about when that might have been. Twelve to thirty-six hours before we found them, they think."

"Told you," Lou said.

"And both docs say they're not ready to decide the cause of death yet."

"Of either victim?"

"That's right."

"What, too many options?"

"That's part of it, I guess. So many injuries, all so"— he looked at Rosie—"what's the word Dr. Stuart kept using?"

"Profound." Rosie rustled through her notes. "About John Doe number two they said, 'Insults to the spinal cord might have been fatal. Damage to kidneys, liver, and spleen could have been fatal. Large number of broken bones could have resulted in shock sufficient to cause death.'"

"Furthermore, my guy was sodomized," Ray said. He

tried to be matter-of-fact, but he had trouble getting the word out.

"So this is a sex crime?" Darrell asked.

"Well, duh," Ray said, "what did I just say? Except John Doe number two wasn't raped." He looked at Rosie. "Isn't that what you said?"

"That's right. No sign of anal intercourse on number two. Which seems odd, doesn't it?" Rosie looked around the table. Everybody shrugged.

"Doesn't seem any odder than everything else about Saturday," Lou said.

"Well, I mean," Rosie said, "they were in the same *barrel* together."

"Rosie, it isn't catching, like a head cold."

"Still," Rosie said. "You'd think whoever…" She let the thought trail off.

"But to get back to cause of death," Ray said, "the main reason they don't want to decide yet is both docs saw reason to believe that many of the injuries might have been inflicted after death."

"After death?" Lou looked up over his glasses. "What kind of sense does that make?"

"Hey, I'm not a doctor, how do I know what kind of sense anything makes?" Ray turned a page, looking his most gloriously gloomy, and added, "Boy, I realized yesterday, those guys live in a whole other *world*. They talk English, most of the time, but still it's not the language of my tribe, you know what I mean?"

"Do I ever," Rosie said. "My notes have query marks all over them." She read a sample. "Bruising shows little QQQsubdural something…contingent upon results of tissue studies from QQQ—" She turned a couple of pages. "Dr. Stuart said both bodies were, quote, extremely difficult to read, unquote"—she looked up from her notes and grinned—"and Pokey said, 'Difficult? Is whole friggin' course in forensics.'"

"Hey, you give good Pokey," Lou said.

"Don't worry," I said. "When they're done, they'll deliver their conclusions in plain English. Mostly."

"But not right away." Ray scowled around the table. "They want to run some further tests, they said. They think they'll have a decision in a couple of days."

"Oh? This keeps getting odder. Tell me again," I asked him, "they think a lot of that body damage—broken arms and legs and so on—that might have been inflicted after the victims were dead?"

"Even number one's broken neck," Ray said. "They agreed it would have been sufficient to cause death, but they didn't want to say it's what killed him, and they found reason to believe it might have been broken after he was dead."

"Same with number two," Rosie said. "'Several spinal fractures which would certainly be life-threatening,'" she read. "But they didn't want to identify any of them as the fatal one. They didn't even want to confirm, at first, that the victim was Mexican."

"Confirm it?" I said. "Who ever said he was?"

"I did." Looking around at surprised faces, she said, "Well, he *looks* Mexican. Didn't you all think so?"

"He just looked very dead to me," Darrell said.

"And totally beat all to hell," Lou said.

"Honestly. Men," Rosie said.

"Whaddya mean, *men?*" Darrell said. "What kinda crack is that?"

"Yeah, Rosie," Lou said. "If one of us said, *'Women,'* like that, you'd have us up on harassment charges."

"Well, I'm sorry," she said, suddenly contrite, "you're right, that would make me mad. But it just seems to me sometimes," she burst out, her voice rising, "like men don't ever want to *notice* anything."

"Notice what, for chrissake, Rosie?" Ray said. "What're you talking about?"

"Think about it," she said. "The way his mustache was trimmed. Longer on the ends than you usually see here, and slanting out across his cheek like this. Remember his hair? Very black and thick, and wavy, not curly, and the way it was cut, that slant across the ear that men around here don't do anymore—and didn't you all see the shape of his forearms?"

"Rosie, his arms were packed into a space the size of a king-size bagel," Ray said.

"Maybe so, but they still had that characteristic curve that mestizo men's arms have," she said stubbornly. She waited a few seconds. "Of course, I saw him after he'd softened up quite a bit," she offered helpfully.

Around the table, male faces regarded her with mounting amazement. Finally Darrell asked her, "How were his toenails trimmed, Rosie?" and everybody laughed but Bo and me. Bo wasn't laughing about anything, and I was thinking that I agreed with her about the hair.

She shrugged nervously and finished, "I asked the doctors what they thought, but they said they didn't know, they didn't care. Pokey said race is a social construct and irrelevant in science. I said, That's good to know, but I'm a detective, and what do you think about his teeth? So then finally Dr. Stuart said, Well, now that you mention it, those gold fillings do look a little offbeat, what do you think, Pokey? But Pokey wasn't interested, so Dr. Stuart called a dentist friend of his, who came over even though it was Sunday, because he got interested. He said he goes sailing every winter in the Sea of Cortez, and after he looked in the victim's mouth, he said he'd bet his Mexican fishing permit those fillings were done in Mazatlán, Puerto Vallarta, along in there.''

Lou French sat back in his chair and said softly, ''I'll be a son of a bitch.''

''So is it confirmed?'' I asked her. ''John Doe number two is Hispanic?''

''Mexican,'' she said. ''I'm pretty sure.''

''Good. Good for you, Rosie.'' I looked from her to Ray, who shrugged and turned his hands up. ''I give. Anything else?'' She shook her head.

''They talked a lot,'' Ray said, turning to another page in his notes, ''about some spots under my guy's eyelids?'' He shook his head. ''Totally threw me a curve. I mean, with everything else that was wrong with this guy? I couldn't understand why Pokey would get all concerned about spots under his eyelids. Then they opened him up and found the same kind of spots on his lungs and a couple on his heart, and they both pointed and said, 'See, see?' ''

''They're considering suffocation,'' I asked him, ''along with all this beating?''

''Ah, you know about these little purple spots, huh? I finally just asked them, what *about* the spots? And they told me they're considering he might have been asphyxiated.''

''Well, he did have a mouthful of money,'' I said. ''Maybe he choked on that.''

''I suggested that, but they said there would have been, uh, emesis—that means vomit—on the money if he choked on it, and there wasn't any. So they think probably the money was put in his mouth after he was dead, too.''

''Jesus,'' Darrell said, ''lotta fooling around with dead bodies here. Booga booga booga.''

''For sure,'' Lou said. ''Make a helluva Stephen King

plot so far. So now, shall we add to the list of things we didn't find in that alley, some kind of a suffocation device? A towel, a blanket? A pillow with the victim's blood and hair all over it?''

''Or a roll of Saran Wrap,'' Ray said.

''Saran Wrap? Would that work? I suppose it would,'' Rosie said. ''You find any wrapping material in that garbage, Darrell?''

''No.''

''We didn't have time to go through the Dumpster, though,'' Ray Bailey said. His crew all looked at him with fear and loathing. ''So I impounded it,'' he said.

''You did?'' I beamed at him. ''Were you able to get it sealed?''

''Yup. The city owns it. It's one of their twenty-cubic-yard roll-off models. Sealed and sitting on the impound lot alongside of three stolen cars.'' He tried to look modest.

''How'd you do all that so fast on a weekend?''

''I got that same answering tape Darrell got,'' Ray said. ''But then I remembered that the manager of Rutherford Solid Waste Disposal is a buddy of my uncle Ed's. Fern Plenge, you guys know him? Taught me how to fish for suckers with worms when I was about seven. Helluva nice guy, I think he's spent his whole life trying to be so nice nobody'll notice that his name is Fern. Anyway! I called him at home. Soon as he heard about my problem he had a crew bring a fresh Dumpster to the alley behind the Lotus Flower, and they picked up the original one and delivered it to us. While he was at it, of course''—he looked morose—''he told me a lot more about solid waste disposal than I ever wanted to know.'' Then he looked around the table and actually smiled at his crew, a big sunny smile that made them all sit up in alarm. "So we're all gonna be going through garbage today."

"Eeooww," Rosie said.

"Boy, it's just one bold career move after another for you, kid," Lou French said, clapping her on the back. "Dead bodies in the alley Saturday, garbage today."

"Besides a pillow or some wrapping material, what else are we looking for?" Darrell asked. "Clothes?"

"Clothes, shoes, wallets, car keys, credit cards," Ray ticked off on his fingers. "All the things those two bodies didn't have on them that they should have."

"Wait a minute," I said, "let's get this straight. Are you looking for something that could have been used to suffocate the man, or are you talking about a device for strangulation?"

Ray Bailey turned his hands up. "They said there weren't any marks on his neck from ligatures."

"I don't get it. I always thought those red marks were from strangulation."

"All I know is what I've got written down here," he said. "Couldn't find ligature marks on the neck, but purple-red dots under the eyelids."

"Shee. Okay, if suffocated, a pillow, a garment, a sack. If strangled, some way that left no marks—"

"Except there were marks all over this guy," Ray said. "You saw him."

"True. So then possibly a chain or cord—"

"But this suffocation deal isn't for sure yet, remember, and primarily we're looking for ID. Also heavy weapons, a pipe or sledgehammer that could inflict massive wounds like we saw Saturday. Remember?" French, Doyle, and Betts nodded solemnly.

"Can we draw some coveralls from the supply room?" Bo asked. It was his first question since we sat down.

Ray's glance, which had been sliding past him all morning, came to rest briefly on his top shirt button. "Sure," he said, keeping his voice neutral, "good idea."

This isn't fair to either one of them, I thought; I've got to let Ray know about Bo's special arrangement.

"Darrell," Ray said, "I want you to finish your Toter inquiry first. Come and tell me as soon as you find out where it belongs. Lou, are garbage fumes gonna make you cough too much?"

"Nah," Lou said, "outside I should be okay."

"Good. Also, Lou, Darrell, Rosie, give all your notes and tapes, from the crime scene and the autopsy both, to LeeAnn for transcription before you start on the Dumpster."

"You serious?" Lou said.

"Sure," Ray said, "this is your bigger, better People Crimes division. We have a full-time steno now, waiting to take routine drudgery off our hands."

"Hot damn," Rosie said.

Ray told them all he would catch up to them at the Dumpster as soon as he made a few phone calls. As his crew filed out, I said, "I know you're busy, but I think we ought to talk a minute."

"Me too," he said. His own new office still had no glass in its surrounding windows, so he followed me into mine and closed the door.

"First, I want to say how pleased I am by the way you've taken hold of this case," I said. "Good work, Ray."

His mouth flattened out in his usual just-barely smile, and he said, "Thanks for not ragging on me about being late."

"No problem. Now. That shirt the number-one John

Doe was wearing, we took it off before we sent the body to the morgue, didn't we?''

"Yes. But nobody thought about it till the BCA van was gone." He looked apologetic. "It's in the evidence room. The shoe, too, the one Lou found."

"Good. The money too? Out of the victim's mouth?''

"Yes. Two fives and three ones."

"Okay. I'd like to have a look at those items today, okay? We can send 'em to BCA tomorrow along with''— I gave him a pussycat smile—"all the good stuff you're gonna find in that Dumpster today."

"I know it's a remote possibility," he said, "but I thought we had to try."

"Of course. Now, about Bo Dooley.'' To tell him about my forty-hour-week arrangement, I had to tell him why I made it.

"I knew about his wife," Ray said. "Everybody knows. Does he really think he can keep a secret like that in a police station? But thanks for telling me about the work arrangement. I can live with it, Jake, for now—''

"I'm starting to wonder if you can," I said. "It puts me between you and one of your crew, doesn't it?''

Ray nodded. "It's gonna have to be one way or the other before long," he said. "Bo's been sort of in a little capsule by himself ever since he came here, hasn't he? And if you were willing to put up with that, the rest of us thought we could too. But now—is he on my crew or not? I can work with one less man, Jake, if you want to keep him in vice detail and let him make his own hours. What I can't put up with is a guy on my crew who doesn't answer to me. It's gonna cause trouble all up and down the line."

"I see that now. Give me a couple of days to work it

out, will you? For right now he's just on garbage detail with everybody else, agreed?''

Deep in Ray Bailey's dark brown eyes, a glint of gratification showed for just a second. Otherwise, his face never changed as he said, ''Right.''

''But the other thing I wanted to suggest is this: as soon as you finish digging out the Dumpster, I think we might want to ask Bo to start calling his snitches.''

''About what?''

''The chief suggested that money stuffed in the mouth and the complete lack of any ID on these bodies seems almost like a mob hit. Or a gang. He seemed to think it had that feel to it.''

''With no gunshots? And all these injuries? Seems to me more like somebody gone berserk.''

''I know. So many details seem inconsistent with so many others. So—if organized crime seems like an unlikely theory to you, let's try to eliminate it first. If we can do that, we'll go on to your idea, the angry rampage.''

''Where I admit right away I got questions. I mean, in the first place, two victims? Not the usual fight. Or the typical jealous husband scenario.''

''No. But maybe some kind of revenge.''

''Yeah. You anxious about this vice angle? You want me to pull him off the Dumpster?''

''No,'' I said, ''I think it would be good for team spirit if he sorted garbage today.''

Ray's a circumspect person who doesn't make eye contact often, but he looked right at me then, nodded in a satisfied way, and said, ''Agreed.''

I powered through a pile of messages before the chief called and asked for a progress report. He was afraid if he didn't keep feeding the media, they'd start trolling again for rumors.

"It's a damn shame they got hold of the news about the money," he said. "Two bodies in a trash barrel had 'em excited enough. Now they're all over me like ants at a picnic. So tell me again, now, what else have you got that you want to hold back on?"

"You kidding? Except for what's already out there, we don't know a damn thing."

"You still don't know who they are? Or have any indication where they came from?"

"Who says they're not from here?"

He chewed on his teeth awhile. "Rutherford folks haven't shown much inclination to stuff each other into trash barrels," he offered, "historically."

"It's been more the exception than the rule in the population generally, I believe."

"No shit?" He kicked his desk. "You feel sure about that?" Kicking doesn't always mean he's angry. His feet are too big for the space under his desk; he's always trying to resettle them.

"There is one thing. Rosie got convinced from things she saw at the autopsy that the victim in the bottom of the barrel might be Mexican. We haven't proved it. It's just an idea."

"Anybody agree with her?"

"The guys seemed to think it was kind of a stretch."

"So really, you've got nothing I don't already know." He shifted impatiently.

"Can't you just *say* we're holding back some details? You know, in order to blah blah blah—" I waved my hands vaguely.

"You mean a few minor details like the identity of the victims and how they died?"

"People have gotten kind of used to hearing it. And it

makes us sound smart instead of dumb. Better than admitting we don't have a clue."

"Damn, Jake, I'm glad you came in here and helped me with this. Go," he said, seeing me look at my watch. "Keep me in the loop, though. Everything, hear?"

"Absolutely."

I went back into my office, called Pokey, and said, "Lunch?"

He chuckled merrily. "You want to pick old Polack's brain, you gotta buy."

"Deal. I thought you were Ukrainian."

"Is border town. Soviet Union, Ukraine, Poland, depends which year."

"Okay. Noon at Victor's?"

"Quarter after. Bring plenty money, hah? Takes lotta red meat to get me through tough hard-hitting probes by keen-eyed detectives." Pokey seemed to find me more than usually amusing this morning.

I went back to my In basket, trying to get a clear desk so I could concentrate on the shirt, the shoe, and the money. Kevin Evjan found me swearing over the last two pieces of paper when he tapped urgently on my door frame half an hour later, saying, "Jake, could you step over to Grant Hisey's office with me for a minute?"

"Why?"

"Because he's got a guy over there—you know how I was gonna put the run on those swindlers with the story in the paper?"

"Oh." I'd forgotten. "And?"

"Looks like I haven't quite succeeded yet." He bounced a couple of times on the balls of his feet and said, "Just come and listen a minute, willya?"

So in the name of being there for my crew, and also because it's hard to resist Kevin Evjan when he's in Roman candle mode, I followed him out of the Rutherford Police Department and across the landing to the Hampstead County Sheriff's Department. Sheriff Hisey, a raw-boned fortyish guy with rough farmer's hands that he earned as a boy on his father's farm and maintains by helping his kids in 4-H on weekends, waved to a pasty-faced bald man standing in front of his desk. "Jake, this is Louie Forsell."

"Louie owns the Chicken Shack," Kevin said, in a kind of proprietary way, as if he were passing me a drumstick.

"Been there many times," I said, shaking hands. The Chicken Shack is a one-room beer tavern with a loud jukebox, several miles out on the Eyota road, one of those places you drive out to when you want to get crazy. All the food there is stiff and salty, and so is the clientele, usually, before the night's over.

"I always seem to end up dancing when I go to your place," I said, "sometimes even with girls." I was watching Grant Hisey for a clue. The Chicken Shack is his turf. Rutherford PD and the sheriff's office cooperate when we need to, of course, but we don't trot cases back and forth across the landing.

"Grant called me," Kevin said quickly, "because I showed Frannie's story to a couple of the guys over there"—by now he had probably shown it to most of Rutherford—"and he figured I'd want to hear about this latest caper. This time I think we can go after these swindlers. We've got a clear case of child abuse, reckless endangerment of a child, something like that."

I could feel my face getting hot. I had just come from two meetings where we bemoaned how little we knew about a grim double homicide. I could not possibly work fast enough to satisfy the urgent demands of my job today, and now I was trapped over here in an inane conversation about an incident that didn't concern me because it was outside my jurisdiction. All this because Kevin had been showboating around the building with his silly newspaper story, flaunting his cases outside the department.

Trying hard to keep my voice even, I said, "Not we. Grant."

"What?"

"Louie's place is in Hampstead County. Not in Rutherford."

Kevin and Grant and Louie Forsell all cocked their heads a little to one side, like dogs listening to distant thunder. Their faces all said I was being a prick about a bureaucratic detail, and they were trying to figure out why any decent person would behave like that. I began counting silently backward from five thousand by fifteens.

"Jake," Kevin said, "Louie took time out of his busy day to come in here and tell us about this incident, because he thought we should do something about this helpless little child being put in a box, in a bar, in the middle of the night—"

I opened my mouth to say, "In the county of Hampstead, not in the city of Rutherford," but I had reached four thousand nine hundred and ten, and the roaring in my ears had quieted down a little, so I asked him, grudgingly, "What do you mean, in a box?"

"Tell him," Kevin said, looking at Louie Forsell.

"About ten o'clock Friday night, this middle-aged man with a red nose—"

"Mr. Murphy Game, again," Kevin said, and I shushed him with my hand.

"—came in with a pretty little girl with blond hair down her back, maybe eight years old. He asked the waitress, was it okay if she had a Coke while he had a beer?

Waitress said sure, and they got their drinks, and he started talking to a couple of guys at the next table.''

Forsell rubbed his face, yawned hugely, and said, ''Fridays we get a rush right after work, then it's pretty quiet till around ten-thirty, when people start gettin' offa swing shifts in town and the games are over, then we're busy till closing. So I noticed the man with the little girl when he first came in; then the place filled up, and I forgot about them. He got her some nachos and I think he had another beer, and by then he was talking to half a dozen people at the tables around him. Everybody was having a good time, so I let him alone.''

When Forsell noticed the man again, he had a couple of dozen people around him, mostly men, all about half in the bag, buying rounds and trading loud jokes. Louie began to keep his eye on the group, which kept growing till almost everyone in the bar was crowded around the red-nosed man, who had begun to talk about some kind of a bet.

A dark-skinned man had joined the crowd around the man and his little girl, and now he went outside and brought back a big cardboard box. When Louie looked up from pouring a half-dozen pitchers, he saw that the blond-haired child was standing on her chair. Her father said something jokingly in her ear, and then lifted her gently and set her inside the box. She looked around at the ring of red-faced beer drinkers surrounding the box, and smiled as if she was enjoying the attention. Her father took off his jacket, and she folded it carefully into the bottom of the box and sat down on it. Somehow then a couple of big rolls of tape appeared from somewhere, and the dark man who had found the box got ready to tape the lid. But the red-nosed man stopped him and said, ''Who wants to bet?''

Most of the drinkers began holding up twenties and yelling. The red-nosed man took their names and wrote their bets in a little notebook he had. Soon he had a fistful of money, and the bettors began yelling that Louie should hold the money. So Louie held the bets while the red-nosed man wrote the names and amounts in his book. When all the bets were in, the dark-skinned man taped the lid shut. He had found some twine somewhere, and he tied that around the box several times, too.

Louie got nervous then and said, ''She's going to run out of air in there before long.''

''Don't worry,'' her father said, grinning, ''she always gets out in plenty of time.'' He said to the man with the tape, ''You got a car here?''

''Oh, sure,'' the dark man said, and the father said, ''Good, you can be the one who gives my baby a ride.'' He yelled to the crowd around him, ''Come on, you better watch me load her in the car so you know it's not a trick,'' and they all followed him outside.

''They made me go with 'em,'' Louie said. ''They said, 'You got the money, you better see this.' Everybody was sorta crazy by then, seemed like. So I called my cook in from the kitchen to watch the bar, and we all went out in the parking lot, and the two men put the cardboard box in the backseat of an old Buick that was there. 'Just drive her over to the city park in Dover,' the father said. 'We'll meet you there in fifteen minutes, and if she's still in the box, I'll pay all these guys double.' They watched the man drive away, and the father said, 'Hey, plenty of time, let's finish our beers first.' So we all walked back into the shack, me still holding this fistful of cash, and the little blond girl was sitting at the table she'd just left, smiling and drinking her Coke.''

''How'd she get there?'' Hisey asked Forsell.

"I don't know."

"Surely your cook saw something," I said.

"He says he was stocking the beer cooler like I told him to, and he bent over to put some bottles on the bottom shelf, and when he stood up, she was sitting at the table."

"You believe him?"

He shrugged. "He's worked for me five years, and I've never caught him lying. Why would he start with this?"

"Okay. What next?"

"Everybody came back in the bar, and the father went over to his little girl and said, 'Boy, you did that fast tonight, honey,' and she smiled at him and shrugged. He laughed around at all the people there, threw his arms in the air, and said, 'I have no idea how she does it!'

"He came over and got the money I was holding, and took his little girl by the hand and headed for the door. But a couple of guys got in front of him and said, 'No, you don't, you're going to Dover with us, and we're all going to look at that box we put in the car.' But just then that old Dodge came roaring up to the door of the shack, and the dark man jumped out of it and came running in, looking scared. When he saw the little girl standing there he fell down on his knees and said, 'Oh, Madre de Dios, thank God you are here,' and he hugged her with the tears running down his face.

"He told us he was driving east on the road to Dover when he heard a little noise like a balloon popping, and he looked in the backseat of his car and saw that the box was gone."

"Come on, Louie," Grant Hisey said, "that's crazy."

"I know it," Forsell said. "Don't you think I know it? But the dark man kept carrying on with all this crying and thanking God, and then he said somebody get him a beer, for the love of God, he was gonna pass out in a minute, and while everybody was crowded around him giving him beer and asking questions, that guy with the red nose took his money and his kid and got out of there.''

''And the dark man, did he—'' Kevin said.

''He stayed for a couple of beers and told the story several more times. Then I called last call, and he went in the men's can, and I never saw him again.''

Kevin was getting excited, saying, ''I think this time we've really got him.''

''Got him where?'' I said. ''Do you know where he is? When you find him, are you going to put him in jail for betting in a bar?''

''But, Jake, putting a kid in a box—''

''Did she scream, put up a fight? Talk to some social workers. Ask them how much documentation it takes to get a child away from even the most abusive parents.''

''In a box, in a bar, in the middle of the night,'' Kevin said stubbornly. ''It's depraved, for God's sake.'' He looked at Grant Hisey.

''I don't like it either,'' Grant said, ''especially when you tell me they're teaching the kid how to steal. Talk to Family Services, why don't you? If you find anybody who wants to move on it, I'll sign the complaint forms.''

When Grant started going over the story again, I looked at my watch, stood up, and said, ''Excuse me, Grant, I've got to go.''

Kevin looked up, startled, as I walked past him. He said a quick good-bye to Grant and followed me out.

''Kevin,'' I said when he caught up to me on the landing, ''you know we're working a new homicide?''

''Uh…yeah, I heard. Right downtown, huh?''

''And two victims.'' I unlocked the door to our side of the building. Inside, I added softly, ''Packed one on top of another in the same trash barrel.''

"Wow. And no ID, I heard."

"Right. So Darrell's had to come back over to People Crimes—I suppose he explained that to you, didn't he? And we'll almost certainly be calling on the rest of your crew for help before long. This is an ugly case, you understand that? The two victims were badly battered, there's a lot of brutality involved, including some sexual abuse. Anxiety will be high, as the paper's so fond of saying. The chief is going to be getting those concerned calls from citizens, and we need to show him we're doing all we can."

"So you're saying—"

"Get your new detectives on the street interviewing whatever property crimes you've got that need follow-up, get current cases caught up as fast as you can. Quit playing cops and robbers with these two-bit grifter complaints and get your desk clear." I gave him a hard stare, the best Frank McCafferty imitation I could manage without Frank's pop-eyed twin blues. "Get focused."

He was shocked. He's always been teacher's pet, bright and energetic, an altar boy and an Eagle Scout. In his whole life, he could probably count on one hand the number of times he's been reprimanded. He hated it; his face got bright red, and his mouth trembled before he clamped it shut.

But ambition had her hook in Kevin too. He wanted that office with his name on the door more than he wanted to argue with me. He swallowed once, hard, said, "Gotcha," turned and went into his office. I heard him yelling, "Clint! Andy?" and his new detectives came hurrying along the hall as I sat down at my desk.

FIVE

BEFORE I WENT BACK into my office, I stopped at the steno desk, one place where reorganization was demonstrably working, thanks to LeeAnn Speer. A single mother in her mid-thirties, left jobless last summer when the computer consulting firm she worked for went belly-up, she had passed a battery of tough tests to get hired for the Rutherford PD support staff. I picked her out of the pool there because her test scores were so high, and her supervisor didn't want to let her go.

Openly pleased to get the small raise I could offer, she jumped at the chance to create a niche of her own. She was a little tense right now from trying to please everybody, but I thought she'd be fine if we could resist piling too much work on her.

Her desk space was a shoehorn job in the hall outside my office. "I hope you don't find the traffic too disruptive," I said when I showed it to her. She pushed her big glasses up on her small nose and said, "No, it's handy to be right in the middle of everything."

I had shoved several gray metal work stands up to the sides of her desk and walled her in behind a word processor, two printers, a copier, a fax, and a big bank of communications gear. She had just room to go in and out of her jury-rigged workstation sideways. Adding shelves, drawers, and corkboard on her side of the barrier almost daily, she was turning herself into the networking wizard of the investigative force. Message clips, in/out markers, and the keys to everything were creeping up the wall behind her desk, and "Ask LeeAnn" had already become the section's mantra.

I told her now, "My office is full of stuff I don't want to move, but I need a clear space to look at some evidence. You know of any spare desks on this floor?"

"I'll find out." She came through my door five minutes later, followed by a maintenance man carrying a folding table. "Will this be okay for a cover?" she said, unwrapping a pristine white paper tablecloth.

"Perfect," I said. "Boy, this is service, LeeAnn. What other magic tricks do you know?"

"Oh, my," she said, "magic. I don't think so." But she smiled, so I asked her to walk over to the evidence room with me and help me check out the items I wanted to look at.

"Shall I bring a box? Is there a lot to carry?"

"It isn't that," I said. "There's a little bit of cash involved, and it takes two people to sign out money."

We walked the long hall together, or sort of together. She dropped behind me every time we met somebody, to make sure they had plenty of room to pass, and then she had to trot to catch up. I wanted to tell her she didn't have to give way like that for anybody but the chief, who really did need a lot of room, but I was afraid of making her more nervous, so I let it go.

Casey passed out the evidence inventory form for the money, and I signed a line on the chain-of-possession grid and passed it to her. "I know it's ridiculous for this little bit of cash," I said, "but a rule's a rule."

"That's okay," she said. "Am I supposed to say how much?"

"It says that up here, see?" I showed her the line for a description of evidence, where it said, "Thirteen dollars." "You just confirm the amount and sign."

"Oh, I see. So, what is it? Two fives and three ones?" She turned the glassine bag over, checking carefully till she was sure it held thirteen dollars before she signed on her line. Her even, flowing handwriting looked elegant next to my terrible scribble.

"Thanks, LeeAnn," I said. "I can do the rest of this by myself." I wanted her to go back to her desk so I would not have to hear her anxious little footsteps pattering behind me all the way back. I still thought she was a helluva find, but everything about her body language kept asking, "How do you like me now?" and I thought I'd try to keep some space between us till her self-esteem recovered a bit of its bounce.

Back in my office, I switched on the overhead fluorescents, pulled on latex gloves, and unbagged the money first. It was the most mystifying evidence we had collected, and I wanted to look at it with fresh eyes. The bills looked gummy and gross on the white tablecloth. Staring down at them, I tried completing a sentence that began, "I've just raped and killed a man and now I'm stuffing money in his mouth because—" I didn't get the answer in ten words or less; I didn't get it in more words than ten. I just didn't get it.

Ray had been careful to leave the bills folded the way they came out of the dead man's mouth. I debated: Should I leave them that way? After a few seconds I decided I needed to look at both sides, so I spread them out flat, faceup, on the tablecloth. What about the amount, thirteen dollars—any significance there? People used to say thirteen was an unlucky number; does anybody still believe things like that? I didn't know. The bills were well worn, not crisp and new. They looked genuine. I turned them over, took a couple of bills out of my wallet to compare with them, saw no deviations. To hell with it, I decided, BCA would make the call on whether or not the money was genuine. I stared at the bills a minute longer, shrugged, and put them back in their evidence sleeve. Money only really talks to people who know a lot about it.

We hadn't proved the shoe had any connection with the case, but I knew the shirt had been worn by John Doe number one, so I concentrated on that next, laying it out as flat as its wrinkles would allow.

It looked filthier than ever on the clean table cover, and smelled like grease and cigarette smoke and sweat. Three of the tiny white front buttons were cracked, but the splinters still clung to the threads. The breast pocket was ripped almost off, and there were several holes and snags across the front of the shirt, roughly in a line about an inch below the pocket.

The collar, when I flattened it out, showed a ring of dirt but was not frayed, nor were the cuffs. The shirt had been beat up, not worn out. I turned it over. The back was just as dirty as the front, but considerably less damaged, with no rips or holes.

I turned it back and thought about what it had been to begin with, an inexpensive dress shirt, medium blue hard-finish cotton with a tiny white stripe, the kind called "wash and wear" that profits greatly from a little pressing but often doesn't get it. It would be sold by low-end department stores to men who wore Levi's for work and play and probably owned a couple of shirts like this to wear with their one Sunday suit. Or guys who lived basically in cars, on the move, might have half a dozen shirts like this one, in a worn suitcase in the trunk. They would wear them with a greasy tie while they sold roofing and siding off the tailgate, or shilled at poker tables in casinos, or telemarketed cancer insurance out of a boiler room. It was a shirt that spoke of marginality.

I packed the shirt back up and opened the shoe. It might have looked pretty respectable once, I thought, a brown wing tip in a decent grade of leather. It was scuffed and run-over at the heel now; the insole was curled away from the sole, and the size and brand worn to illegibility in the lining.

Standing by the table, I dialed Mort Halper, who was keeping his small menswear store afloat downtown by giving exceptional service, something the glossier stores at the mall didn't appear to have considered. I figured a guy who could remember the inseam measurements of half of Rutherford's adult male population could shed some light on these items.

"Jake," he said, "did you get mad at me or quit wearing clothes?"

"It's worse than that," I said. "I bought a place in the country."

"So, shall I tell you about our fine layaway plan?"

"Probably, pretty soon. But today I'm just begging for help." I told him what I needed and asked if I could stop by on my way to lunch.

"Always glad to help out Rutherford's finest," he said.

In his tiny, jam-packed office back of the store, he walked around the shirt while I held it up for him. He put on half glasses and leaned in to read the label. "Turn it over," he said. He squinted at the small print. "Washing instructions. See if there's another little label somewhere in the inside seams." I fumbled, being careful not to let the shirt touch anything, and finally found a tiny, rolled-up tab that when flattened out read, "Made in Belarus."

"Isn't it wonderful? A few years ago we couldn't find that place on a map; now they're making our clothes. We don't manufacture anything in this country anymore; we just buy and buy." He smoothed some hair over his bald spot and said, "I better not start. You'd miss lunch."

He made a note on his desk pad. "It's not one of mine. I carry moderate-priced but not quite this far down-market. This is, like, a knockoff of a knockoff. I'll make a couple of phone calls and tell you this afternoon if it could have been sold in Rutherford. The shoe"—he pondered a few seconds—"opposite problem. So standard everybody sells it. Three of us, at least, here in town. In the Cities, probably a dozen at least. I'll give you the names of the local ones when I tell you about the shirt."

He watched me put the garments back in their bags. "Got a whole rack of jackets on sale, you got time to try on a couple?"

"Thanks, Mort," I said, feeling like a piker, "but I'm already late."

I was, but Pokey was later; I had placed my order and was sampling the bread basket by the time he slid into the booth across from me. The waitress was right behind him with both our plates.

"How'd you do that, get your order in so fast?"

"Came in kitchen door, told cook," he said. "You know him? Mustafa Khan? Kinda crazy, but sure can cook." He took a bite of beef stew and said, "Mmm. Good. Mustafa got tortured by Taliban before he got outa Afghanistan, is why he talks to himself sometimes. Eat enough of his own cooking, oughta be okay pretty soon." He barked one of his short laughs. One of the many things I don't understand about Pokey is how he always seems to know the life stories of people I never heard of, like Mustafa the crazy cook. "So"—he slathered butter on a bun and dipped it in gravy, "somethin' botherin' you about autopsy, Jake? You got questions?"

"I have so many questions I hardly know where to begin," I said. Pokey nodded approvingly. "That pleases you, does it?"

"Proves you're paying attention," he said. "What's first?"

"My first question? Lessee. What do you think about the money in the mouth?"

"Don't think anything about it. Is question for cops, not doctors. Damn good question, though, hah? But don't concern me. What else?"

"What makes you think some of the wounds were inflicted after death?"

"Logical reason. Man dies, heart stops. Heart stops, blood don't flow. Pound on guy who's dead, you make abrasion, scrape, maybe cut, but...won't be much blood in tissue surrounding, understand? Gets kind of waxy yellow appearance, not like regular bruise." He chewed awhile. "Sounds easy, but . . . is hard to be sure, sometimes. Stuart thinks maybe yes on some, maybe no on others. Wants to show to some tissue specialists at lab."

"Both bodies? They both have wounds you think might be posthumous?"

"Yup. More on bottom guy. Is lotta difference in number and types of wounds on these two victims, Jake. Guy in bottom of barrel—you call him John Doe number two, huh? Okay, number two, unless tox scan shows otherwise, is pretty certain he died from series of head wounds, close range, probably made by baseball bat, metal pipe, some weapon like that."

"So then the after-death wounds—"

"Mostly to fit him in bottom of barrel, I think. Some kinda tamper." He illustrated. I felt my appetite for pork cutlet waning, pushed my plate away, and stirred a lot of cream and sugar into my coffee. Coffee drinking, for some reason, feels acceptable during even the grittiest conversation.

Pokey buttered another roll and plowed right along. "So both victims died about same time, looks like, and both had wounds after death, but you need to think about big difference in how these two guys died."

"Okay," I said. "I'm thinking about it. Tell me some more."

"Number-two guy in bottom of barrel, I'm not saying was cakewalk for him, took some hard knocks before he died, for sure, but nothing compared to number-one guy on top. That poor fella was tied up to something while he took his beating—I can't exactly say, a bench or a tree? Had marks like rope burns on his wrists, scrapes all over insides of his arms and his chest and throat—"

"His chest? There are holes across the front of his shirt—" I showed him.

"Uh-huh. Figures. Also was raped, John Doe number one."

"Ray told us. You're sure it wasn't consensual sex?"

He shook his head. "Trust me. Lotta damage."

"But the second man didn't—he wasn't—"

"Wasn't raped, wasn't asphyxiated, none of that."

"Number one was smothered some way?"

He nodded emphatically. "But is puzzling too, dammit, that part." He forked down a big bite of salad, crunched awhile, and said, "Usually, you see petechiae—you know what I'm sayin', little purple-red dots? On insides of eyelids, lining of mouth—this time we saw a few on surface of lungs and heart, too. Usually, you see those dots, you know you got strangulation victim. Hanged, garroted, whatever. But number one don't seem to have ligature marks on neck. Although, damn, so much damage…hard to say. So we look at inside of mouth again and find scrape marks like you get with suffocation. Teeth marks on tissue of cheeks, you know? From being pressed down on like this—'' Obligingly, he suffocated himself with his napkin.

"Anything I can do for you, Doctor?'' our waitress asked, appearing suddenly by his elbow.

"'Nother cup of coffee be wonderful,'' Pokey said, recovering without a blink, "and say, this fella's buying, what kinda pie you got out there?'' Besides the lightning changes in mood he can always manage, like from grim autopsy facts to joshing with a waitress, another thing I've never understood about the coroner is how he can eat like a stevedore and stay thin as a whippet. He seems blithely unaware of the concept of calories; when the waitress brought him peach pie à la mode, he dug into it with happy little cries.

"These marks on the insides of his cheeks,'' I said as he munched his dessert, "any chance they could have been made when that money was stuffed in his mouth?''

He screwed up his face and thought about it. "Don't think so. Was characteristic tooth marks, just along here,'' his fingers traced the line along his dental occlusion, "and money was old, no sharp edges. Didn't cut his tongue or inside of gums.''

"Okay. So number one was strangled and suffocated, he was raped, and most of his bones were broken. Would you care to place your bet on what killed him?''

"Valves in both ventricles pretty well shot. Lotta plaque in arteries leading to heart, coulda been contributing factor.'' He chewed through some more pie. "Was walking coronary, probably, before fight ever started.''

"Fight? You're calling this a fight?''

"Oh, you bet. Had lotta flesh and blood under finger-nails, big gash on ankle mighta been caused when he kicked somebody. Yeah, looks like he didn't give up so easy."

"How come Ray didn't know about the possible heart attack?"

"Ray didn't like how number-one Doe got sodom-ized." Pokey pursed his lips. "Got pretty bummed out, maybe didn't hear good for few minutes."

"I thought he had a hard time talking about it. How'd Rosie do?"

Pokey's face filled up with glee. "That girl! Is like Energizer bunny, huh? So many questions!" He cackled over the last of his pie. "Too busy taking notes to worry about blood and guts. Some kinda writer!" He mimed a manic Rosie Doyle, writing fast and pushing her hair around. It was as good an imitation, almost, as she had done of him.

"Was she right about number-two John Doe being Mexican? You think?"

Pokey's enthusiasm turned off abruptly. "Forensic sci-ence don't give shit about country of origin," he said stiffly. "Is totally irrelevant."

"It's useful information for cops, though."

"S'pose so. Don't mean I gotta care."

"Rosie said Stuart's dentist says yes."

"Uh-huh. Young fella, kinda smart-ass. Enjoyed show-ing off for red-haired lady cop."

"The question offends you in some way, Pokey?"

He stirred his coffee noisily and took a big slurp. "Good thing about forensic science," he said finally, not meeting my eyes, busy chasing the last of his ice cream around his dessert plate, "open people up, can't tell Uz-bek from Italian."

"I see." He clowns around so much, I sometimes forget what good reasons he has to be edgy on matters of race and ethnicity.

"One more thing," Pokey said quietly as I paid the bill. He nodded toward the door and followed me onto the sidewalk. "You gonna be sendin' evidence up to BCA anytime soon?"

"Yeah, we'll have to make a run today or tomorrow, I guess. We need to send up that shirt number one was wearing, and the money, and a shoe we found in the alley. Plus whatever they find going through still more garbage today. Why?"

"Took extra slide of semen from number-one John Doe, got it in my office. Stuart's lab gonna do DNA studies from both victims, but they're so backed up they might take all summer, you know? But Trudy told me she's doin' extra DNA work on Saturdays, up there at ol' Doc Wang's Sweatshop"—Pokey resents the prestige and power of Jimmy Chang and the Bureau of Criminal Apprehension, and retaliates by pretending he can't remember the chief scientist's name—"they got that STR equipment now, very fast. If you took my slide to Trudy and asked her to bump it up the line for us, bet she could get results for you by next week."

"Okay." I tried to read his face, but he was watching the cars in the street. "Am I being dense? Whaddya got in mind, Pokey?"

"Not bein' much denser than usual, I guess." He turned and smiled up at me. "Thank you for very nice lunch."

He told me I could send somebody for the slide anytime, so I called in from my truck and got the shift captain to send a patrol car. Good thing, too, because when I got back to the department, Darrell Betts and Ray Bailey were sitting in front of my desk, looking bleak.

"Tell me quick," I said, "and get it over with."

"That Toter the bodies were in?" Ray said. "That came from Bo Dooley's house."

"Oh, shit." I sat down. "The city told you that?" Darrell nodded. "Just now? They took all morning to find their list?" I needed somebody to blame for this bad news, so I indicted the Solid Waste Department for clumsy record-keeping.

"They told me three hours ago," Darrell said, "but I couldn't believe it, so I made them find the driver. He insists he emptied garbage at Dooley's house Friday and put the Toter back on the sidewalk. They use those big trucks with arms"—I waved my arms impatiently, and he hurried on—"and this morning, it's gone from behind the house where Bo keeps it."

"How do you know?"

"His wife called it in. The company was already looking for her missing garbage can when I called to say we had found a barrel, with that number on the outside and two bodies on the inside. They were, um, shocked."

"I should think. Does Bo know?"

"Probably not," Ray said. "See, Bo wasn't with us downtown Saturday, so I guess…he knows we found two bodies in one trash container, but maybe—"

"Uh-huh. Maybe he doesn't quite realize that container is the one that should be at his house. Since nobody's exactly talking to him this morning."

"And vice versa," Ray said, with a little flash of temper. "We been like a bunch of mute crows out there picking over that damn Dumpster."

"Anything useful out of that yet?"

"No."

"Okay. Go get him and bring him in here, Ray. Sit still," I added hastily to Darrell, who started to follow him out. "You made the find, you gotta be here when we tell him."

Darrell sat back down as if he suspected his chair had grown tacks on the seat. Seeing him squirm there in anticipation of confronting Bo Dooley, it occurred to me that a judgment might be coming up about a possible administrative leave for Bo. If it had to be done, I wanted it quick and clean, so I decided to see if I could get the chief in on this story from the start. I picked up the phone and told Lulu I needed to speak to him, and for once she put me through without giving me a lot of grief about how busy he was. He wasn't delighted to be summoned to my office without knowing the reason, but I conveyed a certain urgency, and he walked in the door a couple of strides ahead of Ray and Bo.

Darrell jumped up and started pulling chairs away from the wall. Bo sat down on the edge of one of them, looking ready to jump out the window if anybody made a sudden move. Bo may not be a great communicator, but there's nothing wrong with his instincts.

I prodded Darrell through the story of his morning again. When he got to the news that the two new homicide victims were in Bo's barrel, Bo, white-faced, pulled out his wallet, flipped it open, and showed his shield to Frank, saying, "Is this what you want?"

"Now, just a minute," the chief said. He raised his hand in a restraining gesture, like a teacher quieting a classroom, and held it there. "No hurry about that."

The chief's size works to his advantage when things get tense. Lou French told me once, "The good thing about partnering with Frank on the street was that I hardly ever had to fight. He could just stand there looking like some goddamn big gorilla, and most people would wait to see what his next move was gonna be.''

So we all sat quiet and waited, and finally he put his hand down heavily on his knee. ''Bo,'' he said, ''you live on Oak Hills Drive, don't you?''

''Well,'' Bo said, ''yes.''

''Way out southeast there? Next to Bryce Park?''

''Uh-huh. My backyard adjoins the park.''

''Didn't you say to me,'' the chief said, turning to me, ''that you thought the alley back of the Lotus Flower was a real poor place for a murder? Said it was too busy back there, no place to pull off a noisy killing like that without getting interrupted?''

''That's right,'' I said, ''and besides, we didn't find any of the trace evidence that would have had to be there. No blood, and there would have had to be blood if they were killed there.''

''But Bryce Park—'' Ray said.

''Would be perfect. A perfect place for a murder. Is that what you're saying?''

''Uh-huh,'' Frank said.

Ray said, ''Whaddya say we go take a look?''

''*Yeah,*'' Darrell said, ''let's do it.''

I asked Frank, ''You wanna come?''

''Uh—'' He looked at his watch. ''Yes. I'll take my own car in case I have to come back before you're done.'' We all stood up when he did, except Bo, who was still perched on the edge of his chair, watching us silently. He wouldn't ask. The chief turned toward the door, noticed Bo still sitting there, and said, ''What?''

''You can have my shield whenever you want it,'' Bo said.

''I know I can, and if I need it, I'll ask for it,'' Frank said. ''But right now there's no reason to declare you a suspect. You never saw the victims before Saturday, did you?''

"I never saw them then," Bo said. "I—"

"What the chief is saying," I said hastily, "is that there's nothing to tie you to the case but that trash barrel. Right?'' I turned to Frank.

"Right," he said, looking from one of us to the other. "So—we might have to assign you to other cases till we clear up the trash barrel thing, but we're not even that far yet. First I want to look at Bryce Park"—he let his eyes rest on Bo for a few seconds with that dispassionate stare that can make the hair stand up on your arms—"and I think you should come too." In the doorway, he turned back and said, "Better call your wife and tell her we're coming."

Bo went to his cubicle to make the call. Ray checked out a department car, and Darrell and I got in; Ray drove around to the front entrance, where Bo came hurrying out and joined us. As soon as he got in, silence descended on the vehicle like a wet wool blanket. After a few blocks, Ray said, "You usually take South Broadway to Thirty-first Street, Bo? Or—"

"Easier if you take a left on Twenty-sixth," Bo said. "Cross the bridge there and turn left at Carson Road, you'll come out on Oak Hills Drive a block west of my house." We rode the rest of the way in silence till we turned in to his block and he said, "Third house on the left there."

It was the smallest house on a street of small houses, a one-bedroom clapboard with white paint beginning to flake. I have never heard Bo complain about money, or anything else for that matter, but looking at his tiny, well-worn house, I realized his wife's crack binges and trips to detox must be a helluva financial drain.

We parked on the street, and the chief pulled in behind us. Diane came out and stood on the cement step in front of the house, a pale, brown-haired woman with the remnants of prettiness in her thin face. She never said hello, just watched us all till her eyes found Bo, locked on his face, and followed him. He went up to her, leaned toward her ear and said a few words, opened the house door, and encouraged her back inside with his hand an inch behind her shoulder blades.

He came back down the steps, saying, "We can go this way," and we all followed him around the side of his house. There was a little swing set in the backyard, and a shed to one side with Bo's old Harley in it. He pointed to a circle of dead grass by the shed and said, "Here's where the garbage can belongs."

A chain-link fence ran along the back of his yard. He unlocked the gate and held it open.

"You keep this locked?" the chief said. Bo nodded. "Then how did—"

"Don't know," Bo said. The chief looked at the gate for a few seconds and shrugged, and we all filed out onto cushiony turf just greening up. A few feet farther out we crossed an asphalt bike path that circled the perimeter of the park. Beyond that, a broad sweep of grass led out to playgrounds, horseshoe pits, and rows of huge old oaks and maples beginning to leaf out. Under the trees, cement picnic tables and benches were set up on pads with outdoor grills nearby. Looking at the shady picnic areas, I recalled Pokey saying, "...was tied up to something...a bench or a tree."

"Let's look around the tables," I said.

"You best come with me, Bo," the chief said.

They started at the east end of the row. The rest of us spread out; Ray headed for the northwest corner, Darrell and Lou split the middle, and I headed downslope toward a group of tables by the duck pond. The sites were numbered, I discovered, and I noted the numbers in my notebook as I finished each one, because they were so close to identical I knew I'd get confused.

I was at the third site when I heard Ray's whistle. He stepped out of a circle of sumac bushes and box elder trees and waved, and the whole team moved quickly toward him, across the dappled shade under the trees. Coming up to him, I saw how his mouth was set in a grim line, and sweat stood on his upper lip. He led us around a screen of bushes and stopped, and we all stopped. It seemed as if the sun went dark for a minute, and I shivered.

"Jesus," Darrell said in a raspy whisper.

"Must be it, huh?" Ray said, watching the chief.

"Yeah." Frank cleared his throat. "I'd say you found it, all right."

It was easy to imagine that yesterday, given a different string of luck, some unlucky local stroller might have wandered in here looking for a family picnic spot and found this awful scene. At first he might have mistaken it for a site where someone with no skill or experience had dressed out wild game, and would doubtless have said, indignantly and with contempt, "Well, what kind of a no-good takes an animal out of season and then leaves a mess like this—" And then with dawning horror he might have noticed that the hair in the clotted blood was human hair, and that the bloody lump on the leg of the picnic table was a fragment of a human ear. I could almost hear his distressing cries as he ran out of the place, arms reaching ahead for help, feet not able to run fast enough to take him away from the horror of it.

"Well," I said, noticing that my voice didn't seem to

be working so well either, ''I better get a BCA crew back down here. If I can.'' I hit the wrong button on my speed dial, punched off, and started again. My hands felt stiff and clumsy.

''I'll get a couple squads out here,'' Ray said. ''I suppose they better bring some kinda plastic cover, huh?'' The flies and ants were busy. ''Crime scene tape. What else?''

''Better notify Parks and Recreation,'' the chief said. Soon we had all turned our backs on the gory crime scene and were talking on cell phones. And shortly after that, the streets around Oak Hills Drive filled up with official vehicles and media vans, and the park was swarming with people who had no time for recreation.

RAY STAYED AT the picnic site, and kept Darrell with him. He said he'd call if he wanted any more help. Bo and I rode back to the station with the chief, who had decided it would be best if Bo was assigned to other cases until the smoke cleared a little on this one. He still wasn't ready to consider administrative leave.

''You're not implicated in any way,'' he said. ''We don't even know the identity of the victims yet. Anybody can see how easy it was for somebody to swipe your garbage can. If I put you on leave, no matter how many times we announce later that you're cleared, it leaves a smear you can never quite wipe away. But just in case''— he didn't say in case of what, and we didn't ask—''it'll be safest if you stay out of this investigation entirely. Work on something else till we see what we're dealing with here.''

Back at the station, Bo went to change out of his garbage-stained coveralls, and the chief said, ''Jake, come in my office a minute, will you?'' As soon as his door was closed, he said, "Okay, let's be realistic. Everybody's gonna want to know, was Bo or somebody in his household involved in these murders? If not, why did they pick his yard to steal a garbage can from? And second, why did they need it at all? Why did they move those bodies?"

"They? You've decided on multiple murderers?"

"You met anybody recently who could overpower two grown men without using a gun, and then beat them both to death while he had sex with one of them?"

"Uh...no. The how and why of everything might get a whole lot clearer if we could find out who the victims are, right? We haven't had any Attempt to Locate notices filed since Saturday, huh? Nobody's looking for these guys?"

"I don't know," he said. "Ask Ed Gray; he's running the shift today."

"I will," I said, "and I need somebody to start checking nationally, too. And we ought to take a look at recent reports of non-firearms homicides in the five-state area, come to think of it. Time to start raiding Kevin's crew, I think. Frank, is there anything else? I need to get going."

"What's this about Bo not seeing the bodies on Saturday?"

I had foolishly hoped he might not have noticed that little slip. "Well, that's right," I said, keeping it casual as if I had just remembered, "he didn't work Saturday."

"Thought you told me you got your whole crew on it. Is something going on I don't know about?"

"No. I'm just trying to leave Bo alone on weekends as long as I can because Diane is—well, you saw her."

"Yeah. God damn, crack is filthy stuff, isn't it? But the question for us is, has her addiction somehow involved her in this homicide? I know you feel a lot of loyalty to Bo—"

"Just what he's earned."

"I understand that. Just don't forget to protect the department first. Be very sure you leave no stone unturned."

"I hear you."

"Okay, get going, but keep thinking about why they moved the bodies, huh? You figure out why the bodies were moved, you'll be close to the rest of your answers." He seemed to have a fully formed theory of the case already. I wished I felt even a fraction of his certainty. All I had in my head were questions and a sense of urgency.

I FOUND BO TALKING on the phone in his cubicle. I sat down on the small chair in front of his desk and waited; he said "Uh-huh" a couple of times and then, softly, "Well, gotta go. Mmm. Talk to you later."

When he put the phone down, I asked him, "Is Diane nervous about staying alone in the house now? I could have a squad bring her downtown—"

"No. She'll be all right." He knows she couldn't stand the scrutiny she would get down here, I thought. He dropped a couple of pencils into the mug on his desk, rocked a couple of times in his chair, and sat back. "I picked that house so Nelly could play in the park," he said. "The house isn't much, but the street seemed quiet and...safe."

"And it has been, hasn't it? And doubtless will be again. Just hang on, Bo."

"Oh, sure." He was wrapped so tight already that it was hard to see how he could be doing anything *but* hanging on. "Well...back to the stuff I was working on before, is that it?"

"Except before you start, I want you to put together a list of your favorite snitches and their phone numbers, beeper numbers, whatever, and give it to Rosie next time she comes up here. She talked to a lot of your guys when you were on leave before, right? And you said she did okay.''

''Yes. What are you—''

''Tell her I want her to check the street for any word that might be out there about this homicide. The chief has a notion it's gang-related, so I'd like to check that out first, see if we can get any support for the idea or get it off the table, whichever way it goes.''

''Seems a little too...over the top, to me,'' Bo said.

''That's what Ray said.''

''But sure, we can ask around. Can't hurt. Does Ray know I'm doing this now?''

''No. But I'll tell him. It's a pain in the butt, having you sidelined like this,'' I said, looking out the door. ''I could use your instincts right now.''

Bo inspected his shoes for a minute. ''Nothing wrong with Rosie's instincts,'' he said, finally. ''She'll do fine with what I hand off to her.'' I went back to my office feeling hot and dissatisfied.

Ray called a few minutes later and said, low and fast, ''Darrell just found some clothes out here, Jake, looks like they might be what we're looking for.''

''Tell me.''

''Pair of pants, socks, shoes.... He'll be there in a minute. I decided I better send them to you right away.''

''Oh? Why?''

''There's a wallet in the back pocket of the pants.''

''You wouldn't shit me, Ray, would you?''

''Nope. I looked at it to see if it was what we've been looking for, and it is, so I put it back so you can see how we found it.''

''Thank you. Where'd Darrell find this stuff?''

''In a bag in the garbage can, next to the table.'' He

laughed a little, excitedly. "Darrell says he's building his career on a solid foundation of garbage."

"Damn straight. Well...I better get ready for him. Find the brass band and all." We both laughed, a little shakily. The zing that hits the solar plexus when a case suddenly starts to move feels like five cups of coffee on an empty stomach. Your gut grumbles, and a little film of cold sweat forms on your upper lip, and you think, God damn. Maybe gonna nail this hummer after all.

The folding table was still standing where LeeAnn had left it. I walked out in the hall and asked her, "Were there any more of those paper tablecloths in the storeroom?" She nodded and started to get up to get me another one, but I waved her back to her seat. I needed an excuse to move around. I could not sit still while I waited for Darrell.

As soon as I'd found the fresh cloth, I walked around the corner and stuck my head in Kevin's door. He was typing furiously, but his desk looked almost clear. I said, "Can you free yourself up in a few minutes to help me?"

Without turning his face away from the screen he said, "Sure."

"Good. I'll call you." I walked away from him quickly, not wanting his unfriendliness to dissipate my optimism.

Darrell was in my doorway ten minutes later, grinning, holding a plastic garbage bag high.

"Damn, you did good, huh? Put it down right here. Have some fresh gloves." I pulled the pants out of the bag. They were dark gray, lightweight wool serge, with two pleats and a cuff. I tried to lay them out flat, but they were deeply wrinkled and stuck together in spots. I sniffed and said, "Blood, huh?"

He nodded and pointed. "And this here's semen, I think."

"Ah. And the shorts are still inside? He got undressed in a hurry, huh?" I pulled them out. They had been white once, so it was easier to see which stains were blood and which semen. "Jesus, plenty of samples."

In the right-hand front pocket of the gray pants, we found three quarters, two dimes, and a cheap ballpoint pen. The left-hand front pocket contained a tightly folded city map and a couple of Spanish pesetas.

The wallet was in the right-hand back pocket. It was old, ragged, and greasy, made of Dacron in a canvas weave. A tag inside said, "Assembled in Mexico." The currency pocket was empty. The plastic sleeves held three credit cards, all issued to John Francis Morgan, and an Illinois driver's license in the same name, with an address in Joliet, Illinois.

I slid the card holder out of the wallet, laid it on a paper evidence bag, and carried it to Kevin's desk. "Got gloves handy? Start with the driver's license, run it through DMV, and bring me everything you get as fast as you get it. Handle with care, please, it hasn't been tested for anything yet."

Darrell had the rest of the clothing out of the bag when I got back. "Holes in the toes of his socks," he said. "Black leather walking shoes, well worn"—he looked inside—"size nine double A. The belt"—he squinted—"looks like there's blood on that too, doesn't it? All scraped up, like—I don't know like what."

I held it up to the light. "Like maybe it was used to tie somebody's hands to a concrete bench?"

"Whoa. Where's that idea comin' from?"

"Pokey said he's pretty sure John Doe number one was tied up to something for a while. Said he had scrapes on his arms and chest like— What is it, Kevin?'' He was standing in my doorway, opening and closing his mouth as if the air had grown too thin on the second floor.

''This license—''

''What about it?''

''Where'd you say you found it?''

''In these pants,'' Darrell said.

Kevin shook his head and looked at me.

''In Bryce Park,'' I said. ''At a picnic site covered with blood, where we think maybe Saturday's victims were killed.''

''I thought you said they were downtown.''

''When we found them. We feel sure they weren't killed there, and we now have reason to think they might have been killed in the park. What *is it,* Kevin? You got a bone in your throat?''

''John Francis Morgan is Mr. Murphy Game,'' he said.

SIX

"KEVIN," I SAID, "I've tried to be patient with you, but you seem to be totally obsessed by that sleazy bastard. I told you we have to—" I stopped because he was waving his arms like a man signaling a fighter plane onto a flight deck. "What? *What?*"

"Can't you just listen a minute?" He was beginning to swell up and turn red.

"One minute." I raised my right index finger in the air. "One! Minute!" I raised my left wrist and glared at my watch.

"The car that took that little girl away in the box? From the Chicken Shack. Last Friday night!" He had begun to nod, as if agreeing with himself was going to convince me. "One of the men betting money wasn't quite drunk yet, I guess, so he wrote down the license number of the car. He gave it to Louie after everybody else left. Louie gave it to me this morning. I ran it through DMV a few minutes ago—" I opened my mouth, and he raised his palms defensively. "It only took a minute! You said I should get my desk clear, and that was on my desk! So I ran it. But I knew you didn't want to hear about it—"

I quit watching my watch. "Now I do," I said.

"Okay. The car was registered to John Francis Morgan."

"Same middle name too?"

"Exactly."

"Still, John Francis Morgan, those are all common names. There could be more than one."

"At the same address?"

"You're sure about that?"

He read it to me. "Three-thirteen South Richards Street, Joliet, Illinois."

"Kevin, this has gotta be wrong. You know yourself the coincidence is just too crazy! Besides, Louie Forsell just came in with that story this morning—"

"But he was talking about last Friday night."

"In the middle of the night, though, you said."

"Well—ten o'clock or so. Okay, maybe midnight by the time the whole thing was over. What time did the dishwasher at the Lotus Flower find the bodies?"

"Eight-thirty, quarter to nine."

"On Saturday morning? Plenty of time."

"I'm not sure. Both docs at the autopsy said twelve to thirty-six hours since death, they couldn't be sure—"

"Oh, you know how they like to cover their asses with those ridiculously huge time frames! Didn't all of you say the little wormies indicated six to twelve hours? That's what Ray told me."

"Okay, but think about it. Mr. Murphy Game would have had to take his little girl home to wherever he lives and go back out and meet the Mexican—"

"What Mexican?"

"I'll tell you later. And go to Bryce Park and get the two of them killed, and not by any nice quick gunshots but slowly and painfully with various heavy weapons, and then get the two of them stuffed into a trash barrel—"

"Which had to be stolen, don't forget," Darrell said.

"Right. Stolen and then loaded into some conveyance and carried downtown and unloaded, which as we know from recent experience''—I nodded to Darrell—''is hard as hell to do—''

"Amen," Darrell said.

"—all before daylight?"

"I grant you," Kevin said, "it's a tight schedule. But then"—he brightened—"everything we've heard about this man has been extremely unusual."

"Come on," I said. "Just because he can sell snake oil—"

"And make his child disappear on command, just like that," Kevin reminded me, snapping his fingers.

"This means he can get himself killed faster than the average asshole?"

Darrell tittered nervously. "World's fastest murder victim, how's that for a piss-poor title?" He met Kevin's eyes, and the two of them began to laugh.

"We could start a new fad," Kevin said. "Least Coveted World Titles—" The two of them began breaking up.

"Okay! Enough!" I said. "I know this is weird stuff, but we're not gonna turn it into a joke, dammit. Darrell, Ray's expecting you back, isn't he? Better go, then. Ask him to call me as soon as he can, will you? Kevin, stay where you are. Don't get comfortable, though; I gotta shitload of work for you to do."

"Citations on the car, that kind of stuff?"

"Eventually. First I want you to run John Francis Morgan through NCIC and MINCIS, look for arrest records, you know the drill. Is your crew in the building?"

"Last I knew."

"Good, have Clint get on the horn with the Joliet PD and find out everything about that Illinois address, what kind of dwelling, whether the post office lists John Francis Morgan as an occupant there, who else lives there, everything he can get. I'm gonna call BCA and see if we can get a match on the prints. Now what?'' He was still in the doorway, flapping his hands.

''When do I get to hear about the Mexican?''

''Oh. Rosie got convinced at the autopsy that her John Doe was Mexican.''

''So you think maybe the Hispanic man with the coins—''

''Uh-huh. And the dark-skinned man who drove away with the little girl in the box—''

''Might be the same guy? And he might be the guy in the barrel? But then it starts to look like everything we've all been working on fits together—''

''With an audible click. Yes. Which is a little too good to be true, if you ask me, but see what you can do.''

He bounded out the door, delighted to be back in his rightful place as a boy wonder.

I called BCA and got Trudy on the phone. ''The van's on the way, is that what you want to know?'' she said. ''Almost there, in fact, they just passed Oronoco. Ted's driving, though, so''—she giggled—''if he doesn't show up at Bryce Park in a couple of hours, you maybe ought to send out a search party.'' Trudy never tires of dissing Ted's navigation skills.

''I'm glad to hear about the van, but I called you about something else.'' I told her about finding the pants with the wallet. ''Have you put Saturday's prints into the database yet?''

''No. There's a long line ahead of you, Jake.''

''And you know I'd never even think about trying to jump that line.''

''Except what?''

''Well, see, we found a wallet in some clothing. And I won't bother you with details right now, but there's good reason to suspect the name in the wallet might be that of John Doe number one, the top guy in that barrel we found downtown Saturday.''

"Oh me oh my. You want me to search on the name?"

"If this guy's who we think," I said, "he's almost sure to have arrest records."

"Heck, that won't take long," she said. "Lemme have it." I spelled everything and gave her the Illinois address.

"Okay, I got it," she said. "Call you back in a few."

"I really appreciate—"

"Just keep your trap shut about it, hear?"

"Gotcha," I said meekly. My phone rang as soon as I put it down.

"It's me," Ray said. "What?"

"BCA van should be there any minute," I said, "and I need to tell you what I just asked Bo Dooley to do." I laid it out for him, my reasons and all.

When I was done, he said, "Uh-huh. Well. So Rosie's tied up for a while now too, huh?"

"Well, yes. But I put Kevin to work running the name on the driver's license through NCIC and MINCIS, and he's gonna have Clint start calling about that address in Joliet." There was a kind of loud silence on the line. After a few seconds I said, "I guess it might have been better if I ran all those orders past you first, huh?"

"Well," he said, "I do need to know what's going on."

"Yes. It's very hard to break old habits, you know?"

"Uh-huh."

"I'm used to just…forging ahead. But you've gotta give the orders in your own section, I know that."

"Be kind of a joke if I don't."

"Of course. We'll get this straightened out! How about

if I schedule a meeting first thing tomorrow morning, just for the two of us, to go over the protocols again?''

''If there's time. I better go, Jake, the van's here.''

I hung up and said, ''Shit.'' I slammed a drawer shut and kicked the leg of my desk and said again, louder, ''Shit!'' I went out to the cooler and drank a lot of cold water and walked back into my office just as the phone rang.

It was Trudy. She said, ''You can go to the head of the class now, Jake Hines.''

''I can? Really? You already got a match?''

''Two of them. Both positives, two full sets. Illinois in '97, Wisconsin in '95. You want the SID numbers?''

''God, yes.'' She read the state ID numbers that we could feed into NCIC to get the details of Morgan's convictions. ''FBI numbers?''

''None attached.''

''Good, that simplifies things.'' I read the numbers back to her, and when she confirmed them, I said, ''You are a beautiful, smart lady, and I love you very much.''

''Wow. Were you that hard up for a little piece of good news?''

''You have no idea. See you in a couple of hours, huh? You won't be late, will you?''

''Not unless some bozo calls and wants a favor,'' she said.

''Who would try such a thing?''

I called Ray and told him the news. His initial reaction was even more dubious than mine had been. ''You saying this beat-up guy in the barrel is that Mr. Murphy Game that Kevin's been telling everybody in the building about? Darrell tried to tell me this, and I wouldn't believe him. It sounds too crazy.''

''I know it does. I said so too. But Trudy's very good

on that fingerprint machine. If she says it's a match, I believe her.''

"Yeah, I know that, but…Jesus, this is freaky.''

"Agreed. But it's what we've got. Will you tell Darrell for me that he's got an attaboy coming for finding that wallet?''

"For sure. Listen, though, if we've got fingerprint ID and we're gonna have arrest records, we're about ready to start thinking about suspects for the murder, huh?''

"Yes. I'll say this, it's gotta be somebody nimble. This crime seems barely possible timewise.''

"I guess I don't see…''

"No, you weren't in the sheriff's office for the story about the disappearing girl, were you? Never mind, I'll tell you later. Tomorrow morning. What I think we better do is expand this sit-down in the morning to include Kevin. The three of us need to go over everything that's happened since early last week, make sure you both have the same facts about the scams that went on last week and the murders Friday night.''

"Yup. And divide up the chores, I guess.''

"Again. Yes.'' I heard Lou's cough coming up the stairs as I hung up. Then Rosie knocked once on my door-jamb and sailed in, disheveled in terrible-smelling coveralls, with Lou behind her, equally rank and wild-haired but looking pleased. Rosie held up an evidence bag and said, "Guess.''

"It looks soft. Like a bag full of bags.''

"Close doesn't count! Look here!'' She pulled a wrinkled mass of clingy plastic wrap partway out of the bag.

"Damn, guys, you think maybe…the murder weapon?''

"If the fingerprint gurus say it is, it is,'' Lou said. "We were careful, and it's covered with prints. You know, if we hadn't talked about how they coulda used something like this''—they looked at each other, grinning—"we'd've passed right by this stuff and never looked at it.''

"Yeah, but see''—Rosie pulled some more crinkled, smeary plastic out of the bag—"soon as I saw it shining there under the rotten cantaloupe rinds, I said, 'Hey, Lou!'"

"And I said, 'Yeah, Rosie, yeah!''' Lou said. They glowed at each other with pride over this brilliant repartee.

"*Bunches* of the stuff!'' Lou said. "Yards of it. And it was all right together.''

"God,'' Rosie said, shuddering, "imagine getting wrapped up in this stuff—'' She made an agonized face.

"Don't think about it. Check it in to evidence, and I'll send it to St. Paul tomorrow. Is this the end of the garbage detail, are you done out there?''

"Yes. Except we don't know what we're supposed to do about getting the Dumpster back to the city,'' Lou said. "But somebody better do it pretty quick, the impound lot is turning into Stink City.''

"I'll ask Ray.''

"Good, then I'm headed for the showers,'' Lou said. "If I came home smelling like this, Mamie might exercise her escape clause.'' He chuckled, the laugh turned into a spasm of coughing, and he turned away with his face in his hands.

"I hope we're not gonna kill him right here at the end of his career,'' I said, listening to his noisy progress toward the locker room.

"Oh, but he's enjoying himself so much! He was *great* out there, you should have heard him, telling war stories''— she giggled—"about old days on the street. Fun stuff! I guess he's already thinking about missing the action.''

"Yeah. Listen, Rosie, as soon as you're cleaned up, will you go and see Bo Dooley? He's got information to hand off to you."

"Oh? How come?"

"He's off the case till we settle the business of how the bodies got in his garbage container. So you're going to talk to his snitches. Oh, you like that, do you?" She had her fist in the air and had just hissed, "Yes!" to herself. "And Rosie—" She turned in the doorway. "That's the last order you're going to take from me, understand?"

"Oh?" She made three syllables out of it. "You retiring too?"

"No. But Ray is the head of People Crimes now, and from now on you're going to get your orders from him."

"Oh." She shrugged. "That."

"Chain of command is essential. Anything else is chaos. It's hard for me to remember, too, but we've gotta make the changeover."

"Oh, I know." She waited a few seconds. "So, what will you do from now on?"

"Supervise." She raised her eyebrows. "Type memos." She flashed a dimple. "Bleed from the pores." Her laughter bounced off the walls as she sashayed down the hall.

The chief was pleased to hear we had an ID on our first homicide victim, till I told him who it was. He refused to believe it. "Go back over the evidence," he said. "You've got something wrong. Why would anybody murder a guy who makes a half-assed living pulling nickel-and-dime tricks on people?"

"Chief," I said, "a match is a match. And Trudy found two."

"It makes us look like a bunch of goddamn Keystone Kops, for chrissake. First we publish that silly story in the paper, and then one of the shysters turns up dead in a barrel? Remember Ole Carlson? He's president of the City Council now. He called me this morning and said, 'What kind of an outfit you running down there?'"

"Frank, we can't choose our homicide victims to please the City Council."

"Ole figures we should do everything to please the City Council. You know what he said to me? He said, 'See here, Frankie'"—Frank's imitation was devastatingly accurate—"'people come to Rutherford to do business, they want a clean, quiet town.'"

"Most days, that's what we give them. Tell Ole Carlson to cut you some slack. You can't control everything that happens."

"Reasonable's not Ole's strong suit." The chief rubbed his cheeks. "He's sure got sanctimonious down good, though." His face was a couple of shades redder than when we started the conversation. I wondered if he was remembering his blood-pressure pills. "What about the second guy in the barrel, then? Who do you figure he is?"

"We think he's the dark-skinned man in all the stories, the coin dealer and the man with the box at the tavern." I told him all our reasons. "Officially, of course, he's still unidentified. And getting a make on him might be pretty tough, given their lifestyle."

"Their lifestyle is why I don't believe this. People don't murder guys who cheat 'em out of ten bucks. Okay, sometimes it was a couple of hundred. Still—"

"Maybe just once he did something worse. The body's here, Frank, we gotta work with what we've got."

"What we've got includes full sets of fingerprints for

both men and plenty of DNA, right? So go after arrest records for number two.''

"Sure. But if he's Mexican, there may not be any. DNA, we won't get any help there unless he's a known sex offender. And it's all gonna take some time. I can't ask Trudy for any more favors right away.''

"No, God, let's not get Trudy in any trouble, she's one of the best resources we have.''

"Amen. Nothing like friends in high places. Which reminds me, I gotta find out what Ray promised his uncle's friend we'd do with the Dumpster when we were done with it." I stood up. "I think I've given you everything I've got, Frank.''

Lou went coughing by in clean clothes, on the way back to his cubicle. Frank inclined his head toward the noise and asked me, "Are you being careful enough with his workload?''

"Maybe not quite. But I've never seen him so happy. And he's a terrific asset on the street, Frank; he sees everything and never forgets.''

"Oh, yeah. Eye like an outhouse rat, always did have. What's he got left, six weeks? If that cough gets any worse, I might dredge up some extra work records, put him on a fast track outta here.''

"He wants to finish by the book if he can. I'll keep an eye on him, Frank.''

"Do it. We were partners once, did I ever tell you that? Back when we were both so young our knees weren't even wrinkled." Frank's face softened. "Lou was very good at calming people down. Almost never had any trouble while I worked with him.''

I went back to my desk and phoned Ray again. He answered, "Bailey," very short and testy, but when I asked him about returning the Dumpster, he said, "Oh, hell yes, thanks for reminding me. I'll call him, Jake, I wanna thank him personally. He really did us a favor, huh? If the stuff they found has some good prints on it.''

"He really did us a favor. Give him my thanks, too. How's it going out there?''

"Slow. We're gonna be here for a while yet. These new guys Ted brought along haven't been out in the van before, and they're scared stiff of screwing up, I think. They're doing their tasks ver-ee sloooow-ly''—he sighed—"being sysss-tem-aaaa-tic.''

"Gotcha. See you in the morning, huh?''

I went back to Kevin's office. He was glued to his console and said, without looking up, "Be patient, be patient.''

"Came to tell you something. Listen a minute.'' He rotated his whole body toward me before he peeled his eyes away from his blinking screen. "What?''

"Trudy called me back. The prints she took off our number-one John Doe match the prints that came up when she entered the name and address of John Francis Morgan.''

Kevin treated me to the handsome poster-boy smile the girls find so irresistible and said, "Oh, shit, oh dear, that's nice to hear.''

"Thought you might like it.'' I gave him the SID numbers Trudy had given me. "Now, listen. We've got a positive ID; now we're looking for a motive for murder and a list of suspects. Your task on that machine is to find everything our John Francis has ever done that got put into the official record. He must have had a very bad habit—or some quite profitable swindle. He did something objectionable enough to get murdered for. Two-bit hustles won't cut it.''

"How do you know? Plenty of people get killed for truly dumb reasons."

"Morgan wasn't just killed, he had the holy living shit beat out of him."

"So, a fight. What's new?"

"No. You haven't seen the body, have you? Get Lou to tell you about it. Mr. Murphy Game got tied up and raped. All his bones are broken, and his mouth was stuffed full of money. Somebody got seriously annoyed with this man."

"Ah. Okay. Well, I'll have found everything there is to find by close of business today."

"Good. Bring it to my office first thing tomorrow morning. You and I and Ray Bailey need to get ourselves on the same page."

I hurried back toward my phone, which was, as usual, ringing. But the answering machine picked it up before I got there, and anyway Clint Maddox followed me through my office door, saying, "Hey, you know that address you told me to check on in Joliet, Illinois?" He wiggled his eyebrows, and his freckles bounced. "Well, there ain't no such place. Any chance you meant some other state?"

"Nope. Illinois's what he used."

"Joliet police say no such address."

"Do they have a record of the driver's license?"

"Yes. With that address on it."

"His car's registered there too. And it's the address that comes up on his prison records."

"I hear you, Jake, but see, it won't come up on any of my street maps, so I called the PD there, and they ran a scan for me and said there isn't any such address. So I said, Well, we gotta body here that seems to have lived there." He wiggled his ears and flashed the loopy grin that makes him look like Alfred E. Neuman. "So they sent a squad to check. There's a three-eleven and a three-fifteen, but no three-thirteen."

"Huh. Well, I guess we shouldn't be too surprised. This Morgan was a con artist. He probably lived under his hat, mostly."

"You know"—he squinted at my desk lamp—"I never thought about this before."

"What?"

"When you go to renew a license, they don't check your address, do they? They just say, Is this your correct address? And when you say yes, they put it down."

"Sure. They figure you know where you live. And they don't have time to check; there's usually a line of people waiting behind you."

"So I could be giving out fictitious addresses?"

"I guess."

"Why would I, though?"

"Because all our systems are set up for people who have addresses. It's the first thing they ask you when you go to license anything."

"So if I didn't live anyplace—"

"You'd have to make up something."

"Huh. You know what, though, that would make it hard to get your mail."

"But if you lived like John Morgan, you might not want to get any."

"BEFORE KEVIN GETS in here," I told Ray Bailey Tuesday morning, "I want to say I'm sorry about any confusion I created by firing off orders like I did yesterday. I never meant to invade your space, Ray." I had rehearsed this speech in the truck on the way to work, and I wanted to get it out quickly before I gagged on it. Getting or giving, I hate apologies, which are demeaning to both sides, and never good enough.

"You didn't," Ray said. "My space is fine. We're just working out the kinks in this new system, aren't we? And there was a lot going on yesterday."

"So you're not pissed at me?"

"Hell, no. Let's quit talking about it and go ahead and work on this homicide."

"You're okay with that?"

"Sure."

"Okay." I flipped a pencil in the air and caught it. Then I said quickly, "Actually, there isn't any question how the chain of command works. I just have to remember to stick to it."

"And I have to remember to step up and do my job. You don't have to take all the blame, Jake."

"Okay. Now I really am going to stop talking about it."

"Fine." He picked a piece of lint off his pants. "I do need to know what's going on with my crew, though."

"Of course." I was really sick of the subject then, so I said, "Now, where's Kevin?"

"Haven't seen the bugger," Kevin said, walking in the door, looking pleased with himself. He sat down next to Ray and made a big show of slapping down a thick stack of report forms and printouts. Ray reached into the inside pocket of his jacket, pulled out a three-by-five spiral notebook, flipped it open to a page covered with tiny script, and stared at it.

I punched the On button on my tape recorder. "You've got the biggest stack of paper, Kevin. You go first."

"Well, to begin with"—he picked printouts from NCIC and MINCIS off the top of the stack—"the two convictions Trudy found for us break down like this: John

Francis Morgan did nine months in Wisconsin in '87 for hanging paper in bars, and seventeen months in '92 for a spending spree on a stolen Visa card. No violence involved before or after incarceration, and time off for good behavior both times.''

"Anything else?"

"One earlier arrest, a dumb little shoplifting charge in Des Moines in the summer of 1985. Charges dismissed when he paid for the item. It predates the other two charges, so it slightly extends the amount of time he's been active in this area. Otherwise there's nothing noteworthy about it except that for some reason he listed a nickname.'' Smiling delightedly, he read from the paper in his hand: "John Francis Morgan, a.k.a. 'Happy Jack.'''

"You're kidding," I said.

"I'm not. Mr. Murphy Game once styled himself 'Happy Jack Morgan.' Does that sounds like a really bad joke now, or what?"

Ray shook his head. "He's been remarkably consistent, hasn't he?"

"Yup." Kevin beamed at the paper. "Relentlessly sleazy."

"Nothing else?" I asked him. "That's all you found?"

"That's all. John Francis learned his lesson by 1992, looks like. Got sick of stints in the pokey, worked up some soft-edge scams with women and children, and kept moving after that."

"Soft-edge scams that somehow got him violently killed. But go ahead, now; tell us all about last week's complaints. When you're done, we'll download Ray about everything since Saturday."

We took the rest of the morning for it because, for once, we *got* the rest of the morning. LeeAnn held our phone calls, and both crews went on about their tasks without needing any help. Kevin worked his way down his stack of complaint forms, reciting the list of last week's frauds and scams, while the tape whispered from one spool to another and I turned it. Freed of the need for note-taking, we talked our way through the intricacies of the coin caper, and then to consensus about the approximate hour—between 11:00 p.m. and midnight—when the little blond girl got into the box and somehow, quickly, back to the bar.

I put in a fresh tape and described the phone call at 9:45 a.m. Saturday when Pitman summoned me from my yard. Then Ray picked up his spiral notebook and, reading easily from his tiny handwriting, reviewed the essentials of the homicide investigation since then. By eleven-thirty, when we broke to answer phone calls and get lunch, we had our three heads full of identical information, with a tape backup.

So we were ready to evaluate the information and divide up the work. At two o'clock, Ray and Kevin came back in my office carrying yellow legal pads, each with a couple of pages of scribbled notes.

"Close the door," I said. "I see you've both got plenty of questions, but I'd like to start with my biggest one. The location question."

"I thought you decided that," Kevin said. "Didn't you say there was no trace evidence to indicate they were killed in the alley?"

"And plenty in the park," Ray said. "If it tests out okay."

"Well, right, and I'm not suggesting we waste time speculating about the evidence in the park. BCA will tell us, soon enough, if the DNA they picked up at the picnic site matches what came out of the bodies in the barrel."

"Well, not soon enough," Ray said, "but eventually."

"Okay. Nothing we can do about turnaround times at the lab. But in the meantime we're assuming, in the absence of any other bodies—"

"Or any more bloodstained picnic sites," Kevin said.

"Yeah. We're assuming that the park is the murder site."

"We're assuming it so that we can do what?" Ray asked.

"Ask the really interesting question about the murder site. Why didn't the killer or killers leave the bodies where they were murdered and just walk away?"

"Why were they moved?" Ray said. "You think that's the most important thing? Why?"

"For one thing, because the chief does. He keeps saying, 'Why did they move them? Find out why they were moved, and you'll probably know who your killer is.'"

"Oh, I don't buy that at all," Kevin said. "Killers do just as many stupid things as the rest of us. More."

"Agreed. But moving added so much risk," I said. "They went to a lot of trouble. It's not something they'd do on a whim, the chief thinks, and I agree with him."

"Okay. What reasons do you like?"

"It has to be one of two things, doesn't it? They didn't want them found in the park, or they did want them found downtown."

Ray cleared his throat. "I don't know which end to start on."

"Let's just take them one at a time. Why wouldn't they want them in the park?"

"If I was doing it," Kevin said, leaning back in his chair for a bone-cracking stretch, "I'd see Bryce Park as an ideal place to stash a couple of dead men. It's one of the quietest parks in town—there'd be a good chance the crime scene wouldn't be found for some time. Bodies harder to identify, a colder trail—what killer wouldn't want that?''

"Unless for some reason the killers didn't want the park identified with the crime," Ray said, looking at the ceiling.

I watched his face. "But then they'd clean up the mess, wouldn't they?"

"You'd think so, wouldn't you? Unless there just wasn't time," Kevin said. I stared at him, and he said, nervously, "Okay, a reason they *did* want them found downtown, then."

Ray drew some stars on his tablet. "Before we leave the park"—he studied his toe—"I think you oughta ask Bo a couple of questions."

It was almost a relief when he said the name aloud. "Oh?" I said. "What questions?"

"Like, is he sure his gate was locked that night? If he is, can he explain how they got through it to take his trash can? If he isn't, does he usually leave his back gate open? To a public park?"

"And does he always sleep so soundly," Kevin said, "that he wouldn't hear a heavy trash barrel being rolled away from his house?"

I stared at them. "Do I detect a little piling on, here?"

"These questions are gonna get asked, Jake," Kevin said. "We better have the answers."

I looked at Ray. "He's on your crew," I said.

Ray drew a little circle around one of his stars. "Not exactly."

I counted backward from fifty by eights. When I got to two, I said, "Okay, I'll ask him. That enough of that? Let's go on. Reasons to want the bodies found downtown."

''To cause trouble for the Lotus Flower,'' Kevin said, ''or the Chow family.''

''It doesn't seem to have done that,'' I said. ''We asked Sam to look at the bodies, and he looked. Asked him if he recognized either of them, and he took his time and said no. You were there, Ray; did you see anything suspicious about his behavior when he did that?''

''Absolutely not. And I know him fairly well; he's in my Elks Lodge. I don't see Sam Chow as a suspect, not at all. Anybody in the world had access to the alley behind his place.''

''Okay, okay,'' Kevin said. ''No offense to Elks intended. Reason two, they'd be found sooner.''

''Why would you want that?'' Ray said.

''I don't know. It's just the only other neuron I've got firing right now.''

''Let's fool around with that one for a minute,'' I said.

Ray drew some more circles around his stars. ''I'm the murderer, and I'm finishing this sentence: 'I want these bodies found downtown as early as possible because—''' He looked up at us blankly.

''—because the sooner they're found,'' I said, ''the faster my message will spread.''

''What message?'' Ray said.

''I don't know. What figures? 'Ivan the Terrible, here's your traitor.''' I scratched my ear awhile. '''Great Gambling Gorilla, the debt is paid at last.'''

''Wow,'' Kevin said, ''I never knew you had all this *flair,* Jake.''

''Make up your own, then. Any number can play.''

''You're not just kidding around, are you?'' Ray said. ''You really like this idea.''

''It works with my Why question.''

''Which is?''

"Why would a consistently sleazy two-bit con artist who styles himself 'Happy Jack' be worth killing?"

We were all listing questions in our tablets as we talked, but now Ray looked up from writing and said, "Maybe he wasn't. What about the guy in the bottom of the barrel?"

"What about him?"

"We don't know who he was, so we don't know what he's been up to. Maybe Mr. Murphy Game just got in the way when payback time came for Mr. Hispanic."

"I kind of like that one, too," I said, "except—" A wisp of a thought floated past my eyes and away, and I finished lamely, "except I'm afraid Mr. Hispanic is going to be hard to identify."

"Maybe so, but we don't know that till we try. We don't want to be guilty of discriminating against the darker victim."

"Absolutely not," Kevin said. "He's got just as much right to be a son of a bitch as anybody else."

"Very cute," Ray said. "While we're at it, let's not be guilty of blaming the victims because they're not here to defend themselves. Maybe they just ran into some very bad guys."

"Possible," I said. "But we know John Francis was a liar, a fraud, a pimp, and a thief. So it's not hard to imagine that he annoyed someone severely. Maybe even some of the people he was traveling with."

"And Mr. Hispanic picked the wrong side in the fight?" Ray got up and sharpened his pencil and thought about it. "But aren't all the other members of the group women and children?"

Kevin considered. "Uh...all we've seen so far, yes. Two women and one child."

"Due respect on all sides—" Ray looked up from his

precise lines of script. "I don't see this as a crime committed by women. There's a lot of hard physical labor involved."

"And a rape, come to think of it," I said. "Unless—" We looked at each other, aghast. "Nah. Pokey would've said if it involved a foreign object. I can check to be sure." I stared at my notes a minute and said, "Who thinks, though, that it would be a good idea to find the females now?"

"Nifty idea," Kevin said. "But if they're still on the planet, the media have told them what happened to their guys. And whaddya bet they've got systems in place for getting out of town?"

"Oh, sure. And a dozen tested hidey-holes to duck into, probably. Still, we have to try on that one, too. We've got pretty good descriptions." I made more notes. The elusive thought was knocking at the inside of my skull, but I couldn't call it back, so I said, "Can we back up a second? Ray, you seem to have clear ideas about what it took to do this killing. What do you think it took to get them moved?"

"In terms of strength again, or—"

"And equipment. A three-hundred-fifty-pound Toter comes almost up to my shoulder, and it's just short of twelve feet around at the top. And loaded—overloaded— with two bodies, it had to be a bearcat to move. We've talked about *why* they did all that in the middle of the night, but *how* did they do it without anybody noticing?"

"In a van. With a ramp." Ray beat a pencil tattoo on his tablet. "Well-prepared murderers," he said finally. "What does that say to you?"

"It says Connections with a capital C," Kevin said.

"Okay." I doodled a house with five windows. "Here's another sentence for you to complete: I'm a member of a well-organized street gang, drug ring, whatever, and I have decided to murder this two-bit grifter because—"

"He's just too tacky to take up space on the planet any longer," Kevin offered.

"Somehow," Ray said, "I can't see the Original Gangsters worrying about that."

"Okay. I'm gonna kill him because he laid the moves on my girl."

"Mr. Murphy Game wasn't much drawn to that, was he?" I added a shade tree by my house. "His schtick was, he brought his own girls and offered to share."

"Money, then," Ray said. "The fool cost me money, so of course I have to kill him."

"I like that one," I said. "Costing people money was Happy Jack Morgan's area of expertise."

"It sounds more like standard Gangsters logic too," Ray said. "Can we get Bo to listen around for talk about that?" He realized suddenly what he had just said and looked mortified.

"Bo can't do it, but Rosie can," I said. "She's working his vice rounds till this is over." I gave my house a brick walk and a cat. "We about ready to divide up the chores?"

Kevin took the search for the females, since his crew had done the original interviews and were in the best position to go back to the merchants with Identi-Kits and more questions, to work up profiles and images we could use for a Wanted for Questioning notice. He would also be talking by phone to property crimes investigators throughout the five-state area, inquiring about scams in other towns.

Ray, besides following up on details of both crime scenes, agreed to initiate the search for Mr. Hispanic, with advice from Kevin on the best people to interview at the Chicken Shack. He would be working up a psychological profile as well as a physical image, and we'd hope to get lucky eventually with DNA results.

I had already agreed to query Bo about his yard security arrangements Friday night, and I would check with Pokey, too, for details about the rape. "Otherwise I'm gonna be gone tomorrow," I said. "I'm making the run to BCA."

Ray raised his eyebrows but made no comment. Kevin looked amused and asked, "You're not allowed to ask your lady for favors in the privacy of the home?"

"Favors?" I said. "You didn't hear anything about favors from me. But speaking of favors—" I smiled at him the way a wolf smiles at the smallest calf in the buffalo herd.

"Oh, shit," he said, "what now?"

"You need to be asking for one. From the managers in those stores that called last week to complain about the scammers."

"Whaddya mean?"

"They were mostly in chain outfits like Circle K and that?"

"Circle K, 7-Eleven, Rexall. So?"

"And the coin rip-off—didn't I hear you say that the Hispanic man made several contacts in the lobby of Methodist Hospital?"

"And the downtown Holiday. Yes. What about it?"

"Don't they all have surveillance cameras?"

"Uh…well. You mean… Aw, Jake, do you realize how many yards of boring film we'd have to look at before we found—" He waited a few seconds and tried another tack. "They probably don't keep those things more than a day or two, do they?"

"The stores will keep the ones from the day of the rip-off, to show their insurance company. Security at Methodist archives tape for a month at least before they recycle it.''

''Time-consuming—''

''Put Andy on it. Get warrants if he needs them. Most of those machines identify the hour on the tape, don't they? So we can find where to start looking. Any luck, we might be able to find one of those scams happening.''

Still reluctant, Ray said, ''You think this is the best use of our time right now?''

''For pictures of the two mamas and the little blond-haired girl? Sure. We could put their pictures on an Attempt to Locate notice. We might even get a picture of Mr. Hispanic good enough to identify the man in the morgue.''

''Okay,'' Kevin said. ''Is that it? That's the two things you want?''

''No, that's all number one. Number two is, if you give the job of scrutinizing the tape to Lou, he's going to piss and moan, but after that, he'll sit at a desk and scroll till his eyeballs fall out because that's the way he is. And what I'm hoping is that, besides possibly finding us something we can use in our search, maybe if he sits still in there and sucks on his inhaler every so often while he scrolls, he still might get to his retirement party alive.''

''I suppose,'' Ray said, ''that would be a good thing.''

''Frank would like it,'' I said.

SEVEN

LAST WINTER while I waited for the funding to expand my staff, I took to walking across the skyway to the library on my lunch break, to browse through self-help books. I was looking for hints on how to ride the wave of growth instead of drowning in it.

The first thing I learned is that for some reason, the people who write self-help books are obsessed with numbers: *Four Ways to Wealth, Six Sure-Fire Weight-Loss Techniques, Eight Ways to Stronger Relationships, Ten Steps to Higher Self-Esteem.* Most of the books are written in simple language with a lot of capital letters and exclamation points, as if the writer suspects that only a gravely retarded person would ever read her book. Or they appeal directly to your inner thumb-sucker; my favorite of these was *The Anxiety Coloring Book.*

I did find one idea that appealed to me: Try, it said, to do the hardest task of each day early, while your energy level is high. On the Wednesday morning after we found the bodies in the barrel, I decided to give that one a shot. So as soon as I finished my e-mail and phone calls, I walked down the hall to the People Crimes section, looking for Bo Dooley.

Thanks to our shoehorn job, Bo didn't really have an office anymore, just a dinky little cubicle with freestanding walls and no door. He had turned his desk around so it faced the blank wall in back. It looked odd at first, but apparently it helped his concentration; he was sitting still as a stone, completely absorbed in the case file he was reading. Then he breathed, and the diamond in his earring caught the light and flared. I tapped on the nameplate set into the wall by his doorway and said, "Bo?"

He turned and saw me, said politely, "Come in," and then, "Have a seat." I walked around him into the tiny, well-ordered space on the other side of his desk and saw at once how his arrangement put the guest at a disadvantage. One straight chair stood against the wall by the shelves where his supplies stood in precise rows; I moved it so it faced him across the desk and sat down. He had the only good light, and I was facing the distractions of foot traffic past his door. Bo hadn't been a vice cop for ten years for nothing. In spite of the limited space available to him, he had fixed his cubicle so he had the high ground during interviews with suspects.

"Couple of things," I said, and told him about Ray's "the fool cost me money" hypothesis.

"Makes sense," he said.

"I thought so. So will you pass it along to Rosie and ask her to start nosing around for street gossip about money grudges?"

"Sure."

"Then, second, I'm going to make a run to BCA, and I need you to come with me while I check out the money."

"Oh, sure. Hey, do you mind taking along the finger-print card I just checked in over there? I was going to send it by mail, but if you're going—"

"Be glad to. Anything I should know about it?"

"Just an old fingerprint from one of the cold cases we talked about last week. Trudy knows about it."

"Okay."

"So, you ready to go now?"

"In a minute. First I need to talk to you about one more thing." I tried to keep my voice as neutral as it had been before, but a little anxiety must have leaked through, because I could see him starting to close up, mentally. He folded his hands together on the desk and faced me attentively, but the light went out of his eyes.

Watching his guard go up like that, I thought, Screw this. I stood up and said, "Come to think of it, let's take a walk," and I walked out his door and into the hall without looking back. He really had no choice but to come along unless he wanted to put his head out in the hall and yell at my back, so after a few seconds he came out and followed me to the stairway. He was only a couple of steps behind me by the time we reached the tall glass doors at the bottom, and I pushed one open and motioned him out onto the front steps ahead of me.

We turned left and walked in silence toward the park. When we were half a block away from the government building, I said, "I can't help it that it was your garbage can the bodies were found in. I don't suspect you of killing them. I know you could do it, and I believe you would if Diane or Nelly needed you to, but I think if you did it, you'd tell me about it and not watch me chasing my tail around you while I tried to figure it out."

We walked along together for a few more steps before he cleared his throat and said, "Thanks." I waited for him to say more, but he didn't, so I stopped and turned toward him. He was two steps past me before he turned and faced me, with the flat planes of his cheeks set so hard they looked like freckled marble.

"I'm doing the best I can for you, Bo," I said, "but I

need you to quit treating me like the enemy now. If you want to help yourself, you've got to help me."

He watched me from under his sun-bleached eyelashes for a few seconds and finally said, "I know it." He turned and watched the traffic in the street awhile, turned back, and said, "But it's hard, you know?" His voice cracked, and he swallowed and worked his mouth a couple of times. "It's just…real hard right now to know the right thing to do."

"I see that. So let's start with questions you can answer yes or no. Was your gate locked when you went to bed Friday night?"

"Yes. Nelly and I went out in the park and played catch for a little while before supper, and I locked it when we came back in. I always keep the back gate locked on account of Nelly."

"What about the front one?"

"Friday night I didn't expect to go out again, so I locked up the front one at the same time."

"You always lock the front gate at night too?"

"Yes. Once we're in for the night, I lock up. The back one, we just keep locked all the time. Nelly loves the park. I'm afraid she might be tempted to go out there by herself sometime and get lost."

"Sure. How about Saturday morning? Did you check your gates then?"

"No. Saturday morning we all got in the car right after breakfast and went to visit Diane's sister in Sioux City. Opened the front gate to go out and locked it right back up again. We got back around nine Sunday night, opened the front to go in, locked it again, and went right to bed. Monday morning was…like most Monday mornings, you know? Big sweat to get Nelly to day care and still make it to work on time. I never looked in the backyard."

"So when did you find out somebody'd been there?"

"Diane called me at work about nine and said the garbage can was missing. I told her to call the city."

It all came out simple and easy and plausible, and I watched him, thinking, If it's as simple as that…. He was watching me, too, and he was a cop, so he knew dubious when he saw dubious. I reasoned that he was obliged to bluff as long as he could, but it was my job to call, so I said, "If it's as simple as that, Bo, why is this so hard?"

He shrugged and went back to watching traffic. I tried another tack.

"Say for the sake of argument a couple of agile guys could jump your fence, or climb over it—do you think they could lift that Toter full of garbage back over the fence? And set it down on the other side so quietly they wouldn't wake you?"

He cleared his throat. "Be kind of hard."

"Uh-huh. Darrell and I loaded it into my pickup downtown. We had to get two uniforms to help us. We unloaded it again at the station by ourselves. It only had a couple of sacks of garbage in it, and we damn near gave ourselves a hernia. We made a lot of noise doing it." The barest shadow of a smile came and went on his face. "Yes, all right, Darrell and I are not well schooled in solid waste disposal. But even so—it was plenty hard dropping it off the back of a pickup. We would not have been able to hoist it over a fence."

His silence suggested he'd rather not comment on my lifting prowess. A nasty little breeze with a cold edge had sprung up; I shivered and said, "Let's walk some more," and we turned toward the lake where the ducks were. People were feeding them on the slope above the water, putting coins in a dispenser to get bags of corn. We stood and watched the birds rushing each corn-thrower in turn, and finally I said, "I don't see anything about this homicide so far that suggests a connection to the drug trade."

"Oh…no, I guess not."

"So…why do you think Diane's involved?"

He looked at me, startled. "When did I say that?"

"You didn't. But why do you think it?"

"I sure don't know where you got that idea."

"Don't shit me, Bo. You're wrapped so tight you can hardly breathe, and I know what makes you get that way. You were ready to hand over your badge when you walked into my office with the chief yesterday. Doing your best to surrender before anybody even thought about charging you with anything."

He shrugged again, that tight little rejection shrug that makes him so hard to talk to sometimes. "Guess I did kinda jump the gun on that."

"Uh-huh. Because you were expecting to be accused of something. Bo, did you ask Diane about the gate?"

"Sure." We watched while a long vee of ducks swam across the lake toward the trees on the other side. "She said as far as she knew, it was locked. I said, Well, how could the garbage can be gone if the gate was locked? She said she had no idea, and why should I think she would know? Then she said she supposed from now on she was always going to get blamed for everything bad that happened in the whole town. Said she wished she knew how long she had to stay clean before everybody would quit watching her. I said, Just try to stay clean today, Diane, and let's worry about the rest of the days later on, okay? After that"—he watched the ducks climb out on the opposite bank—"it was very quiet at my house for the rest of the evening. It wasn't the answer she wanted to hear."

"What did she want to hear?"

He thought about it. "Junkies are very needy and very guilty but sometimes very tricky too. You can't give them enough love and reassurance to fill them up, but if you try too hard, they'll see they've got you going, and start taking advantage of that. So"—he swallowed and waited through a few painful seconds—"what does she want? More than I'll ever be able to give her, I'm starting to think." It was two long speeches in a row for Bo, and he looked very tired by the time he finished.

A gust of wind blew corn chaff in our faces, and I said, "I guess we ought to start back." We walked faster, feeling the wind rising at our backs, watching fast-moving cumulus clouds start to darken the sky.

Bo said, "Looks like we're due for some rain." His voice sounded raspy and raw. Maybe he's getting a cold, I thought, and he'll call in sick for a couple of days. I was ashamed of the relief I felt when I thought of him out of the building.

"Yeah. Well...let's go up to the evidence room and check out this big heap of money, huh?" We stood together at the window while Casey brought the items we asked for. We each signed our own withdrawal slips, and then Bo cosigned on the one for the money and walked away without saying any more. I watched him go, thinking, He never did tell me how he figures the Toter got out of his yard.

I DROVE THROUGH two small fast-moving showers on the way to St. Paul, taking the spray of dirt and gravel from the first gust on the windshield each time, and then the big drops that soon turned into a steady downpour and abruptly tailed off to a sprinkle after a few minutes. The breeze was tricky, easing off some during the hardest part of the rain and then blowing fresh from a new direction a minute after the storm had passed. White smoke from the refinery was blowing across the road at Pine Bend, and a dirt cloud blinded me for a couple of seconds just as I drove off the LaFayette bridge in heavy traffic. I was more than usually grateful to start hunting for a parking spot on University Avenue.

The check-in system at the state crime lab is surprisingly informal. The first time I went there I was prepared to see a high desk like an altar, with robed figures glaring down at waiting lines where humble supplicants like me stood in obedient rows. Instead, there's just a space near the elevators on the second floor, where a couple of reasonable-looking people sit at office desks. I stood in front of a desk where there was only one client ahead of me, and before long I got a seat in front of a guy in gray wool pants and a pocket protector, whose name tag read Bob Moss. He said, "Hi there, whatcha got?"

Bob was friendly and helpful, but not at all casual about the stuff he was checking in. He had the zeal of an inquisitor about the way everything was packaged and sealed. Police work is all about details, so I'm accustomed to careful packaging and meticulous notes, but Bob gave new meaning to the phrase "rigorous standards." He donned fresh gloves and turned every item over critically, sniffing it like a fox, holding it up to the light.

Behind his desk he had bags of every shape and size, paper for biological items and plastic for firearms and ammo. He had scissors, tubes, boxes, bottles, and slides. And tape, all kinds of tape. BCA admissions personnel are like Zen masters in the art of taping. Here, grasshopper, their faces say, as they hand the stuff to you, try again to learn the Tao of Tape.

It feels like they're being arbitrary, but I know they're not. Their first task is to make sure you're not bringing anything into their building that's going to contaminate evidence already there.

My slides and money passed muster, but Bob made me add another paper bag around the clothing packs I'd taken so much care with back in Rutherford. Then I had to tape hell out of them, and of course relabel each one. Finally I was allowed to proceed to Elly, who was operating "the Beast," the big new electronic machine with drop-dead software that spits out case and lab numbers, descriptions of items, and estimated due dates for test results. When the due dates appeared, they were so far in the future that I groaned with disappointment.

"I know, I know," Elly said. "The backlog here is getting ridiculous."

Obviously there wasn't anything she could do about it, but I got progressively grouchier as the Beast kicked out analysis request forms for each package and matching bar-coded stickers for the police report, the case file, and the evidence bag.

"God, it's got a life of its own, huh?"

"I wish. Unfortunately, I have to know which miracles to ask for."

"If you're getting the miracles you ask for, why does this place keep getting farther behind?"

She gave me a cool gray gaze over her granny glasses. "Improved technology is a mixed blessing."

"Oh? What makes you say that, Elly?"

"Well, just for one example, DNA testing is much more precise than blood typing, but it takes a lot longer to do."

"Ah. So the more dazzling we get, the behinder we're gonna fall?"

"I hope it's not that simple, but I gotta say from here it feels that way."

"Life really is a bitch, huh? See ya, Elly."

"Take care, Jake."

I muddled around a couple of turns on the second floor, stuck my head into a storeroom and then somebody's office, rounded a corner, and ran into Megan Duffy.

"Hey, Jake," she said. "You lost?"

"As usual in this building," I said. "You know where Trudy is today?"

"Fingerprints. Take a right at the end of this hall and then—"

I walked away from her, muttering, "Right, left, right—" and found a corner office where a screenful of fingerprints confronted a familiar yellow braid.

"Trudy?"

"Mmmm." She remained absorbed in the screen for a few seconds, and even after she raised her head and met my eyes, there was a scary little moment when she stared at me blankly as if trying to remember where she'd seen me before. Then her mind pried itself loose from whatever it was working on and her cheeks rounded in a big smile. "Jake! Why didn't you tell me you were coming up?" Then, suddenly apprehensive, "Is anything wrong?"

"Nope. Somebody had to bring evidence up, so I looked around for the least essential guy in the building, and here I am."

"Dear me. You're not getting jealous of your own assistants?"

"Jealousy has nothing to do with it. I just can't seem to remember to quit doing their jobs for them."

She laughed. "I never thought about that. I suppose it is a hazard, isn't it?"

"Tell me about it. I screwed Ray over so royally yesterday, it's only because he's a superior human being that he's still talking to me at all."

''Ah. So today you're trying to stay out of the building?''

''Just till everybody gets started. I realize it's only a short-term solution.''

''I should think so. Well…would it ease your pain to hear some delightful gossip?''

''Sure. Dish me some dirt.''

She leaned toward me, suddenly aglow, and murmured, ''Remember the other day I told you Megan got a phone call and left suddenly in tears?''

''Sure. But I saw her just now, and she looked fine. Very cheerful, in fact.''

''She should be. She's married.''

''Megan is? No kidding? Did she marry anybody you know?''

''Well, that's the amazing part. She married Jimmy.''

''Jimmy who?''

''Oh, come on, which Jimmy's in the building? Jimmy Chang!''

''You can't be serious.'' She nodded so hard her braid flew around. ''But he doesn't even like her! You said yourself he's always giving her a hard time.''

''He used to. Not so much lately, now that I think about it.''

''Well, but…did you know they were dating?''

''So help me Jake, I don't think they ever did! Isn't it a gas? Old Jimmy, who never thinks about anything but work. Somehow she must have got his mind off it for a few minutes.''

''Well, but…do you know yet what he said that made her cry?''

''Not yet. All we know is, she came back to work today wearing a gold ring on the third finger of her left hand.''

"Be damned." I hadn't noticed any ring. "So then you asked her—"

"Not me. Alice saw the ring and said, Hey, what's this all about, and Megan laughed and said, It's all about getting married, what would you think? and Alice said, Well, say, anybody we know? and Megan said, Jimmy Chang."

"Well...have you talked to her yet?"

"I tried to, but she kind of sidled away. I can't tell if she means to be secretive or she's just embarrassed to be talking about it at work. So Alice decided—"

"Who's Alice?"

"She's in handwriting analysis. Alice is going to talk her into going to lunch, and I'm going along, and we'll pump the story out of her then."

"Take notes, will you? Bring every juicy detail home to me tonight."

"Trust me."

"Now, I don't want to distract you too much, but could we just talk about DNA for a minute?"

"Why, certainly! DNA is, like, my pet thing in this building right now."

"Glad to hear it. I brought up that extra slide...the one I told you about, remember?"

"The one Pokey made? Yeah. You checked it in, right?"

"Well, sure. But Pokey suggested maybe you could get hold of it and put it into the queue for your Saturday's work—"

"Yeah, he called me, too. Don't worry, I'll take care of it. I told Pokey I'd look after it. What's he bugging you for?"

"For some reason, he's anxious about that one sample."

"Uh-huh. He's such a foxy guy. Listen, why don't I

go get it now, and you come along with me, and I'll show you the sexy machines I've been slaving over every Saturday.''

"Can I do that? They won't throw me out?"

"No, no." She laughed contentedly. "Charlie and Edna are mad geniuses, but they're perfectly harmless." Her extra hours in the lab were making her tired and irritable at home sometimes, but in here it was easy to see she was excited and pleased to be extending her intellectual reach.

We walked along the crowded halls, back toward the check-in desks. I pointed to an architect's drawing of a classy building framed on one wall. "This the new lab?"

"Uh-huh."

"Will it make a difference?"

"You kidding? It's gonna be three times as big as this one."

"But will more space make that much difference?"

"I should hope to shout. Look around! All the labs are so full of equipment, we can't set anything down, and we're fighting like alley cats over desks and stools. Look at all the boxes stacked in the halls! OSHA keeps threatening to write us up, and the director pleads with them, 'Wait, we're moving, we're moving!'''

"I guess that answers the question I've been wanting to ask somebody here."

"Which is?"

"Which is, if you're so flamin' far behind, why doesn't Jimmy clone some more scientists and catch up?"

"Clone some more scientists, jeez. There are plenty of biologists out there. We just don't have a square inch to set them down in. This whole building is gonna breathe a sigh of relief in a couple of months when the lab opens in Bimidji and we ship a few techies up there. It'll feel like taking off a tight girdle.''

"Now, what would you know about tight girdles?" I asked her.

"Mama's got some. Hey, Elly, howsgoin'?" She signed for Pokey's slide, and we took the elevator to the third floor and edged along more halls with boxes stacked along one side, to a bright lab where a man and woman bent quietly over gleaming stainless steel machines that looked like big pressure cookers with many gauges. Cupboards lined the walls, racks of squeaky-clean containers and eyedroppers crowded the counters, and a computer printed out tall strips covered with lines of, well, lines. All the lines had peaks and valleys like the ones you see on heart monitors on TV.

"That's Charlie," Trudy said, indicating the man in the blue shirt, who did not look up. Then she introduced me to the sweet-faced lady named Edna, who smiled at me.

"So, Edna," she said, "have you started the extractor yet?"

"Nope. About four-thirty."

"Oh, good. Can I use one more slot?"

"Uh…yeah, if you've got time to prepare the sample. I'm in the middle of this analysis; I can't stop."

"I'll do it. Thanks." She told me, "See, now, Jake, there's a lucky break to start us off. Extraction takes overnight. This is Wednesday. So tomorrow's Thursday, obviously, and—Edna, you're gonna run quantification on these in the morning, right?"

"Uh-huh."

"That'll take about two hours." Trudy tapped the end of her nose with her index finger, thinking. "So depending what else is going on, she might even get the amplification done in the afternoon. Four more hours. It's possible. Just barely. If not, there's still Friday for that, and then overnight in the genetic amplifier—I could be able to do the analysis Saturday.''

Edna cocked a dubious eye at her and said, "You're counting on a lot of luck, there, kid."

"Oh, I know. But it does happen sometimes, right? That everything goes right."

"Once in a while," Edna said.

"If something goes wrong, is that the end of it?" I asked her. "We're out of business then?"

"Oh, no, we never discard the sample till we see we've got a good test. If I have to, I'll run it again."

"What if you run out of stuff? Did Pokey send you plenty?"

"Oh, more than plenty. Now that we have the thermocycler"—she patted a gleaming pot with numerous dials—"a tiny little dab is all we need."

"Thermocycler. This is the magic replicator pot?"

"Forget magic," she said, "it's all about the heat." She'd been explaining some of her methods to me at home, and now she pointed to a label on the machine and read off the temperatures at which the double helix split apart and rebuilt its two halves by bonding with fresh molecules of protein. "In twenty-eight cycles, we get millions of copies of the fragment we started out with. And then, see, over here's a computer analyzing a test run." The tape made a tiny *shush-shush* sliding noise as it rose through the Plexiglas channel. She pointed again and said, "See how these two fragments match?" One set of inky peaks was repeated by the line below it.

"And you compare, what did you say, twelve places on the string?"

"Thirteen."

"But these locations don't necessarily cause blue eyes or big ears, you said."

"No. We don't know yet exactly what they do cause. What we do know is that these are places on the genetic string where each person has a unique pattern."

"Are you really saying no two are alike?"

"Well, the chances of a duplication are one in so many billion, they disappear for practical purposes."

"Fantastic." Logically, it wasn't hard to understand the functions of the machines or see the patterns in the squiggles on the computer tape. But relating these lab exercises to my own flesh and blood still felt to me like finding myself in a George Lucas movie. Trudy had become matter-of-fact about DNA science, and was simply hell-bent on perfecting her expertise, but I still got awestruck sometimes when I realized the woman I was sleeping with was burrowing her way into life's most closely held secrets. "Now that you're getting all these godlike powers," I asked her as we walked away, "are we gonna still be friends?"

"Are you gonna plow up a garden plot for me next weekend?"

"You drive a hard bargain, but yes, I can do that."

"Deal." She slid her hand under my jacket and tweaked my butt. "In that case we're buds to the end." She took her hand away, and my back felt empty. "I should be home on time," she said. "You?"

"Sure," I said. "My job is purely supervisory now." I headed for what I hoped was the front door. When I had it in sight, though, I changed my mind, took the elevator back up to the third floor, and searched out the head scientist's cluttered office.

Jimmy was sitting on the edge of his chair, leaning toward his computer screen, not typing exactly but punishing the keyboard with those jittery pokes and jabs that scientists seem to favor. Images and rows of statistics danced on his screen at confusing speed.

"Hey there," I said, tapping on his doorjamb.

"Whatever it is, you can't have it," he said, without looking up. "We're too busy."

"Not too busy to chase after the help, the way I heard it," I said, and was instantly sorry, because he jumped out of his chair and faced me with his fists clenched and his handsome face blazing with anger.

I smiled what I hoped was my most ingratiating smile and put my hand out. "And caught one, too, I understand. Where do we send the pasta platters?"

He softened up gradually, starting with his pectoral muscles, luckily, and when the meltdown reached his eyes, he misted up a little and said, "Oh, Jake, I—" and grasped my outstretched hand. "I'm not much good at jokes, I guess."

"You'll get better at it." I put my left hand around our joined hands, and we shook and grinned at each other. "Marriage is mostly a barrel of laughs." At the same second we both got uneasy about holding hands any longer, let go, and stepped back. "So, you made up your minds kinda sudden, huh?"

"Yes, well," Jimmy said, jingling coins in his pocket, "I wasn't really, ah, prepared for any of this...but—" He met my eyes, looked nonplussed, and added, "She—"

"Yes," I said gently, "aren't they?"

"Well—" He dry-washed his small, elegant hands for a few seconds, recovered his composure, and asked, like a department store clerk, "You finding everything you need here today, Jake?"

"Oh, for sure. Trudy even gave me a tour of the DNA lab."

"You notice how small it is?" His normal indignation came back in a blink.

"She seems to love it, though."

"Yes, well, good. Because I need to find about twenty more DNA-lab lovers and get them trained in the next year and a half. In that little soup kitchen? How do you suppose I should do that?"

"What happens in a year and a half?"

"The new building comes on-line! Don't you read the papers? Get Trudy to show you the plans." I opened my mouth to tell him she just had, but he swept on. "The legislature finally voted the funds for the new lab we've been begging for for eight years, but in the session before they voted for the lab, they passed a bill that said from now on we're not just going to keep DNA records on sex offenders, we'll keep them on people convicted of all violent or predatory crimes, murder, robbery, assault—"

"You don't like that? Everybody in Rutherford's been cheering—"

"Easy for you to say." Jimmy does contempt very well. "In a stroke, they increased our DNA workload by four. Plus we're supposed to test all the felons now in prison before they're released—"

"Cops love that part."

"I expect you do. Your life's getting easier every year. Ours is getting harder."

"Life's a bitch," I told him, "but hey, you just found the answer to that, right?"

He blinked at me. All his haughtiness left him for one memorable moment, and he said softly, "I sincerely hope so."

I bopped him on the shoulder the way guys are supposed to do, said, "Wish you the very best," and got out of there. Something was bothering Jimmy Chang beyond normal wedding jitters, I thought, and I doubted I was equipped to deal with whatever it was.

The weather had cleared; the sky was clear blue all the way around, birds were flying everywhere trying to make up for the hours they'd spent hiding on the lee side of tree trunks, and the smell of hamburgers being grilled somewhere nearby turned me into one big shameless appetite. I grabbed takeout lunch at a shack that boasted about its burritos, slathered a lot of hot sauce on everything because I love the stuff, and drove to Rutherford doing my best to digest it before it set my chest on fire.

I walked into my section dreading a rush of anxious questions, but there was total silence at Kevin's end of the hall, nobody in his office or the cubicles around it. LeeAnn was transcribing a tape in her bunker in the hall. I asked her, "Everything okay?"

She pulled one earphone away from her ear and said, "Mmm?"

I waved, "Nothing," and went on.

The only person I found in Ray's part of the building was Lou, who was set up at the new meeting table, sucking on cough drops and watching fuzzy black-and-white images cavort on a tiny tape monitor.

"Howsgoin'?" I asked him.

Without removing his eyes from the screen, he lifted his right hand with the middle finger extended.

"Knew you'd make the best of it," I said. I went back in my office and worked my way to the bottom of my In basket, brought up my e-mail and answered it all, logged off, and made some phone calls, including one to Pokey to ask for more details about the rape.

"Far as I know," he said, "was all done by one murderous bastard with own personal Johnson."

"So we're looking for a sociopath with a sore dong?"

"You detectives always lookin' for excuse to make prisoners strip down, ain'tcha?"

At five o'clock I walked out the front door of the building, got in my pickup, and started home. I kept expecting to hear sirens behind me, but nobody ever came and carried me forcibly back to the government center, and by the time Trudy got home, I had the table set and the grill started and was opening a bottle of wine.

"Wow," she said when I handed her a glass on the doorstep, "it's not my birthday, so it must be the Fourth of July."

"This is the new, cool Jake Hines," I said. "Successful bureaucrat and world-class off-loader of odious chores onto the backs of his underlings."

"I can live with it." She watched me carefully while she tried a sip. "Can you?"

"Damn right. I have reserves of ruthlessness you haven't even suspected yet."

"Whee. I've always wanted to sleep with a rogue. What do you have in mind for the grill, rogue?"

"Couple of potatoes baking on it right now, and"—I lifted the cover off a marinating steak—"this in half an hour."

"Super. Shall we start a little fire in the kitchen stove? Then I'll make a salad—"

"All in good time," I said. "You promised to bring me home a story."

"Have no fear." She pulled spinach out of the crisper. "It's just what I thought—Megan is pregnant."

"Whaat? You're kidding me." She shook her head, grinning. "That dog," I said. "That miserable hound!"

She gave me an ironic look. "I had no idea you felt so strongly about premarital sex."

"That's not the point!" I said. "I went up to his office

after I saw you, to congratulate him, and he shook my hand and stood there looking all discombobulated and demure, and he never said *one word* about how he'd already slid into home plate!''

Trudy curled her lip disgustedly, set down her glass with a little sharp click, and said, ''God, men are pigs.''

The phone rang. ''If that's the Rutherford Police Department,'' Trudy said, backing toward it, ''I'm gonna tell them you drowned.'' She picked it off its cradle on the wall, said hello and then, ''Oh, hi, Oz.'' She listened a minute and put the phone against her chest. ''Ozzie and his brother want to come over after dinner and make an offer.''

''Okay with me if it is with you.''

''Sure,'' she said into the phone. ''We haven't had supper yet, though. Can we…eight o'clock is fine.'' She hung up the phone, stood looking thoughtful, and said, ''We haven't talked about this in a while. Remind me, what are our bottom lines?''

''I just want to get as much as we can with the little we've got. Have you still got that price list of materials?'' She dug it out of the knife drawer and flipped it open. We sat down at the kitchen table and went over it again while the potatoes baked. It hadn't shrunk any since we looked at it last; it was going to take all our available cash and some credit card debt. So all while we ate and washed up, we debated again, If we have to do without something, what shall it be? We settled it just before the Sullivans drove into the yard: Forced to the wall, we'd take the new roof and the insulation, and let the wiring go till next year.

Trudy had made a fresh pot of coffee after dinner and put out a plate of peanut butter cookies. Ozzie ate two cookies while he unfolded two sheets of paper covered with figures. ''Dan and me been over this several times,'' he said. "We're pretty sure of our values. Let's take the rental on your land first." He laid a sheet in front of me. "You can check this out if you want to—"

"I already did," Trudy said. "May I see too, please?"

"Oh, sure," Ozzie said, startled. He pushed the sheet closer to Trudy. "Who'd you, uh, talk to?"

"Bestway. Sherman Brothers"—she named the two farm realtors in Mirium—"and Condon and Price."

"Those Twin City guys? They're too far away to know what people are doing down here."

"They have an office in Rutherford," she said, "and one in Cannon Falls. This is pretty far on the low side, guys." She dug notes out of her purse and showed them her estimates from the others.

"Well," Ozzie said, looking a little alarmed, "we're only talking about a swap here! I'm sure we can arrive at a rate of exchange that'll keep everybody happy. What say we look at the work on the house?"

They didn't have the three jobs figured separately. "We were kind of thinking we might have to leave one out," I said.

"I really think that would be a mistake," Ozzie said firmly. "You save so much time if you do all three together; the price would be a lot higher if you broke out any one of these and did it separately. Understand what I mean?"

"Sure. But—so this is the total number of hours? For the two of you?"

"That's right."

"And this down here is the total price." The difference between the price for the job and the rent on the land, I saw, was amazingly close to the figure I had been thinking of quoting for my five-year-old aluminum boat.

"This right here is the hourly rate?" Trudy asked him.

"Yup."

"Let's see now," she said. "Is that the rate for carpenters or—"

"What we did," Ozzie said, "is we averaged the rates for roofers and electricians, and figured the insulation at carpenter's rates."

"But you're not actually any of those things, are you, Ozzie?" Trudy said, suddenly looking him full in the eyes. "You're a bartender. Sort of."

"I'm a farmer, if you want to be that way," Ozzie said, turning red. "Dan is the one in the building trade. Listen, if you're not interested in this deal—"

"Oh, we're interested," Trudy said. "We're just trying to understand this rate of exchange you mentioned. Do amateurs get paid union scale out here in Mirium?"

"Tell you what," Ozzie said, looking huffy, "what you better do, you better think about this, do some more checking around." He reached across the table to pick up his two-page estimate, but Trudy gripped it firmly and would not let go. Ozzie pushed back his chair abruptly and stood up, and Dan, who I thought looked more amused than anything, stood up too. "And then you can call me later if you want to talk about it some more."

"Exactly," Trudy said, smiling at him brightly. "That's just what I thought we should do." They filed out the door without saying any more, got in Ozzie's old car together, and spun out of the yard, throwing gravel at the front of the house.

"Well," I said, "I guess that's the end of that."

"You think so? I don't. I think we're just getting to know each other."

I watched her fold the Sullivan estimates around the other papers she'd collected and tuck the whole bundle carefully into an inside pocket in her purse. "What are you doing with those?"

"I'll have time to make some more phone calls on my lunch hour tomorrow." She gathered up plates and cups and began rinsing them in the sink. "I'm gonna find out the going rate for apprentice carpenters. And while I'm at it, I'll check these materials estimates again, see if there's any wiggle room there."

"I had no idea you were such a shark." Standing beside her at the sink, drying dishes, I gave her a bump with my hip. "I got kinda turned on watching you beat up on Ozzie like that."

"Hey, that was just practice." She bumped me back. "I can play much rougher than that."

"Shall we go upstairs? I wouldn't want to break up the kitchen."

Later, on the edge of sleep in contented darkness, I heard her murmur, "It's just crazy how happy she looks."

"Hmmm?" I patted her arm. "'Cha talkin' abou'?"

"Megan." She rolled over and nested her backside against me. "In some ways her situation is terrible. Jimmy's family's on a rampage, totally opposed to the marriage. And she says that hurts him, he's always been the favorite, and now everybody's mad at him."

"Is that why she cried that day?"

"No, she cried because the night before, they had made up their minds they couldn't get married in the face of all this opposition, they'd just have to break up and have an abortion. Jimmy was supposed to be downtown arranging the financing. But suddenly that day he called her at work and said, 'The hell with this, it's our life and our baby. Do you love me?' And—you remember how I told you she said, 'Yes,' and then listened some more before she hung up and started to cry? Well, when she said, 'Yes,' he said, 'Then come to City Hall right now and marry me.'"

"Imagine old Jimmy saying that," I said.

"I can't." She breathed a couple of times, thoughtfully, and then said, "She seems to be in this amazing state of denial. They're living in her little room-and-a-half apartment because all he had was his bachelor pad at the university. They don't have a home or any furniture or dishes; his parents won't speak to them because she's not Chinese. Her mother's dead, her father's in the army in Guam, she's expecting a baby in a little less than seven months, and you know what? She's so happy she can hardly contain herself."

"Crazy," I said. I was definitely drifting off.

We lay in contented silence while the old house creaked and settled around us, and then from what seemed like a long way off, I heard her say, "It must be chemical, I guess."

"Mmff?"

"Women, when they're first pregnant. They always look like they've just learned some wonderful secret that the rest of us are too dumb to understand." She twitched a couple of times more, and then fatigue overcame her restlessness, and she slept.

EIGHT

"HOW'RE YOU COMING WITH the merchant interviews?" I asked Kevin Thursday morning.

"Andy and Clint are out now doing the last two. We're not learning a whole lot we didn't know before."

"But the pictures, are they working with the Identi-Kits? Coming up with any likenesses?"

"The blond woman, yes, guys who saw her remember her well. Although they mostly say pretty generic stuff like, Wow, whatta pair of knockers. Gets to the nose and eyes, they go vague on us."

"The little girl? Everybody seems to be able to describe her well enough."

"And we've worked up a portrait. But you wouldn't be able to tell it from a thousand other small, blond girls with blue eyes. Probably blue eyes. Might have been hazel. Could have been green." He shrugged. "You know how it goes, Jake. At the end of the day, what they really remember is how she *annoyed* them."

"Uh-huh. And the plain brown-haired woman, I suppose that's harder yet."

"You got it. Medium build, medium complexion, medium medium medium."

"Well, soon as Maddox and Pitman get back, though, you're going to fix up something, huh? And put out an

Attempt to Locate? Ray, anything at all on the Hispanic guy?''

''I've found three of the customers Louie Forsell definitely remembers being in the bar that night. I talked to them all, and they were adamant, they do not want to go to the morgue with me. They gave me descriptions of the Hispanic man, and we worked up a composite photo—''

''Ray, that's not the way to go. You've got a body in the morgue. You've got to get them in there and get them to say yes or no, it is or isn't the guy they saw in the Chicken Shack.''

''They really dug in their heels,'' he said unhappily. ''They want to help, but they want to do it with the Identi-Kit.''

''Do they seem pretty certain about the image you're creating? Are you getting pretty much the same picture from each of them?''

''Well, they all agree he carried some extra flesh, had a fairly big nose, and his hair was beginning to go gray.''

''It was? I don't remember any gray hair on the guy we pulled out of the bottom of the barrel, do you?''

''No. But we were all so surprised, and there was so much going on. Come to think of it, though, Rosie talked about his hair the morning after the autopsy, didn't she?''

''Yeah, she did. Have you showed her the likeness you came back with?''

''No. Is she around?'' He went to see, came back, and said, ''Not at her desk. I'm paging her.''

''Anything else about this guy? Anybody ever see him before that night?''

''No. Except Joe Schermerhorn said there was something odd about his Spanish accent.''

''Odd how?''

"Well, he couldn't seem to say, just that he never heard one quite like it before."

"Hmmm. How many Spanish people does Joe see in an average day?"

"He works at Methodist Hospital. Probably quite a few."

"Ah. Well, big nose, gray hair, funny accent, it's better than nothing. I suppose you could—"

Rosie walked in the door. "Ray, you call me?"

Ray handed her the composite picture he'd created. "Does this look like the man you watched getting autopsied on Sunday?"

She squinted. "The nose seems kind of big. And the hair isn't wavy enough, but of course people—who helped you with this?"

"Three guys who were at the Chicken Shack last Friday night."

"There you go," she said, spreading her hands, "guys and hair."

"You know what I think you ought to do," I said, "before we go back around that argument again, is the two of you take that picture over to the morgue and compare it to the body that's over there. If it's not a good likeness, work on where you think it's wrong."

"I never tried to ID a dead guy from a picture before," Ray said. "How much change do I have to allow for?"

"From when we saw him on the street? Hardly any. He went straight to the morgue, he was autopsied right away and then embalmed. The swelling may have gone down a little from some of his injuries. Otherwise…he'll be a little more sallow, his eyes may have sunk a little. Your main problem is the picture, not the body. Your picture's probably not very accurate. But go ahead, give it a try."

When they were gone, Kevin said, "Did you get a chance to call Pokey? About the rape?"

"Yup. Pokey believes that the job was done with an unassisted male member."

"Ah, good. At least we don't have to start looking for tools. I was dreading that. I hear my guys coming back, excuse me."

The chief called me then, and I went into his office and brought him up to date on where the investigators were and what we had given BCA.

"Actually you've got all your investigators working together on this now, haven't you?" He was rubbing his nose, thinking. "Except Bo Dooley. Is he covering new calls?"

"And working on cold cases. You know, though—" I repeated what I'd said to Bo, that if he had done this crime, he would say so.

"Oh...well." Frank stared out the window. "I'd be careful about thinking you know *that* about anybody. We probably don't even know it about ourselves till the time comes."

I stared at him, shocked. His phone rang. "Tell him to come in," he said, and Lou French walked in, wearing an uncommonly smug expression.

"What'll you give me for a nice home movie of a quick-change hustle?" he said.

"Lou—" I grinned so wide I hurt my cheeks. "You found one, no shit?" The chief came with us to the conference table in front of Ray's office. Kevin and Darrell were already there, and I went and got Bo to come out and watch too.

Lou had found the segment in the Rexall store, with the flashy blond loading up a couple of bags of toiletries, the child touching and grabbing things, asking for this and that, making a pest of herself. There were a few other customers in the store, and you could occasionally see the store manager waiting on them while he tried to keep an eye on the troublesome child.

The climax was the money-shuffling scene at the cash register, when the woman appeared to count her money and protest about the change, and the child suddenly went from mildly annoying to rudely disruptive, pawing through packaged items on a freestanding rack until she toppled the whole display. We watched that part twice, because we missed the money grab entirely on the first run-through. The child played her part so well, it was almost impossible not to watch her even when you knew your eyes belonged elsewhere.

The second time Lou spotted the moment and said, "There!" He stopped the tape and backed up to the frame in which the woman's hand moved to the shelf above the cash drawer where the owner had laid the money he was making change for. We ran it twice more at normal speed and never could be sure we saw the snatch, but we knew where it was now, and each time we went back to it and slowed it down, there were those three frames where her white hand reached, grabbed, and palmed the cash.

We were all high-fiving and grinning around the conference table by then. Ray and Rosie walked into the space just as Darrell, high-fiving Kevin, said, "Jeez, it feels good to feel good for a change."

"Well, duh," Rosie said. "You guys do something clever?"

"Lou found a tape of one of the quick-change hustles," I said. We ran it again, and as soon as they'd seen it, we all helped pick the best views of both the woman and child for our Attempt to Locate notices.

Lou marked them and the money-snatching frame and

said, "I'll take it out to Greg to get prints made." We've got a photo-enhancement guy on staff who can show you the whiskers on the guy at the back of the auditorium in the picture, if you give him a few minutes.

"Good," Ray said, "and tell me now, how many more surveillance tapes have you got to go through?"

"Shit, all but three," Lou said. "Three is all I've done. It takes fucking forever."

"Let's get you some help," Ray said. "It's time-consuming, but it pays off big when you get a hit, doesn't it? Darrell?" Darrell pretended to hide under his jacket. "Get LeeAnn to find you another viewer."

"Welcome to the club," Lou said. "You can have the other end of the table."

"Okay," I said. "Now, Ray and Rosie, come in my office and tell me what you decided at the morgue."

"The body doesn't have gray hair," Ray said. "Definitely."

"And the hair in the picture isn't wavy enough," Rosie said. "And the nose in the image is all wrong. But people's descriptions...you know yourself, Jake—"

"Yes. I do. So what I want you to do, Ray, is go back and find those three guys, and tell them you'll get a subpoena if necessary, but they have got to come and view the body at the morgue and decide if it's the man they saw last Friday night at the Chicken Shack. Or not. Quit being Mr. Nice Guy, get 'em in there."

He gave me a bleak look but nodded and went out without another word. Rosie, cheerful as a bird, went back to downloading Bo and his snitches.

I bounced around my office a few minutes, feeling scattered, trying to decide what to do next. I need a boost, I decided, so I called the best booster I knew.

Maxine Daley said, "'Lo?" in the minimalist speech of the day-care provider.

"Lunch?"

There was a funny little pause, and she said, "It's almost two o'clock, Jakey."

"Oh…well, so it is. I guess I got sort of wrapped up in law enforcement here. So, have you got time for a cup of coffee?"

"Yes. I'm just putting my babies down for a nap. Now's a good time. Don't ring the bell, huh? Just walk in."

Maxine's working day is governed by the urgent needs of small children. To maintain a friendship with her, you have to be willing to talk in short bursts between mop-ups. I stopped at a 7-Eleven and bought strawberry ice cream.

Nelly and Eddy, the two "big kids" in her care, were looking out the front window when I drove up. Nelly was Bo Dooley's daughter; three and a half going on forty, pushed toward early maturity by her mother's drug habit. She looked like Bo, with auburn curls lying close to her head all around and a slight overbite, and she was poised like him too, but more talkative.

"Hi, Jake," she said, hugging my leg.

"Hey, Nelly, how's my bud? Howya doin', Eddy?" He didn't answer, but he took my hand and smiled, sort of, at his shoes. Eddy was seven, small for his age, Maxine's newest foster child. He arrived suddenly on a weekend two months ago, shell-shocked and silent in the wake of a ghastly family tragedy. His father had suffered a psychotic break, during which he shot and killed his wife and all their other children. Eddy escaped by a fluke.

Maxine had agreed to take on the exhausting labor of tending him while he healed. For weeks, he had hardly slept. Maxine stayed by him through those terrible nights, reading to him, singing nursery rhymes, till he could drift off. The first time he spoke, she cried.

He still couldn't concentrate on anything complicated, so helping Nelly play was just about right for him. He would hold a doll for her, or hand her Legos and tiny dishes, and Nelly would spin her busy fantasies around him while he watched her silently. Some days, fear and horror still pursued him with iron teeth. Then Maxine would tell Nelly, "Eddy needs to be quiet today. Let's sit by him, and I'll read to you."

Easing him back into life was going to be dicey work for a long time. I knew Maxine could do it if anybody could; she had been my foster mother for the six best years of my childhood. Health and Human Services dragged me away from her, kicking and screaming, the year I was nine, because her hapless husband had taken to drinking up the aid money. I went through some rough patches in households where I didn't fit before I got lucky again. A talented teacher showed me how I could save my own life in school, and I studied my way out of juvenile delinquency. Years later, when I made the police department, my spare-time hobby became an ongoing search for Maxine.

I found her by accident last winter. After an initial outburst of hugging and crying, we had settled quickly into hastily snatched give-and-take, the gabbing, nagging, and small favors characteristic of grown family members anywhere. By unspoken agreement, we had never discussed our future, but we both knew wild dogs wouldn't tear us apart again.

She came out of the bedroom now and said, "Hi, honey."

I handed her the ice cream in a brown paper bag and said, "After-nap treats."

"Oh, thanks," she said, moving toward the refrigerator.

Nelly, quick as a cat, asked, "Can we have some now?"

"Better wait; you had a cookie after lunch." Maxine slid the box into the freezer. "It won't be long. How about if you and Eddy play with toys for a while, and let me enjoy a cup of coffee with Jake? Here, I'll give you some privacy." She slid the folding door between the living room and kitchen almost closed. Clearing a place for me at her cluttered table, she said, "I warmed up some soup for you."

"You didn't have to—" She shushed me with her hand and ladled out a bowl. "Good," I said as soon as I tasted a spoonful. "Oh, it's good," I said again, suddenly ravenous. She brought crackers, and coffee for both of us, and sat down with a sigh.

"Nelly doesn't nap anymore, huh?"

"She did, till Eddy came. Now she'd rather stay up and keep him company. Of course, she's at that age…. I let her skip it unless we go to the park in the morning, then she gets too tired."

"Speaking of tired, you look kind of bushed yourself."

"Eddy woke up crying last night. Bad dreams, I guess. He couldn't seem to say. It took him a long time to settle down after."

"I thought you were going to quit taking care of the babies. Isn't it enough, the aid money for Eddy plus what Bo pays?"

"I could get by. But my other two mothers both have jobs they just love, and they keep pleading with me to stick with them till they can find somebody else as reliable."

"Fat chance of that."

"Well, there's some good ones out there. They're just all full up right now." She stretched and yawned. "Enough of that. Tell me how you're coming on your house."

"We've got a couple of guys from the neighborhood working up a bid."

"They know anything about fixing houses?"

"One of them does. And the other one's his brother."

"Jake, it's not like blue eyes, it doesn't run in families."

"Oh, well, I know. But they work together quite a bit."

"What does Trudy think of them?"

"Right now I think Trudy would settle for having the whole problem go away. We thought that house was going to be so much fun, and now it seems like it's just a bunch of hard decisions."

"Ain't that life? Want some more soup?" She got up to fetch it, glanced through the opening she had left in the folding door, and froze in place, watching. I could hear Nelly through the cheap plastic sliding door, talking to her toys.

"Now, don't you worry if I don't come home," she was saying. "I just have to go with the man sometimes." From where she stood by the stove, Maxine crooked her finger and beckoned. I got up quietly and moved to stand beside her. Nelly took the blanket Eddy was holding for her and tucked it carefully around a doll, a teddy bear, and a giraffe that she had laid out side by side on a pillow. She talked to them while she worked. "You just be good kids now," she said, "and take care of Daddy till I get back."

Eddy had been standing as usual, quietly watching her. Suddenly he began to pace back and forth in front of the blanketed toys, saying in a loud, angry voice, "Something's gotta change here!" Startled, I turned to Maxine, who was watching him, horror-struck. "I'm gonna put a stop to this!" Eddy shouted. He picked up a small broom, one of Nelly's playthings, aimed it like a gun at the row of toys lying under the blanket, and made loud firing noises. "Bam! Bam! Bam!"

Nelly looked distressed.

Maxine slid the folding door open and said calmly, "Listen, kids, you know what? Jake says he thinks it would be okay if you two had your ice cream first, before the babies wake up."

"Raaaay!" Nelly said, and ran for the table. Eddy hung on to the broom a few seconds, looking dazed. Finally he dropped it quietly and came toward his chair. By the time Maxine set the bowl in front of him, his expression was pretty much what you'd expect on a kid looking at ice cream. It was hard to believe that you had just watched him play assassination.

"God, that was well done," I told Maxine a few minutes later when we stood on her front step saying good-bye. "But you're worried, aren't you?"

"He's going into the next stage, I guess. Coming out of the deep freeze and starting to act out. They warned me about this when I took him."

"Isn't this kind of complicated? Don't you need help?"

"His caseworker has been urging me to get him started in counseling. I kept putting her off, saying Let the poor little guy heal up a little. But looks like we better get started before he murders a couple of Nelly's toys."

"Yeah. About Nelly's toys…was she telling them she had to go?"

"Uh-huh. Nelly knows things she can't say, I think."

"Like maybe her mother's getting ready to take another hike?"

"Looks that way."

Through the bedroom window beside the door, I heard one of the babies begin to whimper. "Jeez, Maxine. You're running a school for the walking wounded here, and mothering babies on top of that." I gave her a hug. "I wish I could stay and help you."

"Oh, c'mon now, don't start worrying about me." She pushed her hair back in an impatient gesture I remembered. "Survivor is my middle name, remember?"

"That's right. I forgot that!" I laughed. "Maxine S. Daley."

"And you were Jake T. Hines, remember?"

"For Trailblazer." I laughed again. "I forget, what was Patsy?"

"Patricia G. Daley. For Gorgeous. So she could wear that old pink satin dress she liked the feel of so much."

"You know, I can't remember much about that game except I liked it, and for a while we played it almost every day. What did we do that was so much fun?"

"We each did whatever we wanted to do. That's why I invented it, so you two could play it while I was cooking supper. Patsy would swish around being a beauty contest winner, and you'd climb on the furniture and discover the North Pole or something."

"Oh, yeah, I remember now. Once I got as far as Australia, and got attacked by a kangaroo." We stood together on her crumbling front step in the sharp April breeze and laughed, remembering. The details of Maxine Daley's life sound tragic—well, they are tragic; her husband was a drunk, but she loved him too much to leave him; the state took me away from her; and she had to put her daughter Patsy in a boarding school for blind kids in order to get her a life. So it's curious that when I'm with her, I always have a good time, and when we talk about the years we lived together, we usually laugh.

I WENT BACK TO the department and made the rounds. Kevin and his crew were out of the building. Ray was sitting in his windowless office, talking on the phone. I stood and waited till he hung up, and said, "Howsgoin'?"

"They're all dodging me now," he said, quietly furious, "but I'll get 'em."

Rosie and Bo were in his cubicle, turning over a stack of three-by-five cards, commenting on each one, and occasionally pulling a card out of the big pile to add to the small one growing by Rosie's elbow. I waved to them and went on, making a note to myself to needle Bo again about making peace with the computer. Ever the contrarian, he was still fighting a rearguard action against the concept of sharing what he knew with a machine.

Lou and Darrell faced each other at opposite ends of the conference table, scrolling and chatting idly. I asked them, "Anything more?"

"Darrell's got one possible segment of the coin caper," Lou said, "but it's almost out of the frame, and in bad light. We marked it in case we don't get a better shot."

"We can show you everything we've got in the morning," Darrell said, "if we get through the tapes this afternoon."

"Right," Lou said, winking at me, "or if not, then not."

"Yeah, well, that's police work for you," Darrell said, "never a day the same."

Lou hugged himself and rocked silently for a few seconds before he said, "Ah, Darrell, what in the world will I do without you when I retire?"

"Heck," Darrell said, touched, "we can still get together every so often."

I was in my office a few minutes later when Trudy called me and said, "I think I've got enough new information to have another go at the Sullivan brothers. Okay if I set something up for tonight?"

"Sure. Let's make a deal." My life felt a lot easier to me since my visit with Maxine; I wanted to quit bellyaching about our house and fix it.

"Good. I'll see you at home," she said, and she was already there, starting rice and a stir-fry, when I drove into the yard.

"What's this under the towel?" I said. "Apple crisp? Oh, yum. How come dessert on a weekday?"

"That's for later," she said. "The Sullivan boys seem to like baked goods."

"Uh-huh. Is bartering making you devious?"

"Probably not as devious as Ozzie Sullivan, but we'll see." We had the dishes done and the floor swept by seven o'clock. Trudy set two pairs of chairs facing each other at the kitchen table, and dug out the papers she had folded into her purse after our last meeting with the Sullivans. When she unfolded them, I saw she had added several sheets.

Old internal combustion engines develop signature sounds, I reflected when Ozzie turned his Chrysler into our driveway. I knew without looking whose car it was, and if I listened a little longer, I thought I'd be able to say which piston was misfiring. Trudy dished up the apple crisp and put out cream and sugar.

Dan Sullivan came in first. This time he was carrying the folded sheets of paper and a ballpoint pen. Ozzie followed, holding an armful of pussy willows, which he handed to Trudy, saying, "Here, I brought you a present."

"Oh, how very nice," Trudy said. She stood with her arms full of the fuzzy gray bouquet, doing her best to look pleasant but really not very pleased at all; she had prepared carefully to have the upper hand at this joust, and she did not want to be stuck at the sink arranging flowers when the discussion got started.

I grabbed the branches out of her arms and said, "Here, I'll put 'em in water."

She threw me a look of grateful surprise but said, "Uh...no water. They last better dry—but there's a tall vase there on the bottom shelf of the sideboard." She went back to the chair where she had stacked her estimates and said, "Now, who wants coffee?"

Getting the tall vase out meant getting down on my knees, taking out all the shorter items that were in front, and replacing them after I found what I wanted. I had the vase set up on the drain board by the sink and had my arms full of pussy willows again when the phone began to ring. I crammed the branches into the vase, grabbed it off the wall, and said, "Hines."

Kevin Evjan said in a strangely guarded but absolutely serious voice, "How fast can you get to Fillmore Field?"

"Oh—" I brushed leaves and fat gray buds off my shirt. "About half an hour." I didn't even think about asking why.

"Try to make it a little faster. We'll wait for you if we can. We're in C section, top row."

The phone went dead. I got my side arm and shield out of the pantry. "I gotta go to work," I said, buckling on my Glock. "Sorry. Go ahead and—" I waved vaguely at the three astonished faces around the table, walked out the door, and climbed into my pickup.

I covered the forty-one miles from my door to the baseball diamond in northeast Rutherford in twenty-six minutes. The highway was almost empty, and nobody made a move to intercept me till I was three blocks inside the city limits and slowing down. Then Vince Greeley squealed out of a side street, recognized my pickup, and fell in behind me. He jumped out of his blue-and-white and trotted quietly beside me toward the gate, saying, "Plenty of us out here, Jake, just say when."

"Okay." I had no idea what we were talking about. I showed my shield discreetly to the middle-aged woman in the admissions booth, went through the turnstile, and scanned the bleachers, which were only about half full. The scoreboard said the game was starting the top of the seventh, tied one-all. The visitors, the Saint Cloud River Bats, were just coming up to bat, with two batters out of the dugout taking practice swings. The Rutherford Blue Herons were warming up on the field, burning fastballs at one another while canned organ music rattled the speakers.

Kevin was in the top row, wearing a loud T-shirt and a baseball cap backward. As soon as I started climbing toward him, I saw Ray, two seats to his right, in nondescript jeans and a no-color sweatshirt.

While I climbed toward them, the Herons' pitcher threw three straight balls so high and outside the batter just stood and watched them pass, then two good breaking balls that he swung at and missed. Just as I reached the top row, the pitcher threw high again, and the batter trotted to first while the crowd began that restless patter that starts when a runner gets on base in a tight game.

I stepped across Kevin's knees and sat down between them, panting a little. Kevin said, softly, "Ray and I came out to watch a ball game. He likes the top row. The first couple innings were slow, so we got to looking around."

The second batter was ready at the plate, and the pitcher threw a slider that he swung at and tipped foul.

"A little to our left," Ray said, hunching a little closer to me, "top row in the second tier, the platinum blond in the pink blouse and tan skirt."

"I see her." It was the woman we had watched on the surveillance tape that morning, but better in living color, her bright blouse snug around her full breasts and her hair shiny as a beacon in the glaring lights.

"Watch her a minute," Ray said. The second pitch was low and outside, but the batter swung anyway, and the crowd reacted as he missed it by a mile.

The blond was sitting in the third seat to the right of the aisle. A large raffia purse stood upright on the folded-down seat left of her, a satchel with a flat bottom and stiff sides, open at the top with its handles hanging down. A pink sweater that matched her blouse was draped over the back of the seat next to the aisle, and the seat was down as if she was saving it for someone. Somebody would probably have been giving her grief if the bleachers had been full, but there were plenty of seats available, so nobody was challenging her appropriation of two extra ones. The rest of the row, to the right, was filled with fans enjoying the game.

As I watched, a man in a blue shirt and khakis sat down in front of her pink sweater in the seat next to the aisle and smiled at her in a friendly way. She smiled brightly back at him, and they began to chat as the pitcher threw two balls and the crowd began to shout advice. The man in the blue shirt laid his right hand flat on the seat next to her purse, with a little edge of green showing on the side nearest the blond woman. By the time the pitcher threw a third ball, the woman's hand lay next to the man's hand on the seat, with what looked like a sliver of plastic between her ring finger and pinkie. The pitcher threw a fastball, a little high and inside, but the batter swung anyway and knocked a high fly into left field. The crowd stood up to watch the ball climb steeply up against the lights and then drop neatly into the left fielder's glove. When everybody sat down again, the man in the blue shirt was gone, and the blond woman's hands rested in her lap.

"She's dealing dope in the ballpark?"

"She's dealing something," Ray said.

"How's business?"

"That makes ten sales since she got here in the second inning."

"Have you figured out how she's getting the word out?"

"She's got two helpers working the crowd. One's got a tray of popcorn—the guy in the red apron down there by the third-base line, see him?"

"Uh-huh." He was bending across a couple of fans to pass bags of popcorn to children.

"The other one's over by the men's room. He's behind a pillar right now. Don't worry about him, Andy's got him covered."

"Okay. Is it just me, or does this setup smell funny to you?"

"Odd as hell," Kevin said. "Three people just to peddle a little dope at the ball game? C'mon."

"So what are you thinking?"

"We are puzzled."

"That's why we wanted to get you in here," Ray said. "We thought maybe you could figure it out."

"So far, I'm as confused as anybody," I said. The next man was getting set in the batting box. "You got a plan?"

"I thought maybe you and I might go make a buy," Kevin said. "We've got Clint and Darrell across from us, ready to grab the popcorn salesman, and Rosie's off to our right, covering Andy Pitman's behind. Andy's gonna get the asshole by the men's room.''

"Uh-huh." I looked at Ray. "And you?"

"Ray's gonna stay up here and scan the whole thing," Kevin said, "because he's a good scanner, and we both think this is flaky."

"You're in touch with dispatch, right?"

"Sure, that's why we gotta move—we got most of the uniforms in Rutherford hanging out there in the bushes, and traffic control is going to hell."

"Okay. Well—" The batter laid down a bunt, but the third baseman, playing in, scooped up the ball and made the throw to the shortstop covering second, who stepped on the base and still had plenty of time to throw the batter out at first. As soon as the double play was complete, the stands exploded in a roar and then became quickly chaotic as the seventh-inning stretch was announced. The canned organ played "Take Me Out to the Ball Game," and a thousand fans stood up and milled around.

"Let's do it," I said, and Kevin and I went down the steps with a stream of people heading for the bathrooms and concession stands. Kevin peeled off at the landing above the second tier and crossed to enter the top row from the right side. I slid into the seat in front of the pink sweater and smiled at the blond woman. She didn't look quite so young and glossy close up. In fact she gave off an obscure whiff of something toxic that made my nose itch. She smiled back at me brightly until she felt Kevin on the other side of her, squeezing across the knees of the people in the seats next to her, ignoring their glares. When she looked up at him, startled, he looked directly into her eyes and did not smile.

She turned back to me, awareness growing in her eyes.

I laid my wallet, open to the shield, on the seat between us and said, ''Let's make a deal.''

''Thank God you've come,'' she said. ''Will you help me get away?''

NINE

"YOU DON'T NEED to do that," she said when we put the cuffs on her. "I want to go with you."

"That's okay, lady," Kevin said, "it's no trouble."

"Let's go," I said, grabbing her sweater and purse, anxious to get her out of the crowd. Angry people yelled, "Hey, cut it out," and "Whaddya *doin'?*" as Kevin pushed ahead of us to clear a path. When they turned and saw me hustling the handcuffed woman past them, they gawked and nudged one another.

We passed Andy Pitman holding a thin pale boy by the throat against a concrete piling. "Soon as you put your hands behind your back, buddy," Andy said, "I'm gonna let you breathe."

Outside in the chilly dark we fast-walked the blond woman toward the waiting squads, Darrell and Clint right behind us pushing the popcorn salesman, who was scattering popcorn everywhere and yelling at the top of his lungs, "Be careful, you'll break my tray!"

"If you don't shut up, I'm gonna bust it over your head," Clint said. Standing by Vince Greeley's squad, he got the tray off somehow and put it in the trunk, then shoved the kid into the backseat and climbed in after him. Andy jumped into Manahan's car with the thin kid, who was looking sick. Kevin inserted the blond woman deftly into Buzz Cooper's backseat, one hand on top of her head

and another under her elbow. The squads turned their ro-
tating lights on and hit their sirens a short pop, clearing
a swath out of the parking lot that closed behind them as
soon as they were gone.

I stood by Ray in the parking lot, watching the crowd
thin out. ''Well, so you scanned,'' I said. ''Did you see
anything?''

''Surprised fans wondering why we were kidnapping
their popcorn salesman.''

''No lurking hoodlums, no setup?''

''Nothing but baseball fans—that I could see.'' He
yawned. ''Maybe the blond lady's gonna explain how she
affords all that help.''

''Given her MO, she probably just skips without paying
them.'' I yawned too and said, ''Let's leave the questioning till morning, huh? Charge her with dealing and put
her away. There's nothing here big enough to justify an
all-nighter in jail.''

''Fine,'' he said. ''As it is, we'll be lucky to get 'em
printed and booked by midnight.''

I took forty minutes to go home. There was a lot of
traffic, and I was too bushed to play road warrior. Trudy
was in bed, asleep, when I got home. I took pains to slide
in beside her without waking her up. It felt like my alarm
went off fifteen minutes later, but Trudy was getting up,
so I checked my watch. I shook it several times, but it
still said six-thirty. Reluctantly, I decided that must be
why the sky was getting light and stumbled into the
shower.

Drinking coffee in the kitchen as gold slanted across
the yard, Trudy asked me, ''Was that big trouble, last
night? The Sullivans were very impressed, by the way.''

''Very small trouble, it turned out. But puzzling. Sorry

I had to run out on you. What do you think, should we forget about those guys?''

"Oh, no, no," she said. "We had a good long talk. I think we're getting close to a deal we can all live with.''

"You mean it? I thought Ozzie kind of pissed you off with those pussy willows.''

"Isn't he the crafty one?'' She smiled at the fuzzy bouquet, which was now on a doily on the sideboard. "He comes down to earth when he sees you're onto him, though. And that Dan, now, he really knows what he's talking about.''

"He talked to you?''

"He doesn't talk a lot, but when he does, it pays to listen. He knows a lot about building.''

"Son of a gun. I thought Ozzie was the big mover and shaker.''

She shook her head. "Dan's the heavy thinker. Ozzie's just his helper.''

"I'll be damned. I think from now on,'' I said as we went out the door together, "I'm gonna start calling you Cool Hand Trudy.''

She poked my arm. "Wait till you see if you like the deal.''

"If it puts a roof on this house, I'm gonna like the deal.'' I had come a long way in the last couple of days; I was learning to say, whenever my brain produced a picture of Ozzie Sullivan sitting in my boat, "Who has time to fish?''

Trudy tossed me a cheery wave as she drove out of the yard ahead of me. It's too bad I don't own more stuff, I thought; dickering over it seems to agree with her.

I got to work on time, but Kevin Evjan was already pacing in front of my door and followed me into my of-

fice, saying, ''Ah, finally you're here! I've already got Ms.
Morgan in my office.'' He wasn't tired; he was all aglow.

''Can't wait to get started, huh? You think talking to
aging blond con persons is fun?''

''She's not blond anymore.'' He smiled so widely I saw
all his teeth. ''And furthermore, she's got a lot less front
bumper than previously advertised.''

''What?''

''Before she got into that nice orange smock they give
them at the jail, she took off a wig, and a number of
undergarments Deputy Frieda believes came from Fred-
erick's of Hollywood.''

''Is that a fact? So now she's—''

''Greatly changed.'' He bounced on the balls of his
feet. ''She's the other lady now. Ms. Medium Medium.''

''You serious?''

''Totally. And so is she. Serious and nondescript.
Wait'll you see.''

''You've got her over there in your office?''

He nodded happily. ''Ray's with her. Can you come
over?''

''Yes. But wait a minute. How much marijuana did she
have left in her purse when you booked her?''

''Six nickel bags.''

''That's all? You checked it into evidence?''

''Last night, sure.''

''Did you run a Valtox test on it?''

''Uh…no. Ray said you thought the technicalities could
wait until morning.''

''I said the questioning could wait until morning. Let's
keep our priorities straight here. You booked her for dealing, didn't you? We better make sure she had what we
said she had.''

I walked to the door of Kevin's office and said, ''Ray?''

The woman watched him as he got up from her side and came out in the hall. "Go find Bo, get him to help you test the dope we took off this woman. Come back with the test results ASAP. In the meantime," I told Kevin as Ray hurried away, "let's cut to the other chase. Take the prisoner in the conference room and get Lou to set up that piece of tape where she swipes the money. We'll have her watch it with us, and then we'll talk, huh?"

"Gotcha."

She was seated at the head of the long table when I got there, looking calmly from Kevin to Darrell to Lou, taking her time, getting to know them. As soon as I saw her plain sallow face and slender shape, I understood what had made my nose itch last night. The woman in the bleachers hadn't been a blond wearing makeup, but a nondescript con artist in deep disguise.

As soon as she saw me, she said, "Are you going to help me? I've been so scared."

Her voice hadn't changed. It was spooky hearing it come out of a different face. I said, "Maybe we can help each other," and nodded to Lou. "Let's roll it."

He stood beside her and operated the viewer. The rest of us stood along the table watching her as her blond bombshell persona appeared on the screen. Her face remained a cool blank as she watched the shopping scene unfold, but I thought I saw a spark of pride in her eyes at the moment of the money snatch. It was only a nanosecond, gone before I could be sure, and when Lou stopped the tape, she looked around at us with a vaguely curious expression, like, "Yes? What?"

"You want to tell us about it?" Kevin said.

She shrugged. "I thought he shortchanged me. I still think maybe he did. But then my little girl made him so mad by tipping over that candy rack, he was yelling at us so much I could see it was no use trying to reason with him, so I just took my stuff and left.''

''We've had several complaints of similar rip-offs from other merchants,'' I said. ''In fact, you pull this scene frequently, don't you? It's a steady source of income for you.''

''My gosh, no,'' she said. ''Why, what a thing to say.''

''Where's your little girl now?''

''Oh—'' She waved vaguely.

''What does that mean, 'Oh'?''

''I'm not exactly sure.''

I looked at Kevin. He sat down next to her at the table, pulled out his notebook, and said, ''Was John Francis Morgan your husband?''

''Jack?'' She licked her lips. ''Jack was...we weren't exactly married.''

''You gave your name downstairs as Jane Morgan.''

''Oh, ah, yes.''

''So you were using his name and traveling with him?''

''Um, yes. We were, like, common law, I guess you'd say.''

''Who killed him?''

''Well, see, that's what I've been trying to *tell* you—'' She teared up a little. ''Jack got in some trouble with these guys in Miami—''

''What guys?''

''Well...I don't exactly know their names. I mean I bet they each have several, I wouldn't be surprised. Bad, mean guys—''

''What was he doing in Miami?''

''We were there for the winter,'' she said. ''Jack felt he needed some sun.''

''Just a pair of snowbirds, huh? What did Jack do to get in trouble with the mean guys?''

"I don't know the details. Something about a card game. He came home one day really happy, said he won a terrific pot off this big-timer in the drug business—"

"The drug business? Like the drug business you were in last night, Jane?"

"They made me do that." She looked at Lou. Looked at Kevin. Looked at me. She was a plain woman, and the orange shift did nothing for her, but there was something that happened when she met your eyes directly, a little rush of blood to the ears that was reflected a second later in the groin.

"Who's they?"

"These guys that followed us up here from Florida," she said, "after they saw that story in the papers down there."

"What story?"

"The one from the paper up here—" Kevin's eyes gleamed with triumph; I watched him struggle to keep the happiness from spreading to the rest of his face. "You know, that sneering story about these merchants who claimed some people had tricked them out of money."

"You saying it wasn't true?"

"Just a lot of media hype, I thought." She had perfected the art of the casual banality. If I looked away from the Hampstead County smock, I could have been convinced I was listening to a Rutherford matron in the checkout line at Wal-Mart.

Kevin asked her, "What exactly did they do that threatened you?"

"One morning we got up and found a dead cat hanging from our doorknob."

"You have a doorknob? Where is your doorknob, Jane?"

"Oh...I believe we were in Mankato at the time."

"Are you saying the mean guys from Miami followed you around Minnesota?"

"Or they hired somebody to. I was never sure."

"It never occurred to you maybe somebody just wanted to get rid of a dead cat?"

"Jack was scared. I saw right away that he thought it was serious. I kept asking him, 'What's going on?' But he said never mind, he'd take care of it. Always so sure he could take care of everything," she said, sounding, for the first time, like a wife.

"Then what happened?"

"Well, you know the rest. You found Jack's body downtown in a barrel."

"How do you know it was John Morgan we found?"

"He didn't come home. And the paper said…all that about finding his wallet and then matching his fingerprints."

"Ah, you read all that. So. If we take you to the morgue at Hampstead County Lab, Mrs. Morgan, you think you'll be able to identify your husband?"

She looked into the corner of the room for a minute, biting her lip. "If I have to."

"Well, yes, I mean…I assume you want to be sure we've really got your husband there, Mrs. Morgan, right?"

"Well, um, sure."

"Any reason you might not be able to tell who it is?"

"No. If it really is Jack Morgan, of course I can identify him."

"Yes. And the other man, do you think you can identify him for us, too? The, uh, the Hispanic man who worked with your husband, did the coin caper thing?"

"Did the what? Oh"—she squeezed her eyes shut for

a few heartbeats and seemed to be thinking—''you mean Antonio? If that's who it is, sure I can identify him.''

Ray came back then and stood behind me, saying softly, ''Jake?'' I followed him into the hall, where Bo stood, looking puzzled and mildly amused.

Bo said, ''Hell's going on, Jake?''

''Bo says it's oregano,'' Ray said, looking mortified, ''in those bags.''

''Oregano?'' I looked at Bo.

''Smells like it. Sure as hell not marijuana, anyway. What's going on with you guys?''

''What's going on with Jane Morgan?'' I said. ''And her little helpers down there in the cells, what the flaming hell is going on with them? You know what you better do,'' I told Ray, ''is bring them out of their cells and put them in the interrogation rooms at the jail—I'll send somebody down to help you in a minute—and each of you take one of them and ask them, 'How long have you known Jane Morgan?' and, 'What the fuck did you think you were doing last night?' and a few reasonable questions like that, and see if you can get them to talk some sense to you. We sure as hell haven't been hearing any from the Queen of La-La Land in there.''

I stood beside Bo in the hall, watching Ray Bailey walk away from us with his back very stiff. Then Bo, looking almost cheerful for the first time in weeks, asked me, ''Has she got any Rolexes for sale?''

''Don't start,'' I said, and went back into the room where Kevin was saying, ''Tell me again about the phone call yesterday. This man called, a man you didn't know—''

''I'm sure I never heard his voice before,'' she said, ''and I'm good with voices.''

''I bet you are. And he said what?''

''He said a man was coming with the, uh, the supplies, and I was to do exactly what he told me to do with the stuff, or in five minutes I'd have two broken arms.''

I stood in the doorway and said, ''Kevin.'' He left her sitting with Darrell and Lou and walked out into the hall. ''Bo says the dope we took off this woman is oregano.''

''Oregano?'' He slapped his forehead. ''Shit, we should have tested it last night. Why didn't we? It was so late, and we were all convinced there was something else going on— What about all her customers, though? What about her helpers?''

''All good questions.'' I told him what I'd sent Ray to do. ''I want you to go on down to the jail and help Ray lean on those two boys until you're both persuaded they've told you everything they know. Then come back up and see me.''

''What are we gonna do with Jane Morgan?''

''Before you go downstairs, find Pitman and Maddox and send them in here, will you? I'll have them take her over to the morgue and see if she'll identify the two bodies we've got there. After that, I think we'll put her away for a while and let her think some more about the big picture.''

''Yeah. Does this mean we have to change what she's being charged with?''

''Don't know yet. I can go into court with this Monday if I have to. She was ostensibly selling a controlled substance, and who's to say some of the earlier packets weren't the good stuff? Maybe she just ran out.'' As we turned to go back in the room, I saw Jane Morgan leaning toward Darrell Betts, looking straight into his eyes, talking earnestly, and I saw him start to melt gradually toward her. ''Better be quick, before we have to send old Darrell to the showers.''

Kevin left and came back in a minute with Maddox and Pitman. I walked into the room with them and said, "Okay, time to go."

"What?" Darrell said.

"Time for Mrs. Morgan to go to the morgue. Andy, I guess you'll need to put the cuffs on her again for the trip. Be sure she identifies both bodies, okay?"

She said, "Don't you want me to tell you the rest about the gamblers who threatened—"

"Oh, I think we've heard enough about that for today," I said. "When you're done at the morgue, Andy, you can take her back to jail." Jane Morgan looked at me as she went out, but this time she was trying to read my face instead of doing that tricky business with her eyes.

Darrell said, "What's up?"

"It was oregano. In the little packets Jane Morgan was peddling at the stadium last night."

"What?" He buried his head in his hands. "Aw, jeez, I feel dumb."

"We all do."

"So now what? Don't tell me we got nothing on her?"

"I won't. If we have to, we can say we watched her sell packets of twenty-dollar dope, and I doubt if there'll be a big rush of customers into court Monday to complain about buying a cooking spice. We'll see. We might want to skip the dope sale and go for the fast-change hustle; I'll show the tape of the money snatch to Milo. You heard her ready-made explanation for it, but I think he'll say the picture's clear enough so he can make it stick, especially with the testimony we can bring in from other merchants."

"Well," Lou said, "meanwhile, back to the old tapes, huh, buddy?" He popped a fist gently off Darrell's shoulder and said, "That's police work for you, never a day the same. It's sure not as much fun as lettin' that lady give you a stiffy, though, is it?''

"Come on, Lou,'' Darrell said. "Jeez.''

I was ten steps from my office door when I heard my answering tape starting to say I was away from my desk blah blah blah. I sprinted across the space and said, "Hines.''

"Grant Hisey, Jake,'' the sheriff said. "Say, you know, we been helping circulate that Attempt to Locate notice, with the two women and the little girl and the kind of Spanishy-looking guy? Yeah, well, Jim Nixa just called in, you know him, one of my part-time deputies—''

"Sure.''

"Well, he's out on the Dover road right now, and he just showed the circular to Glenda Ferris at that Trail's End trailer park out there? And she says some of those people checked in there yesterday. Yeah, really. Their Winnie is parked in Space 26.''

"How much support has Jim got out there, Grant?''

"Well, that's the trouble. I'm spread pretty thin, you know, there's really nobody close to him at all.''

"Ask him to hang on till I get over to your office, will you?'' I ran across the landing and into Grant Hisey's office, got on the mike, and asked Nixa, "Where is this place, exactly?'' He gave me directions, and I told him we'd have two squads out there in fifteen minutes. "Do you see anybody moving around the rig?''

"No.''

"There may be nobody there,'' I said, "but just in case…can you stay far enough away so they won't hear your radio, and still keep 'em in sight?''

"Oh, yeah, plenty of space out here, no problem,'' he said.

"Good. I'll let you know when your backup's on the way."

"Not to get too picky, but if we find any suspects, what are we charging them with?"

"Oh. Sorry. Uh…reckless endangerment of a child, I think, for now. But treat as armed and dangerous. One or more of them might turn out to be a murder suspect."

"Copy." I called dispatch and asked for two officers to aid a sheriff's deputy on the Dover road, ASAP.

"Hold your horses," Schultzy said. "Everybody's working a call right now. Is this serious police business or just some kind of a favor, Jake?"

"He's apprehending a suspect for us," I said. "Is that serious enough for you, Schultzy, or do you need to see somebody bleed?"

"Whee," she said, "we're testy today. Okay, Brennan just called in, and I'll find you a second man in a jiffy. Where did you say, now, on the Dover road?"

I gave her the directions, called Nixa back and told him backup was on the way, thanked Grant, and walked back across the landing. Back inside the department, I walked into the chief's office and told his secretary, "Need to see him."

"Can it wait?" Lulu looked at my face and said quickly, "No. Okay. Coupla do-gooders in there bending his ear, lemme see if I can—" She buzzed and said something softly into the phone, and a couple of minutes later the chief opened the door to his inner office and stood in it, shaking hands with a man and woman, telling them how glad he was they had stopped by and how seriously he was going to think about their idea. This part of his job he does about as well as it can be done, I think, and it's not his fault I hate to watch him do it. He was my field training officer when I joined the force, and I still like to think of him as a damn good street cop.

When they were gone, I said, "You know we picked up Mrs. Morgan at the ball game last night?"

"Got the report here," he said. "Any trouble?"

"No. Except this morning Bo tested the weed she was peddling, and he says it's a kitchen spice."

"The hell."

"Yes. And now—" I told him about the call from Grant Hisey and the two cars on their way toward Dover.

"Well. God, I hope this is the last of them. It seems to me every time you tell me something about these people, it's something loonier than the last thing you told me."

"Yup. Crazy City. That's why I'm trying to keep you in the loop."

"So we can both look dumb when the whole case falls apart, huh? No, no"—he saw me getting ready to protest—"I know you gotta do what you gotta do. Just lemme know right away if you arrest any little people in peaked hats, will you?" His phone rang; he answered it and said, "It's for you. Wanna take it on Lulu's phone?"

Ray said, "Jake, I'm sorry to bother you, but I just remembered I promised to meet Roy Beale at the front door, about fifteen minutes from now."

"Roy Beale is—"

"One of those guys from the Chicken Shack that I've been trying to get to come to the morgue with me and identify the bodies there. He said he and Artie Simpson would meet me here and go with me to the morgue. And now that I finally got them to say they'll do it, I don't want to let them get away."

"No, of course not. Well…are you getting anything out of those kids?"

"My guy says his name is Jeffrey Tanner, lived in

Rutherford ten years, never saw the blond lady before Sunday night. Says she offered him ten percent of everything he steered her way, he was supposed to keep track of it and let her know. Such a deal, huh? He's just a dropout with no prospects, been working odd jobs for minimum wage, and I think she gave him a hard-on besides. The other kid is his buddy—Kevin's getting essentially the same story out of him. They both say they never had anything to do with drugs before. Not sure I believe *that,* but essentially I think these two are pretty harmless."

"Uh-huh. Especially when they're selling kitchen products."

There was a little silence, and then Ray said dryly, "So, whaddya say about Beale?"

"Put Tanner and his buddy back in their cells and come on up. We can decide later if we want to hold them."

I hung up, put my head back into the chief's office and told him what Ray said, and walked back to my office, thinking, I should make a chart. And some lists. I felt a need for devices to bring order out of this growing bucket of shit.

The next time my phone rang it was Brennan, saying, "We're bringing your suspects in now, Jake, if that's what you call 'em. Where do you want 'em?"

"Uh…bring 'em up here to me, will you, Marty? How many…uh—"

"Two kids and one baby-sitter's all we could find. Was there supposed to be somebody else?"

"Two kids and a baby-sitter? What in hell did you charge 'em with?"

"I charged the baby-sitter with child endangerment, just like you said. I told the kids they'd be needed in town to testify, and they came with me willingly. Wasn't I right?"

"Uh…okay, I guess it's all right. We'll figure it out when you get here. Did you lock up the rig?''

"The owner of the park's doing that, and she's got the key. They owe her money, so—''

"Gotcha. Okay, bring 'em on in.'' I hung up and thought, Two kids and a baby-sitter? What the hell? The members of this clan, if that's what it was, seemed to shape-shift in and out of middle-class respectability. I remembered Jane Morgan saying, about Florida, ''Jack felt he needed some sun.''

My phone rang. Milo said, ''Hey, I hear you caught a blond cutie in the stadium selling drugs. Am I right she's part of that bunch of hustlers that was pulling all the funny money stuff? The outfit that ended up with two of their guys in the barrel?''

"Yes. And I owe you a whole new rundown on the entire case, Milo, but right now I've got two more carloads of suspects coming in.'' Two carloads of suspects sounded okay; I thought I could explain to him later why I sent three heavily armed officers after two children and a baby-sitter.

"You guys are having a lot of fun with those roughnecks, aren't you? I should have gone into police work,'' Milo said. ''Around here it's just dusty law books and drudgery.''

"Couple of slots open up every month or two, Milo, if you want to take the tests.''

"Yeah, well. Call me when you can talk.''

I walked out to the head of the stairs and saw, through the second-floor windows, two squads pull into the parking lot and up to the tall front doors. Jake and Kevin came out the front door of the jail and walked up the sloping sidewalk toward the entrance where the cars were parked. Brennan opened the back door of his squad, and I could see a middle-aged man in handcuffs sitting there, looking straight ahead. This was the baby-sitter? He made no move to get out of the car. His dark, graying hair was worn a little long, and a purple birthmark covered the bridge of his nose.

Just then another man, about the same age, got out of a ten-year-old Chevy in the parking lot, walked up to Ray, and stuck out his hand.

"Oh, hi, Mr. Beale," Ray said, "glad to see you."

"Can't say I feel the same way," he said, "but let's get this over with, shall we?"

Brennan got his prisoner out of the car and helped him straighten up. Beale looked at the prisoner, puzzled, turned to Ray, and said, "Oh, he's here, huh? What happened to his nose?" He kept looking from Ray to the handcuffed man. "I thought you said he was *dead*."

"He is," Ray said. "The man I want you to identify is. He's in the morgue. This is somebody else."

"No, it isn't," Beale said. "It's the Mexican guy that gave the little girl a ride in the box. Only that night his skin looked darker. And I don't remember seeing that mark on his nose."

A square-built man got out of a red Escort nearby, fed the meter, and walked over to us saying, "Hi, Roy. We ready to go?"

"Not sure," Roy said. "This is Ray Bailey that I told you about. Ray, this is Otto Krutzberger, he was there with me at the Chicken Shack last Friday night."

"Glad to meet you," Ray said.

"He says we have to go to the morgue," Roy Beale said, "but I'm trying to tell him this is the man right here."

"Sure it is," Krutzberger said, "except it's funny, for some reason that night he looked like a Mexican. Didn't he? His skin was darker. And I don't remember that mark on his nose. I thought you said the guy was dead.'' Krutzberger turned to Beale.

"They said he was. Some police work, huh? Can't tell a dead guy from a live one?''

"Then they wonder why we're losing respect,'' Krutzberger said. "Wait a minute, I know how to settle this.'' He pointed at the man with the birthmark. "Have him say something.''

"Say what?'' Ray said.

"I don't care, anything. Have him say, 'Oh, thank God you are here.' ''

"Okay,'' Ray said. He turned to the prisoner and asked him, politely, "Will you say those words, please?''

The gray-haired man said in a bored monotone, "Oh, thank God you are here.'' His voice was uninflected, flat middle American.

"Well, now,'' Beale said, looking puzzled, "that's not the way he talked, is it?''

"Sure isn't.'' Krutzberger wasn't satisfied. "Is that your regular voice?'' he asked the man in handcuffs.

"Only one I got,'' the man said, looking contemptuous. Beale and Krutzberger turned to each other, anxious and dissatisfied.

"I don't get it,'' Beale said.

"Me neither,'' Krutzberger said, "but I could swear that's the guy that took the box away and then came back.''

"Jake,'' Longworth said quietly, nudging my elbow. He gestured toward his blue-and-white, where the tops of two small heads showed above the edge of the door. "Where do you want me to put these kids?''

"Be right there,'' I said, and turned to the rest of the group. "Okay, everybody listen up! Ray, take Mr. Beale and Mr. Krutzberger to the morgue the way you planned, let them look at both bodies and tell you if they're the ones they saw in the Chicken Shack last Friday night. Kevin, take this man''—I pointed to the man in handcuffs—''into the jail, be sure he's been read his rights, and charge him with reckless endangerment of a child—''

''What the hell are you talking about?'' the prisoner said. ''I was taking good care of them! Ask the kids!''

''—and get him printed, and stay with him till I get there.''

I stepped around Brennan's car to Longworth's, and opened the back door. Two little girls looked out at me, pretty girls about seven or eight, with blue eyes and curly blond hair down their backs. They looked exactly alike.

''Um, hello,'' I said. ''Are you twins?'' They nodded brightly and smiled. Their smiles were identical.

''Well, lookit here, will ya?'' Roy Beale said, behind me. He and Krutzberger, standing side by side, stared at the two little girls and then at each other, and said, in unison, *''So that's how they did it.''*

TEN

ROSIE CAME DOWN to help me with the two little girls. Beale and Krutzberger wanted to stay and talk to them, get them to explain how the scam worked. But Ray insisted that the man they needed to identify was at the morgue, and eventually they left with him, grumbling. Rosie took the children upstairs and called Victim's Services. It was stretching a point, a little, but eventually she persuaded a social worker to take the girls to a shelter for battered families. They were well-behaved while they waited, she said, accepting her invitation for treats from the vending machines but never asking any questions or answering any either.

"I couldn't even get them to tell me their names," she told me as we stood on the front stairs, watching them climb into the social worker's van. "Do you suppose nodding and smiling is all they know how to do?"

"More likely they've been taught not to answer any questions," I said.

"Wow. Weird. Such pretty little girls, too."

"They look well taken care of, don't they?"

"Absolutely. Clean and tidy, and all that hair brushed out so nice."

Maddox and Pitman came into my office five minutes later to report that Jane Morgan had positively identified her husband and the Hispanic man in the morgue. "She says his name is Antonio Cisneros,'' Andy said. ''She doesn't know where he's from or anything about his family. He's just somebody who's been traveling with them for a while, she says.''

''Yeah,'' Clint said, turning to a page in his notebook to read me a quote. ''She said, 'Jack always made friends easily, and he liked to have people around.''' He wrinkled his nose and said, ''She made it sound kind of like a traveling picnic. She's funny, isn't she?''

''A real comedian,'' I said. ''Did you ask her how long this Cisneros had been with them? Or how he earned his keep?''

''She can't remember how long they've known him. And she's totally vague about their sources of income. Jack always handled the details, she says.''

''Good thing, huh? Since she seems to be totally clueless. Well…you got her put away all right?''

''With no problem,'' Andy said. ''I think she's the friendliest prisoner I ever dealt with.''

A lot of talk and stomping was coming up the wide front stairs. I stuck my head out and saw Ray Bailey coming toward me, with Beale and Krutzberger crowding and bumping him along the hall, waving their arms and arguing.

''What's going on?'' I asked him.

''They came back with me to sign their statements.'' He was red-faced and grinding his teeth. ''They want to dictate them right now and read them over before they sign.''

''Because he's trying to get us to say something that isn't true, goddammit,'' Krutzberger said, ''and I'm not gonna do it. This is still the United States of America, isn't it? And nobody's gonna tell me to—''

"Otto, I don't think that's what he said," Beale said, trying to quiet his friend down.

"I know what he said. He wants me to say I'm not sure. But I *am* sure."

"All I said," Ray said forlornly, "was that if the skin and the voice aren't the same—"

"Okay. OKAY!" I pointed to Ray's end of the hall and said, "Tell Lou and Darrell to work somewhere else for a while and put these two men at the conference table. I'll get the deputy to get the prisoner out of his cell and bring him up here. They can take another look at him before they make their statements."

The sheriff's deputy said it would be fifteen minutes or so. While I waited, I called Milo and told him about the oregano in the little glassine packets.

"Jesus, she's lucky you picked her up," he said. "Cheating on dopeheads can get you *hurt*."

"My theory is, she was on her way out of town, probably, and she just stopped off at the stadium to pick up a few bucks for the road."

"Sounds reasonable. What about her husband's murder? Are you developing anything to tie her to that?"

"Only that he was her husband. That's usually pretty good grounds for suspicion, isn't it?"

"Sure. Grounds. Now get me some evidence."

"Okay. What would you like?"

"Evidence prepared while you wait, huh? I hope nobody's recording this conversation."

"If we were, you'd know it—all our recording equipment is ten years old and hums. We just brought in her two children and their baby-sitter; you think maybe I could hang it on one of them?"

"She has two children? I thought there was one child and two women."

"Milo, you know, before you go to court with these two on Monday, you and I are going to have to sit down and have a long talk."

"That complicated, huh?"

"More twists than a platter of pretzels. And probably gonna get more so right now, because I hear the next prisoner coming to be interrogated." Chains clinked past my door.

"Sounds like it better be Monday. Around nine-thirty, that all right?"

"Uh…yeah." I wrote Milo's name and the time on my calendar and followed the shuffling prisoner into the People Crimes section. The deputy took off the handcuffs and looked at Ray. Ray nodded, and the deputy removed the belly chain and leg shackles as well. "Call me when you're ready, and I'll take him back," he said as he left. The prisoner sat quietly, rubbing his wrists and flexing his ankles. He's worn chains before, I thought. There's a certain initial outrage that wears off, after a few times.

We asked Krutzberger and Beale to take seats near the other end of the table, where they'd have a good view of the prisoner. Ray and Andy, Kevin and Clint, and I took the remaining seats.

"All right," I said. "Mr. Beale, Mr. Krutzberger, take a good look now, and we're gonna go over this again. You saw the man in question at the Chicken Shack, last Friday night, for how long?"

"Well, it was just a few minutes, off and on, while they were taping up the box with the little girl inside," Beale said.

"Yeah, but after he came back," Krutzberger said, "after the little girl reappeared and the other man, her daddy that's over there in the morgue now, he took her and the money and left, but this man"—he pointed to the prisoner—"he hung around, drank beer with all of us, told the story again a coupla times."

"But he musta had something on his skin, is what we figure now," Beale said. "Makeup or something. Because he looked darker, and his birthmark didn't show."

"And he talked different. But we been thinking about that, too, and what we think is, if he's a con man, he probably has a lot of different voices he can use." Krutzberger made a fist and shook it at the prisoner. "I bet if I had him alone, I could get him to do some of them for me."

"Why are you trying to hang this poor excuse for an ID on me?" the prisoner asked. "Look at me. Do I look Mexican? My name is Art Brown—is that a Mexican name?"

"He's the man who drove the car," Beale said, stubbornly, "only his voice is different, and something's happened to his skin."

"They were in a bar." The prisoner shrugged. "They were probably drunk."

"Okay, okay." I tapped my pen on the heavy oak table; it gave back a nice, solid clunk. "What do you say about the two bodies in the morgue?" I asked Krutzberger and Beale.

"The one with the big nose is the man who had the little girl with him," Beale said. "He's beat all to hell, but he's the same man, no question."

"But the other one, we never saw him before."

"The dead man's wife says he's her husband's assistant," I said.

"She does? Well, but so what? Aren't they all a bunch of thieves and liars? Whose word you gonna take?" Krutzberger was getting openly hostile, and Beale was sneaking peeks at his watch.

I took Ray and Kevin out into the hall and said, "Better get their statements and get them out of here."

"I'd like to have Clint and Andy do that," Ray said, "and the three of us talk to this Art Brown some more."

"Agreed. Has anybody searched on that name, by the way?"

"I'll do it," Kevin said. He took a sheet of paper to the prisoner and said, "Write your full name." The man wrote two names in block letters.

"No middle name?"

The man wrote a third name on the line below. Kevin went out, telling me, "I'll be quick."

We took the gray-haired man into my office. Ray carried the chains along and dumped them in the corner. I put him in the middle of three chairs in front of my desk, and Ray sat down on his right, took out his little pocket notebook, and turned to a fresh page. I got the tape recorder set up. Kevin came in, shook his head once in the doorway, closed the door, and took the last chair.

I turned on the tape, said the date and time and our three names, and asked the prisoner to state his.

"Arthur Brown."

"Middle name?"

"Harris."

"Age?"

"Forty-seven."

"How long have you known John Morgan?"

"Couple of months."

"What was your relationship with him?"

"Relationship?" He raised his eyebrows. "I didn't have any relationship with him. I'm just the baby-sitter."

"Is that so?" Ray and Kevin, sitting on either side of him, turned from watching him with interest to watching me. Their faces plainly registered, Are you really going to swallow that? He was a middle-sized man with some extra flesh around the middle and the beginnings of a double chin, who looked close to his stated age. I wouldn't have expected him to win the 5K in his age group, but he was not in any obvious way disabled either; he looked as if he might be a day laborer, a reasonably capable guy who enjoyed a few beers after work. "Is that what you usually do?"

"With these people, it is."

"Have you worked as a child-care provider before?"

"No." He waited for the next question. I turned my hand over in a gesture that said, "So?" and he added, reluctantly, "Got to talking to them in a bar. Mentioned I was unemployed, and she asked me, how would I like to watch her kids for a while?"

"And you said yes? Just like that?"

"Figured it beat doing nothing."

"What did they pay you?"

"Eight dollars an hour. But I got to eat whenever I fed the kids."

"And you didn't have any trouble taking care of two little girls?"

"No." He shrugged, as if middle-aged male nannies of female children were commonplace, and added, "They're good kids. We always got along fine. I don't know where you got this idea I wasn't treating them right."

"Teaching them to steal, you think that's treating them right?"

"I never did that. What makes you say that?"

Ray and Kevin were beginning to shift in their chairs and scratch their ears. I nodded to Kevin first, and he said, "So, Art, the little girls are twins, aren't they? What are their names?"

"Millicent, they call her Millie, and Margaret. They usually call her Maggie."

"Can you tell them apart?"

"Oh, sure."

"Really? They look identical to me."

"Oh…well, when you know them, you can tell the difference."

"I see. When you got them ready to go in the bars and do their magic trick, you had to be sure to have them dressed exactly alike, right? Everything identical?"

"They always dressed alike. I don't know anything about what they did in bars."

"You don't? They never told you why they were taking their children out in the evening, keeping them out till the middle of the night?"

"I told you, I was just the baby-sitter. I took care of the kids when their parents were gone. What they did when they were all together was none of my business." Kevin nodded at Ray and sat back, looking thoughtful.

"The other man who worked for the Morgans, did he live in the RV too?" Ray said.

"What? Oh…no, there was no room for anybody but, uh, them."

"So you didn't sleep there either?"

"No, there wasn't…the rig is just big enough for four."

"So you had to what, get a room nearby?"

"Sometimes. Lot of RV parks have those little log houses there at the park that you can rent, or sometimes a room or two over the office."

"Must have been hard to pay that, though, on eight dollars an hour."

"Oh, they always paid."

"I see. Who took care of the kids while you were selling the coins?"

It was a nice try, but Art wasn't having any. He turned a puzzled face to Ray and said, "Coins?"

We tried for another half hour, going over the details of his hiring again, in a bar in Eagan, he said. Was that his hometown? No, he just happened to be there when the last job ran out. Like Jane Morgan, he seemed to inhabit some mysterious region where reality could dissolve unexpectedly into mist. We talked sensibly for a while, about the size of the Winnebago and the needs of small children, but when we circled back to the scams they'd been pulling, he gave us a blank stare and said, "Murphy game? What's a Murphy game?" Finally we put the chains back on him and sent him shuffling back to his cell.

"I brought sandwiches," Kevin said. "You want one? I told my mom it was going to be one of those days, and she sent enough to hold me till next week sometime." Perhaps because women chase him relentlessly, Kevin is unembarrassed by being, in his late twenties, still at home with a mother who does his laundry and fusses over his food. We hunched around my desk, wolfing down egg salad and cheese.

"I don't buy it," Kevin said finally, passing fudge brownies.

Ray squirted water into his mouth from a one-liter bottle. "Art Brown, you mean? Or Beale and Krutzberger?"

"Art Brown. I just don't buy him as a baby-sitter."

"Except that when we found him," I said, "he was baby-sitting."

"Well"—he jiggled his right knee in frustration—"you're right, he was. Today. But all the time? A full-time nursemaid? That's baloney. I can feel it in these wise old bones."

"What do your wise old bones feel about Krutzberger and Beale?" Ray asked him.

"Why would they lie? They just wanted to say what they saw and get out of here."

"But Brown is right that they coulda been drunk. And they admit his appearance and voice are a lot different than the man they remember."

"I know, that bothers me too. But at least Beale and Krutzberger are trying to tell the truth, I think, but Brown is trying not to. What about the morphing mate, anybody got a read on her?"

"Jane Morgan?" I blew up his brown paper lunch bag. "That's easy. Every word she says is a lie, and if she writes it down, the punctuation will also be false." I held the bag on my desk and smashed it with my fist. It made a loud, satisfying pop.

"Gosh, Jake," Kevin said, "why don't you tell us how you really feel?"

"I agree with him," Ray said. "Jane Morgan is a three-dollar bill."

"Oh, so do I. I've been thinking back over the scams, though. Consider this: The fast-change hustle was done by Jane and one of the girls. The Murphy game by Jane and her husband. The coin caper by Morgan and Mr. Hispanic. The magic girl by Morgan, Hispanic Man, and one child. No, wait, both children." He mused, popping his tongue against the roof of his mouth. We all seemed to be descending through layers of preteen behavior. "You see any times in there when Jane Morgan and Hispanic Man were working together?"

"Ah...well. No." I swept crumbs off my desk. "So he could be doing both jobs, is that what you're saying?" I squeezed my eyes tight shut, opened them, and enjoyed the haloes that formed around the ceiling lights. "I'm trying to conceptualize that hiring conversation. 'Your job will be to cheat widows and orphans part-time, and otherwise split the baby-sitting chores with the little woman here.'"

"Except that Brown says he was hired by the wife." Ray poured the rest of his water into his throat and gargled with it.

"Yeah, well, why should we believe that if we don't believe anything else he said?" Kevin balanced a cookie on his forehead, raised his head abruptly, and flipped it into his mouth.

"Right now we have one pressing problem." I stood up to put a stop to this tree-house conduct. "I can get a judge's order tomorrow to hold these people over the weekend, but by Monday I better have physical evidence that ties them to the homicide. Otherwise, we're stuck with trying to hang a reckless endangerment rap on a man who swears he was taking good care of the children—and they look as if he was—and hoping to persuade a judge that Jane's sale of a few packets of oregano was criminal behavior. If we fail to make either case, we will have to let that person go."

"Shit," Ray said, "they'll be over the hill and out of sight before the cuffs are cold."

"Exactly. So what *my* wise old bones are finally getting up off their dead asses and telling me, is what they should have said this morning as soon as we got this Brown and the kids in here. We need to get out there and search that motor home. And the extra room. And their car—there must be a car there."

"You're right. Absolutely. Right now, today, this minute." Ray got up too and turned back into a grim-looking forty-year-old man. "My job, huh? Warrant, I need a warrant."

"Friday lunchtime? Good time to catch a judge before he gets back into court."

"Darrell must be close to finished with those tapes, huh? I'll take him with me. Lessee, mainly I'll be looking for blood-soaked clothing, blood spatters on the car, weapons? What else?"

"Exotic coins. Makeup. Wigs. Interesting undies." Kevin's eyebrows did a Groucho Marx.

"Lock picks, maybe? Extra license plates. Don't forget to take plenty of evidence bags." I watched Ray finish his list and leave, then went to tell the chief what we were doing. Kevin rounded up Clint and Andy and put them to work on the break-ins and stolen bikes we'd been neglecting all week.

I was back in my office, looking through my phone messages, when Bo appeared in my open doorway and said, "I think I got something."

"Oh? Come in." He came and stood by my desk. "Sit down," I said, so he did, just barely, in the nearest chair. He looked like he might be holding the bare end of a wire that somebody had just plugged into the wall. "What is it?"

"When Rosie started talking to my snitches," he said, "I took over her cold case files. It was just something to do. But I got interested in the one from the winter of '96."

"The liquor store robberies?"

"Yeah. Three in one weekend, and the third owner got shot."

"Ernie Brotzman. We put in a lot of hours on that one. Don't tell me you found something we missed?"

"No. But there was a print lifted off the open cash drawer that wasn't Brotzman's, didn't match his wife or his clerk or the swamper."

"We searched on it for months," I said, "sent it to the FBI—"

"I saw that. Did I ever tell you I used to be in Records and Investigations?"

"I guess I forgot." It seemed a queer job for Bo. "In St. Louis?"

"For a year and a half. Before I got into vice."

Before electronic fingerprint databases came into being, if you wanted a national comparison, your prints had to be mailed to the FBI, and we waited months, sometimes years, for them to get around to comparing them manually to the gazillions of prints they had on file in D.C. But for a search of smaller scope, of a county or state file, every police station of any size tried to keep one officer trained to compare fingerprints, using a magnifying device called a loupe. The officer got an extra rating on his service jacket and was usually called, around the station, "our R and I."

"That job," Bo said, "you look at enough prints, you get an eye for them, and the unusual ones jump out at you. Soon as I looked at the file on the '96 robberies, I saw that the fingerprint from Brotzman's store was an X."

"It was?" A small minority of fingerprints are so unusual they're called "accidental," and fingerprint technicians shorten that to "X." Trudy always tells me when she scans an X; it makes her day. Go figure.

"Yup. A loop and whorl."

"Wow." I've never caught this virus, so I had to ask, "That's a doozy, huh?"

"Very rare. So, remember, in 1996 we didn't have electronic access to a national database of fingerprints yet. So I got thinking, wouldn't it be a kick in the shorts if we ran this baby through AFIS and got a hit? I called Trudy, and she said she couldn't put it ahead of new cases, but send it up and she'd put it in the queue.''

"So that's the one I took to her the other day?'' I yawned, wishing I hadn't enjoyed so much lunch.

"Uh-huh. But—Jake, you with me?''

"Yes. I'm sorry.'' My eyes were glazing over, and I really wanted him gone. But Bo had taken so many hard knocks lately, I hated to turn him off when he was excited about something.

"Frieda—at the jail?—she knows I like to look at rare prints, so after she fingerprinted Art Brown, she called and said she had a treat for me. I went down to look, and by God she had just taken a perfect set of loop and whorl prints off that guy. You don't see that many accidentals in a set very often. I took a good look, and I'm pretty sure they match the one I sent to Trudy.''

"Bo.'' I sat up, no longer sleepy. "Wait. Are you saying we might have Ernie Brotzman's killer sitting over there in jail? The baby-sitter?''

"The what?''

"I'll tell you in a minute. Did you make a copy of that fingerprint before you sent it to Trudy?''

"Of course. In fact, it's the copy I sent.''

"So you've still got the original here?''

"Yup.''

"Come with me.'' We walked to the chief's office, where I asked Lulu, "You want to see the chief of police kiss a cop? Get us in there and watch.''

She shook her head and said, "No way. No, sir. He's got *engineers* in there.''

"Call him anyway,'' I said. "I'll explain it to him.'' She shook her head some more, her face like mean granite. I continued to smile brightly at her and nod. She shook her head a while longer, finally sighed with exaggerated impatience, and said, "This better be good, Jake Hines." She pushed a button and handed me the phone.

McCafferty said, short and sharp, "Yeah?"

"Bo Dooley and I have good reason to think we might have Ernie Brotzman's killer sitting in jail on a different charge. We need your help to prove it before I have to let the bugger go."

There was a little silence while I held my breath. "Hang on," he said, and hung up.

"He'll be out in a minute," I said, and smiled at Lulu some more. She turned her back on me and began typing furiously. I told Bo about the baby-sitting gig while we waited for Frank. Lulu's back looked like it was growing ears.

The chief came out, closed his door carefully as if the engineers might be trying to escape, and said, "Whatcha got?" Bo told his story again. The chief started losing interest about where I had, so I nudged Bo, he fast-forwarded to finding the matching X's in the jail, and Frank began to smile all over his big face.

"God damn," he said, "is this possible? All those months we searched. Jesus—" He looked at me and asked again, "You think it's possible?"

"Yes. But we gotta be quick. Can we send these prints to St. Paul electronically now? Is that system ironed out yet?"

"No."

"You mean it? We can scan electronically, but we can't send them that way?"

"There's a glitch in the interface between here and St. Paul."

"Aw, Jesus, Frank, that's *pitiful*."

"The day they told me about it," the chief said, "I used up my entire stock of words meaning feces."

"So you're saying we scan them electronically here, and then we have to send them to St. Paul by mail?"

"Don't say it again, I'll probably puke. They're gonna fix it soon, they said."

"Well. Okay. I'll drive the son of a bitch to St. Paul myself if you'll call the director at BCA and plead our case. Get him to say they'll compare these prints tomorrow—"

"This is Friday," Bo said.

"Don't worry about that," the chief said. "They'll come in at night or on weekends for a potential fingerprint match on a homicide. But now, tell me again—you don't have enough other evidence to hold this man?"

"We might not have. We picked him up in a sweep of the motor home that we think belonged to the victims in last week's homicide—"

"The two men in the barrel?"

"Right. An entirely unrelated case, see, and so far we've got no physical evidence that ties him to that killing. None. We've charged him with endangerment of a child, but he claims his only function with the scammers' group was baby-sitting."

"Baby-sitting? Christ, why does it always have to get weird?"

"I don't know. But listen, Frank, I can keep him over the weekend for questioning, but if he walks out of here Monday, he's gone. These people have no ties to the community, and moving around fast is their specialty."

"Okay. I buy your argument, Jake, but every department in the state is pressing Pat for extra speed, every day, so I don't want to ask him unless—are you pretty sure about this print?" he asked Bo.

"Sure as I can be without the magnifying doohicky— what did we call it?—loupe, I need a loupe," Bo said.

"I wonder if we might not have one of 'em still around? Why don't you call Ollie Green? He's a saver." Ollie's our current version of an R and I officer, an expert in arcane arts like making footprint casts and running the Super Glue fuming box, which makes fingerprints show up on small objects.

"Oh, you betcha," Ollie said when I asked him if he had a loupe. "Soon's I heard we were phasing out that system, I copped that baby for the collection." Ollie's not just a saver; he's a painstaking preserver of outdated law enforcement items that the rest of us consider junk. One cupboard, of the many that line his workroom, is labeled "Memorabilia." He keeps it padlocked and opens it only for people who show proper respect for department history.

"We need to use it for a few minutes," I said.

"Well—"

"We won't take it out of the room. You can watch us."

"Okay."

"Can we come over now?"

"Sure. You need any help? You wanna compare a print?

"Yes. And we'd appreciate your help. Thanks."

"Lemme know," the chief said when I told him. "I gotta do this—" He went back into his office, his face indicating that these engineers had better keep it crisp.

Bo fetched the print from his cold case file while I went over to the jail to get copies of Brown's prints. By the time we got to Ollie's workroom, Ollie had the loupe out, polishing it, and a piece of clean butcher paper laid on one end of a central counter. Bo arranged Brown's prints in neat rows and laid the single print from the cold case file next to them.

"It's not quite complete, the old one," Bo said, worried now, frowning. "It was lifted off the side of the cash drawer. But I can tell it's not a thumbprint—" He squinted anxiously. "I think it's an index finger."

Ollie Green stood next to him for a minute, his eyes jumping from the single print to the set, and finally said, "Uh-huh. Left one, I think. Now, see, this here—" He showed us the magnifying glass. It looked like the inverted bottom of a Coke bottle, suspended over a metal tube that flared a little. The bottom of the tube was shaped like a horseshoe, with the open end at the bottom so you could see to line it up straight with the print. He set it down above the single print and said, "Have a look."

Bo bent over the counter, moving the glass a fraction of an inch from time to time, making those tiny sounds like *mmp* and *hnnt* that Trudy makes sometimes when she works. People who perform complex technical tasks seem to talk to themselves subverbally, and the tougher the job, the better the conversation. After a few more mews and grunts, Bo straightened and handed the glass to Ollie, saying, "Classic loop and whorl in both. And seven matching minutiae, that I can see."

Ollie peered into the glass, said, "Uh-huh," and a little later, "I'm pretty sure I see eight. Three broken lines—"

"I found those."

"—branching line just outside the whorl—"

They nattered on contentedly in their special lingo for a few minutes, passing the magnifying device back and forth. Finally they passed the loupe to me and leaned on either side, talking in both my ears, urging me to see what they saw. I did see most of it, I think. It was definitely not as easy as looking at Trudy's big screen in St. Paul, with the green electronic pointers guiding my eyes, and her talking me through it. But in a few minutes, we agreed we were confident enough to justify asking for a priority verification by one of BCA's experts. I called the chief.

He came right away, moving carefully once he was inside the small workroom full of things that mustn't be broken. He stooped, grunting, over the delicate swirls of ink, his massive hands moving the loupe carefully. He said, "Uh-huh, uh-huh. Okay," as Bo and Ollie showed him how the loop wrapped around the whorl, and pointed out the minutiae. When he was satisfied, he straightened, shook Bo's hand, and said, "By God, Dooley, that's a damn good piece of police work." Bo quit punishing his jaw muscles for a few seconds and actually smiled.

Frank turned to me with his big face flushed with pleasure and said, "Goddamn, Jake."

I nodded, happily. "So you'll call Pat Delaney?"

"Right now. Yes." He turned to go.

"Uh—"

He stopped and asked, without turning, "What?"

"Well...would it contaminate the evidence if I was to give it to Trudy to take up with her tomorrow morning?"

He rubbed the end of his nose and thought about it. "No. Just be sure they're sealed properly, and you preserve the chain of evidence. You sign off when you give them to her, and she signs on."

"And then she's got to check them in up there, right?"

"Absolutely. Make sure. We've waited long enough for this break; let's not give any lawyer a chance to take it away on a technicality." He started out, turned back, and asked me, "Why's Trudy working Saturday?"

"She's training in the DNA lab. But if Pat gives our fingerprints priority status, he'll get another expert to come in and do the screening, won't he?"

"Yup. That's what he's always told me; you need it faster in order to nail a guy, we'll get it out. I'll let you know as soon as I've talked to him." From the doorway, he nodded again to Bo before he left.

Walking back to our side of the building, Bo said, "I've got time to get the prints ready to go. Want me to?"

"That'd be good. Thanks." It felt good, being comfortable with him again. I asked him, "Do you buy the idea of a holdup man with at least one killing in his past who hires himself out as a baby-sitter?"

"Is that what he said?"

"Yes. They got talking in a bar, he said, and they offered him a job. For eight dollars an hour. He thought it sounded better than nothing."

"I think that too. As an alibi, it sounds just a little bit better than nothing."

"Except it isn't even working as an alibi for him now, is it? We're charging him with endangerment of children. Claiming he's the baby-sitter just gets him deeper in the shit."

"Unless he's guilty of something worse. Even if you can prove substantial harm to the kids, which it sounds like would be hard to do, the most he can get for endangerment is what? Five years or ten thousand dollars? And most of them get a lot less."

"Okay. But what's he dodging that's worse? Killing a man in a liquor store holdup? If he really is our man, he's been running from that for over five years. Why would he turn himself into a baby-sitter now?"

"Maybe he's had a change of heart. Got religion. Discovered he likes small girls." He looked at me, suddenly horrified. "Ah, shit, I wish I hadn't said that."

"Does that shelter automatically do a physical exam, I wonder? I better check." We were near my office now, and I said, "Imagine that, my phone is ringing."

The answering tape told the caller to leave a message

and beeped, and I heard Ray say, "Okay, Jake, here's the deal—" I ran and picked it up and said, "Ray? Ray?"

"Ah, good, you're there. We've searched the motor home thoroughly, looked underneath and climbed on top. There's absolutely nothing here that ties this place to the murder, that I can see. Maybe BCA could come out here and spray a lot of Coomassie Blue around, bring up some blood spatters, but honestly I doubt it. No bloodstained clothing, no weapons."

"How about the other stuff? Coins? Wigs?"

"Oh, yeah, plenty of that kind of crap, mostly in one closet and a drawer. Well organized, gotta give 'em that. The woman was prepared to be a redhead, too, looks like. And push-up bras, some kind of a girdle thing with extra padding, it's a shame I didn't bring Kevin along."

"Bring it in. What else?"

"All kinds of playing cards, marked decks and sets with eight aces, looks like they did a lot of crooked card games. Otherwise…just what you'd expect for a family living in one of these things. Inexpensive clothes and dishes, toys and books for the kids."

"No gun?"

"Gun? Since when are we looking for a gun?"

"Since an hour and a half ago." I told him about Bo's surprise fingerprint discovery. "So now we're looking for that Dirty Harry Special, remember?"

"Oh, the Smith & Wesson, right. Well, I sure haven't found it here, Jake."

"How about in the extra living space, you look there?"

"The woman who owns the park says these people checked in yesterday afternoon and never asked for any extra space."

"Car?"

"Yeah, there's a car here. Nothing fancy, '94 Buick Century. No blood on it that I can see."

"Does the license match the number we've got here?"

"Not sure. I'll write it down and check when I get there. Otherwise...well, we can check for prints."

"But nothing in the car?"

"One roll of duct tape in the trunk."

"Bring it in. But listen, go over the RV and the car one more time, will you? Look at the undersides of everything, any place where you could tape a gun. Then, when you're sure it's not there, put a crime scene tape on the Winnie and the car both, lock 'em up, and bring the keys in with you."

"The owner wants to keep the keys. She says it's the only security she's got for the rent on the space."

"Tell her we're making a case against these people, we don't expect they'll be released anytime soon." As soon as I put the phone down, it rang again, and the chief told me the director of BCA had okayed a priority screening of our prints for tomorrow morning. "Good. I'll take 'em home with me tonight," I said.

"I asked Pat if they would give us a call as soon as they were sure, and he said they'll do that. I told him to call you, is that okay?"

"You bet. Shall I call you when I know?"

"Would you? Thanks. Can you believe this?" McCafferty said. "All those months of work, and we never got one inch closer to that bastard. And now we find him by accident?"

"Not really by accident," I said. "Bo was doing his job."

"Doing a damn fine job, that's true. I believe you're right about Dooley, he's worth the extra trouble."

"And one of these days, if his wife gets straightened out, he won't be any trouble."

"Yeah. Don't hold your breath on that one."

ELEVEN

SOMEBODY NAMED MARIE answered the phone at the battered women's shelter, listened to the request I shouted against a background of harsh disruptive noises, and said, "I'll put you through to Angela's office, Lieutenant, she's the social worker in charge here today." Angela took six rings to answer and sounded breathless when she said hello, but listened patiently and finally told me, "We don't have a full-time doctor on staff, but Margaret Elliott works us in around her private practice. I expect her later today. Do you have a particular reason to suspect sexual abuse?" I told her the children's nanny was a middle-aged man, and gave her a brief history of their apprenticeship in thievery and fraud.

"Wow. Hoods in training? Where's Charles Dickens when you need him, huh? It sounds mentally abusive anyway, though not necessarily sexual. We'll certainly check, though. I have to say," she added thoughtfully, "they appear very well cared for."

"I thought so too." I put the phone down and thought about it some more. Ray walked in five minutes later and found me still sitting there, with my hand on the phone, staring at the wall by my door. He peered around the doorjamb at the wall and said, "What is it?"

"Nothing. I'm thinking," I said. "You bring back bags of stuff?"

"Including one special bag," he said, "with a 44-mag Smith & Wesson in it."

"You mean it? You wouldn't shit me?" He shook his head happily, unable to restrain a gleeful un-Bailey-like grin. "It's on the conference table, you wanna see?"

"God, yes. Kevin!" I yelled from the hall. When he bounced out his door, I said, "Go get the chief, bring him to the conference room, tell him Ray found ol' Dirty Harry!" As we passed Bo's cubicle, I roared, "Come out here, Dooley!" startling him halfway out of his chair

"It was taped to the back side of the kitchen sink," Ray said, pulling on fresh gloves, "way up in there above the trash can and the soap." He took the bulky package out of its plastic bag, unwound several layers of oily rags, laid the big revolver gently on top of an evidence bag, and stood back, admiring its finely checkered walnut grips and darkly gleaming blued-steel barrel.

"Here's the ammo I found in it," he said, lining up six gleaming brass cartridges with copper-encased bullets. "Few more in here." He set an oblong cardboard box down with a metallic *chink*. "I wasn't even looking for a gun, till you said—" Ray's face maintained its usual moody contours, but his voice had a little quaver of excitement. "I mean, our victims were beat to death, right?—so I was hunting for a bloody tire jack, maybe a sledgehammer."

Frank came in, excited, looked and said, "Oh, Jesus, you found it."

Kevin walked around it once and said softly, "Fan-fucking-tastic."

Bo gazed at the weapon raptly, his hands tucked into his armpits to keep himself from touching it. Ray nudged him and said, "I think from now on we oughta take you

off the case oftener.'' Bo looked up, surprised and
pleased, and smiled.

I squinted at the inch-and-a-half-long cartridges. ''Two-
hundred-and-forty-grain Remingtons with jacketed hollow
points. That match the bullet they took out of Krotzman,
Bo?''

He went to find the file. ''Anyway, now we know why
he wore that Band-Aid, I guess,'' Ray said.

''Be damned, that's right,'' I said. ''I always figured
that was there as a distraction.''

Bo came back, and read, ''Remingtons, estimated to be
either 240-or 250-grain, depending on how much was lost
from fragmentation when bone was struck.''

''All these years,'' Kevin said. ''Why the hell didn't
he get rid of it?''

''Probably couldn't,'' Ray said. ''I expect it's his favorite thing.''

''Well, we'll have to get the lab to check the ballis-
tics,'' I said. ''But it's starting to look like we got this
guy, Chief. Huh?''

''Sure does,'' he said happily.

''So maybe in the morning, if the lab confirms the
match on the prints, I oughta talk to him again. Once he
knows he's dead meat, he might quit telling foolish lies
and explain how the last two murders went down.'' I
looked around the table. ''Whaddya think, Ray?''

''Why would he cop to three murders instead of one?''

''Milo might make him a deal if he cooperates now.''

''What's your hurry?'' the chief asked me. ''Don't you
still have lab reports coming in?''

''Sure. But the last two victims didn't live here, there
are no eyewitnesses, the crime looks like it might be gang-
related. We could work a long time and get nowhere.
What I'm thinking is, right now Brown doesn't know we

have the prints or the gun. If I blindside him with all this evidence and then offer a deal, I might stampede him into telling the truth.'' Ray and Kevin looked dubious. ''Anyway, something closer to the truth than what we've been hearing.''

''Think about it overnight,'' Frank said. ''I gotta get back to work.'' In the doorway he turned, said, ''Nice job, guys,'' and left.

As soon as he was out in the hall, Kevin collapsed onto one of the elegant new chairs and said, ''Where's my day shrinker? I'm ready to go home.''

''Forget it,'' I said. ''Don't sit down, don't even think about resting. We need you to check the car license number Ray brought back, find out if it belonged to John Francis Morgan. And there's another thing I need urgently, too—what was it? Oh, yes, who's on duty tomorrow? One of the new guys again?''

''Ah…yeah, it's Clint Maddox's turn.''

''Okay, so find Clint and talk him through the basics of getting Probable Cause to Arrest orders signed by a judge tomorrow, so we can hold prisoners over the weekend.''

''Oh, that's right, we're gonna need that for both of them, aren't we? Jane Morgan and uh—''

''And her helpers—''

''Oh, damn the stupid little helpers, I forgot them. Right, Jane Morgan and her idiot elves, and what's-his-face—what is his name? I keep forgetting.''

''Arthur Brown.''

''What a fakey name, no wonder I can't remember it. You believe that name?''

''I don't know. Did you check his driver's license when you booked him?''

''Of course. But I didn't find him in MINCIS or NCIC,

did I? How does that figure, when he's got recidivist felon written all over him?''

''Good question, Kevin, and I encourage you to follow through on it in due time. But right now you better think about the fact that your life will not be worth a plugged nickel around here if Clint Maddox doesn't get Probable Cause forms signed tomorrow, so that Arthur Brown and Jane Morgan and those two teenage boys are still in their cells when it's time for their court appearances on Monday.''

Kevin got up reluctantly and asked Ray, ''What's happened to Jake? He was reasonable at lunchtime.''

''He's been thinking,'' Ray said. ''I caught him at it.''

I went back into my office and thought some more. Early-spring dusk darkened the cars in the parking lot while I cleared my desk. When the shadows began to creep up the side of the library, I called Angela at the shelter.

''The twins are physically unhurt,'' she said, ''and the doctor and I agree, they don't exhibit any of the behaviors we associate with sexual abuse.''

''That's very good news. Now, Angela—'' I needed her help for what I wanted to do in the morning, and just as I expected, she took a good deal of persuading. I rubbed my aching neck while I assured her of my good intentions and described all the safeguards that would be in place. Finally she agreed, and I went home.

''Ah, good, you're here finally,'' Trudy said, dropping pasta into boiling water as soon as I walked in the door.

''Are we late for something?''

''No, no. I was just hoping to make it an early night; I've got a ton of work to do tomorrow, and I'd like to get going early.''

''Aw, heck,'' I said, lying down on the doormat and

closing my eyes, "I was counting on taking you back in to Rutherford for some square dancing."

She laughed. "Are you implying that your day was somewhat hectic?"

"Just a spot." I put my fist behind my neck and rolled my head around, feeling the knots in my neck muscles start to ease. I took a deep breath, held the smell of onions and tomatoes inside my head as long as I could, and let it out slowly.

"But you must be pretty excited, too, aren't you? Pat Delaney called me and said be sure to get the fingerprints you were bringing home, said you found something wonderful—"

"Bo found them. If he's right, we're gonna nail a killer and make Frank McCafferty very happy." I told her the story.

"Wow. No wonder the big cheese himself is coming in to check them in the morning."

"Who's the big cheese?"

"Fred Welch."

"Oh, him." He's BCA's head fingerprint genius, Trudy's teacher when she started, a bearded, noisy, gregarious man.

"So, you did bring them, didn't you?"

"Right here in my briefcase. I'm gonna get up and do the paperwork any minute now." I opened my eyes a crack. Trudy was walking back and forth across my line of vision, putting salad and bread on the table. "You know something, babe? Watching your soft places jiggle from down here is the most incredible turn-on."

"You better get up out of there before you make the cook forget what she's doing." She kissed me, though, when I stood up, and after that we were both trying to get to bed early.

SATURDAY MORNING at nine, Fred Welch's basso profundo, even over the phone, rattled the kitchen windows. "One of your hotshot investigators spotted this print match, is that what I heard?"

I moved the receiver an inch away from my ear. "Yes."

"Well, you can give him an attaboy. He's right on the money this time."

"Well, you know, Fred, that is really outstanding news."

"Yeah. Well, tell him not to get too puffed up about it. Be a pretty dense R and I guy if he didn't remember a full set of loop and whorl. How often do you see one of those?"

I had no idea, but I agreed anyway and thanked Fred for coming in so early on Saturday. He said, "That's okay. Trudy Hanson let me breathe in her ear," and chuckled merrily as I hung up.

Trudy and I promised each other, early on, never to set foot on the jealousy path. Less secure lovers might dream of squashing Fred Welch like a bug. I counted down from a hundred and sixty-two by nines, phoned the chief, and made him a happy man. Then I called Ray.

"I'll tell Kevin and Bo," Ray said. "You gonna talk to Art Brown now?"

"Damn right."

"Me and Kevin want to be there, okay?" They were waiting in bright sunshine outside the tall doors of Government Center when I arrived. We stood together in the conference room watching as the deputy brought the prisoner up from jail and unchained him. He looked a little older and bleaker than he had yesterday. County jail isn't hard time, but it's no fun either. The deputy said call when we needed him, and Art Brown sat down where we told him, at the far end of the table facing the hall. We took the three chairs nearest the door, facing Ray's office. Brown's face clouded as he watched us; he could see we had something. "Art," I said, "you remember Ray Bailey?"

Ray told him about finding the gun behind the sink. Brown did a good job of masking the pain he must have felt and told us, deadpan, that he didn't own a gun, so whatever we had found must have belonged to Mr. Morgan. We didn't let him waste too much time on that before we told him about Bo's fingerprint hobby and the confirmed match with the print from Ernie Brotzman's cash drawer, and our expectation of more matches off the gun and ammo box.

The birthmark on his nose flushed darker red, and his no-color eyes turned to gray ice. "That shot was self-defense," he said. "I never meant to shoot anybody, but the fool went for his gun—"

"Hang it up, Art," I said. "There was no gun in the store. I can bring in a dozen witnesses who knew Ernie Brotzman all his life and will swear he never owned a gun."

"Did I know that? He reached for some weapon—"

"Like the cash register key? The drawer was open, and his hands were full of cash."

"You're gonna hang it on me no matter what I say, aren't you? Where's the lawyer you promised me? Said I was entitled—"

"You'll get a lawyer Monday. Pro bono lawyers hate to work weekends, Art. But in the meantime, we thought you might like to tell us the truth about how you murdered John Morgan and the man who was underneath him in the trash container."

He actually looked surprised. I wondered, How does he

do that? ''Is that what this is all about? You're gonna try
to stick that mess on me, too? What is it with you guys,
you can't find anybody else in town to persecute?''

''Art, do yourself a favor,'' Kevin said. ''We've got
the gun and the prints; we'll get the other two store owners you robbed that weekend to identify you. You're toast.
The only way you're gonna make this any easier on yourself is to cooperate now.''

''And then you'll tell the judge what a good boy I am?
You watch TV every night and memorize what they say
on there, is that it?'' Art Brown crossed his arms and
glared. ''Go fuck yourselves,'' he said. ''I want my lawyer.''

''Okay,'' I said. I got up, telling a surprised Ray and
Kevin, ''I'll be back in just a minute.'' I walked out into
the hall and along it to the landing at the top of the stairs,
where Angela waited with the two little girls.

They were self-possessed and quiet, holding hands as
they walked down the long hall. I opened the door to the
People Crimes unit. They went through it and stood looking around uncertainly till they spotted Art Brown at the
far end of the table. Then they streaked across the room
to him, calling happily, ''Daddy!''

TWELVE

"How did you know?" Ray asked.

"We all kept saying they looked well cared for," I said, "and there wasn't any extra space rented at the RV park."

"Why'd you bring the mother in, though?" Kevin asked. "I was kind of surprised by that."

"Because I wasn't sure she was their mother. And I knew I couldn't believe anything she told me, so I thought I'd better go by her first reaction."

"Well, you must have been plenty satisfied by the one you got. I don't think I've ever heard a sound like that from a woman before."

"I made certain the man and woman never got near each other in jail," I said. "So I was pretty sure she didn't know we had them."

When Jane Morgan saw her daughters sitting on their father's knees, she had given vent to a shattering cry of utter despair, and run toward them with her arms outstretched. They reached up to her, and she spread her arms around the three of them and held on. For several minutes they blended together in one gently heaving, murmuring mound. None of them ever made another sound above a whimper. We gave them some space and time, and they used it, as far as I could see, to hold each other and whisper, push hair out of each others' eyes, and pet each other all over.

Finally, Angela said, "Jake, I can't—" and I nodded. She walked to the family, said something softly, and began gently tugging on the girls. The mother got up and organized their departure, putting their two hands together and following them to the door. All the way, she asked quick little questions of Angela and got soft answers. At the door she stooped, whispered something in each girl's ear, and got a quick bright nod in reply. They each took one of Angela's hands and walked away down the hall with no fuss. When they were gone, their mother had turned, given me a look that scorched the skin on my nose, and walked back to Art Brown.

"If that is his name," Kevin said now. "I still don't believe it. They haven't scanned his prints into the databases yet, have they?"

"No. And I have no idea what name she'll use when I see her again." I thought it would be a waste of time to talk to her that day, so I asked the matron to take her back to her cell. The three of us sat down around Art Brown again, and I said, "Okay, we're gonna try this one more time. Obviously, you're not the baby-sitter. So now, what was your relationship with John Morgan?"

"He was my wife's uncle."

"Your *wife's* uncle? Ah. And how long have you traveled together?"

"Since the—the accident in the liquor store," he said. "Neva was scared—"

"That's your wife's name?"

"Yeah. She said, We've got the babies now, and I don't want you to do this anymore. Said, I'll find my uncle Jack, he'll help us."

"How did she find him?"

"I don't know." The answer was a little too quick; I made a note. He wiped his hand across his mouth and went on. "Jack liked to brag, and he wanted to run everything, but he said there wasn't no need to take fool chances with guns, and Neva thought that sounded good. He taught us what to do, and at first it was okay, we got along all right, and Neva and the kids liked the traveling." Like his wife, Art Brown had an uncanny knack for presenting their outrageous life as a lark.

"But the last couple of years"—Art Brown frowned—"Jack started drinking more, and his gambling got out of control. We'd make a score, he'd disappear, and when he got back the money would be gone, we had to go right back to work to get grocery money. Then he got into that screwup in Florida—"

"This was last winter?"

"Yeah. Jack was gone two days, come back one morning acting kind of crazy; I think he had a couple of lines of coke in him. Threw a pile of money on the kitchen table and walked around it drinking rum out of the bottle, bragging how he took these Cuban gamblers for a big pot, and from now on we were gonna live on easy street. Neva and me said, 'You crazy? We gotta get outa here right away.' He was too drunk to stop us, so we packed up and hit the road, and for a while up here we thought maybe it was gonna be okay, but—that story in the paper—"

"Somebody in Miami read it?" Kevin's normal cynicism toward prisoners' testimony evaporated when he heard his brilliance had done the trick. He barely kept his face straight.

"Yeah. We woke up one morning in Mankato and found a dead cat on the doorknob." Mankato again, by God, I thought, and there's that same dead cat.

Brown echoed what his wife had said: "Jack was scared." He studied our faces, saw that Kevin's smile was fading and Ray and I looked outright dubious. "You ain't gonna believe anything I say, are you?'' he asked me, scowling. "The hell with this. Talk to my lawyer on Monday.''

Ray, who had been quiet ever since the girls came in, leaned forward suddenly and asked him, "Why didn't you leave?''

"Leave where?''

"Rutherford,'' Ray said. "When you heard about the killings, why didn't you get out of here?''

"We did.'' He shrugged. "We were all the way down to—'' He realized he didn't want to tell us where they were. "But Neva...she had a new wig ordered here in Rutherford, light brown, and blue contacts from some eye doctor. Said she decided to go for a more natural look.'' Ray nodded sympathetically, giving no sign that he believed, as he told me later, that he had just heard the most incredibly stupid statement of his entire life. "She kept saying, 'What would it hurt, to run up there just for a day so I could get my things?''' Art Brown shrugged again, like, Whaddya gonna do?

"And then once you were here,'' Ray said, "it seemed like a good idea to send her to Fillmore Field with fake dope?''

Art looked pained. "No. But we blew a tire a few miles south of Byron,'' he said, "had to call a tow. Used up all our cash, almost.''

Ray made a little choking sound and said, "Tough luck.''

"Kinda goes in streaks, seems like,'' Art Brown said. "Been one damn thing after another here lately.''

I told him he'd be arraigned on Monday afternoon and could expect to see an attorney sometime before then. We called for the deputy to take him back to his cell. When he was gone, we walked outside together into the breezy April morning.

"Enjoy the rest of the weekend," Kevin said, and sprinted to his car, still elated over the news that his newspaper gambit had worked.

Dodging through heavy traffic in the northbound lanes of U.S. 52, I rolled down my window to let in the spring smells, punched buttons till I found a country station, and treated a field full of sleepy-looking black Angus to Ol' Willie singing "Blue Eyes Cryin' in the Rain." In Mirium, I wheeled over to the farm implement store and rented a power garden tiller. At home, I made a power garden tiller's enormous corned beef sandwich and washed it down with ice water instead of the beer I wanted because I had been warned by the store owner that careless weekend tillers were at risk of having fewer toes by Monday. I marked out the edges of the garden Trudy wanted, took a deep breath, and pressed the power button.

The machine had torque to spare, but I managed to stay out of its way while it made short work of a big patch of sod. By the time Trudy drove into the yard at six-thirty, a big new garden patch was steaming next to the pasture fence, and the tiller was back at the store. I had the grill started and was treating my lower-back pain with a glass of wine. I poured one for her and walked her out to the wide strip of freshly turned earth, where she chirped agreeably about what a great sod buster I had turned out to be.

"Now that it's too late to change," I said, "this looks like a ridiculously large garden for two people. Are you sure you want this many veggies?"

"Trust me," she said. She strolled happily around it, sipping her wine and muttering to herself about what to put where. When she finished her crooning, she set her glass on a fence post, stretched and yawned hugely, and said, "Aaahh, what a day. But boy, have I got results for you. You want to hear about 'em?"

"What's the matter with me?" I said. "Of course I want to hear! Tell me."

"Let's start with the weirdest part. That slide Pokey sent me, you remember what that was?"

"Sure. Semen out of John Morgan's anus."

"Uh-huh. And it matches all the samples from the man that was underneath him in the barrel."

"What? Wha-a-t are you saying?"

"That number-two John Doe did number-one John Doe, sometime before they died."

"Oh, for Christ's sake. The rapist was underneath the rapee? I can't believe this."

"I couldn't either. So I went over my results again. Several times. And then got Edna to check all my work."

"Wait now. You mean"—I peeled some bark off a fence post—"maybe after all what we have here is some kind of a lovers' quarrel?"

"Some quarrel," she said, "if they ended up offing each other." She sipped her wine. "How is that possible, though?"

"I have to think." I turned my back on my new garden and my clever mate, and stared out at County Road 82 while I rolled my tired head around on my shoulders. An ancient pickup was laying down a trail of dust all the way to the southern horizon. Finally I said, "You know what I think? I think we should put the chops on the broiler and pour another glass of wine, and promise each other not to talk about work again until Monday."

"I'm for that. But shouldn't you call Pokey first? He's got a gloat coming."

Pokey didn't gloat much, just made one little chuckling

noise deep in his throat and then said, "Ah, yah," with that all-purpose sigh of his that seems to cover earthquake, pestilence, and all possible forms of unspeakable human behavior.

"You don't seem surprised," I said.

"Kinda hard to surprise old Ukrainian."

Trudy hummed some wordless tune of pleasure, Sunday morning, making cinnamon rolls with sunshine gilding her yellow hair. They smelled so good coming out of the oven, I couldn't stay in the kitchen without eating them all, so I went out and raked the garden patch till the Sullivan brothers' old motor signaled their arrival.

I poured coffee and put out plates for the rolls while Trudy dug her ever-thickening stack of papers out of the knife drawer. Dan opened his pocket-size spiral grid-lined pad, covered all over with drawings and numbers, and I folded a sheet of letter paper and got ready to take notes. Ozzie's role seemed to be munching up the baked goods and talking.

"Let's take the big-ticket items first, okay?" he said, and we all nodded solemnly.

The ten-acre field and the pasture were the big assets on our side of the ledger. The hundreds of hours of labor needed to wire, insulate, and reroof our house were theirs. Trudy had managed to dicker down Ozzie's working wage considerably, but even so there was a considerable disparity between the value of our assets and the cost of their labor. It was this difference that my lover had worked all week to whittle down.

"About the boat," she said, "we've agreed, Jake, that Dan and Ozzie don't really want to own it."

"They don't?"

"No. Taxes, insurance, licensing, those are cash-flow items they can't afford. They just want to *use* a boat sometimes, and here's the amount we've arrived at, for them to have the use of your boat two weeks out of three, from May through September. We won't have time to get out on the water every weekend anyway, and they agree the boat is totally ours for our two-week vacation in August.''

''Well, now. That's...original,'' I said. ''About wear and tear—''

''We replace anything we break,'' Ozzie said. ''We sign a thing—''

''Rental agreement,'' Trudy said. ''I'm drafting it.''

''Plus we give you a list of the best fishing spots in a forty-mile radius.''

''In whose opinion?''

''Dan's. He's a fishing wizard.''

Dan sucked on his pipe and looked at his hands.

Then Trudy listed our contribution of sweat equity. Large portions of the stupendous garden she had asked me to create were intended for Sullivan tables—bushels of potatoes, baskets of carrots and pole beans, bags of tomatoes and lettuce. ''Plus, you help Ozzie put up the hay crop in both fields, and they store it in our loft.''

''Trudy,'' I said, ''did I mention I'm not a farmer? I know about as much about hay baling as I do about arctic exploration.''

''Fear not,'' Ozzie said, looking hugely pleased with himself as he snarfed up another cinnamon roll. ''I'm gonna teach you everything you need to know.''

I met Dan Sullivan's eyes. He winked.

''We only get two cuttings a year,'' Ozzie said.

''So see, in three years that's only six times you bale hay,'' Trudy said.

''We do all this for three years?''

''That's how we got it to come out even,'' she said, and showed me the multiplication.

"Well, and then there's a few incidentals down here," Ozzie reminded her, pointing.

"Oh, yeah. They get two pickings apiece off the asparagus bed," she said, "and a quart of fresh raspberries apiece. Also I'm going to plant a couple of extra zucchini vines, and make each family twenty-five loaves of zucchini bread for the freezer. Dan's wife has four kids besides a full-time job, she doesn't have time to bake, and Ozzie's wife doesn't like to."

"And what Ozzie's wife doesn't like," Ozzie said, "Ozzie's wife doesn't do." Trudy clucked sympathetically and showed me the descending totals by which she had reduced our deficit to zero.

"Now—" She sat back and smiled at Dan. "Did you say you had a bonus for me?"

"Yup." Dan picked a cardboard rectangle off the floor, laid it on the table, and broke open the bubble wrap to display a glass tube. He winked at me again. Winking seemed to be one of his best things. "I noticed, while we were up in the attic looking at the roof, that the gauge glass for your expansion tank was broken."

"You mean that old tank up there is part of the furnace?"

Trudy said, "Cammy told us, remember, Jake? 'Whatever you do, don't turn on the furnace. Jeff tried it and it floods the whole house.'"

"In a gravity-flow hot water system like this," Dan said, "hot water comes up from the cellar to the radiators. The hotter it gets, the more it expands. Gotta have an expansion tank in the attic to make it work right. I can't guarantee this is the only thing wrong with your furnace, but I'll replace it this afternoon, and the next time I'm over here, we'll put a little fuel oil in the tank, and we'll fire 'er up. If you got any loose joints in the pipes," he said, "now's the best time to find 'em, before we fix everything."

Trudy beamed at me and said, "Didn't I tell you Dan was a very smart guy?"

"So are you. I mean it; I'm impressed how you put this all together. Looks like we got a helluva deal here. Oz," I said, shaking hands with both brothers, "this hay business, I hope I'll be more of a help than an obstacle."

"It's just donkey work, Jake, I can show you in half an hour. Don't expect to love it, though," he said, in a sudden burst of candor.

"Rats, I was counting on you and me singing some of those Russian harvest songs together. Excuse me," I said, as the phone rang.

Ray Bailey was calling from Methodist Hospital to tell me Jane Morgan, a.k.a. Neva Brown, had hanged herself in her cell. "They think they found her in time," he said. "She's on a respirator now, but the doctor in the triage unit says he thinks she'll be off that in a few hours and we can talk to her by morning. She's sedated now and sleeping, but I put a suicide watch order on her anyway, and there's a deputy outside her door."

"What did she use?"

"To hang herself with? Bedsheet."

"But I mean there's nothing—no overhead pipes or—"

"She tied it to the top bunk," Ray said, "and hooked her toes over the basin somehow and let her head and hands hang down."

"Jesus."

"Took determination, gotta give her that. The deputy says the woman in the next cell heard choking noises and called the guard, or she'd've been gone in a couple minutes."

"I'm just so...surprised. She doesn't seem like the suicide type."

"I guess you never know."

"Yeah. Well. Nothing more to do tonight, huh? Thanks for calling, Ray."

MONDAY I PUT OFF the staff meeting till afternoon because Milo was anxious to have my help with the Brown case. By the time he got to my office, he'd heard about the wife.

"So we'll only be taking one prisoner to court this afternoon." He pulled a legal tablet out of his briefcase. "Just as well, actually. He's the big cheese, after all, the man who shot Ernie Brotzman. I bet McCafferty's happy, huh?"

"Yes. He asked me to tell you, anything you need help with—"

"Don't worry, I'll call. So now, okay by you if we remand the two boys to juvenile court?"

"Sure, fine. And the woman—"

"What did I hear, she's in the hospital?"

"She was. They went in with the breakfast tray this morning and found pillows rolled up in the bed."

"What the hell? She went out a window?"

"Not at Methodist you don't; they're sealed shut. Somehow she got past the deputy."

"Who'll never make sheriff now, I guess. Does he have a story for this?"

"The usual. He was never away from the door. He must not have covered all his potty calls as well as he thought. Or, to be fair...this lady probably knows more than one use for a bedsheet."

"What does that mean?"

"If I was guarding Neva Brown, or whoever the hell

she really is, I wouldn't be surprised if she appeared before me as the Maharanee of Whatsistan and sold me a precious nose jewel before she talked me into holding open the front door for her and hailing a cab.''

"See what I mean?'' Milo said. "You guys have all the fun.''

We took our time and checked everything twice because we both knew Frank McCafferty would flay us alive if Art Brown's indictment failed to stand up to a judge's scrutiny. When it was ready, we invited the chief in to look it over.

"Good,'' he said when he finished reading. He put his glasses back in the case, smiled, and said, "Some days, this job is a pleasure.'' He looked at me and raised his eyebrows. "But you're still not happy, huh?''

"We're no closer than ever to finding the killers of the two men in the barrel.''

"So? It's an open file, we'll keep working on it. What else is eating on you? You look like you ate some bad fish.''

"We look dumb letting the woman get away.''

"That wasn't us, remember? Meaning no disrespect to our colleagues in brown, but this happened on the county's watch. And we'll find her before long. However''—he cleared his throat—"I have to point out that you stretched the hell out of every visitation rule we've got, Saturday morning. Out of hours, and allowing physical contact—''

"They weren't in the jail, and I ascertained that the children weren't armed.'' He made a sarcastic face. "They're all habitual liars, Frank. I was looking for a way to surprise some truth out of them, and it worked. For a few minutes.''

My phone rang. I picked it up and heard a woman, crying. I said, "Hines."

"Oh, Jake, it's Angela." She blew her nose. "Oh, dear, my nose is bleeding. Hang on a second—" She banged the phone down. Several people in the background were slamming things and shouting, and I heard someone close by say, "God, Angie, here, it's getting on your sweater—" and a quick rush of water out of a tap. Frank and Milo were watching me, mystified; I held my hand up and mouthed, "Wait."

Angela had her voice under control when she picked up the phone again, but she started in the middle of her story. "See, I didn't even know the mother was out of jail," she said. "Why didn't anyone call me? She came here while we were serving breakfast, said she had to see her daughters right away, it was an emergency. I said, you can't expect to just come in here whenever you like, I have to see a visitation order, but she started to cry and said, 'Their father is desperately ill, please, I must talk to them,' so I went and got them from the dining room and put them in the parlor with her and stayed to watch, of course, but then—" Her control broke, and she began to weep again.

"It's all right," I said. "We should have told you, you should have had more help."

"We never do," she said bitterly. "They expect us to do this terrible job, and there's never enough help, never enough anything." Bitching worked for her; her voice steadied up, and she was able to go on. "The girls ran to her, and for a minute or two they did all that patting and whispering, the way they did at the station, you know? Then—just in a second!—they started this terrible fight, screaming at each other, throwing things—they broke a lamp—" She took a deep, shuddering breath and went on. ''I ran to get Betsy and Grant to help, and while I was gone, the woman and her children ran out three different doors—we ran out after them, but they all darted through hedges into other people's yards. We really couldn't run through the neighborhood after them; some people around here are already petitioning to move us out. So I called nine-one-one, but by the time a patrol car arrived, they were all out of sight.'' She sniffed a couple of times. ''So I called you.''

''Are you hurt? Do you need help now?''

''Oh, no, that was just—one of the books they threw hit me in the face, it's nothing. I'm just…I feel kind of pissed, you know?''

''Believe me, Angela,'' I said, ''I do know.''

The weekly staff meeting finally convened on Monday after lunch. Everybody was there but Bo Dooley, who had called at 8:00 a.m. to say, ''Diane's gone. I need today to do a few things, okay? And I'll be back tomorrow.''

''Do what you gotta do,'' I said. ''Are you going to try to find her?''

''No. I told her yesterday, when she started blaming me for everything, and I could see she was working herself up to this, 'If you leave again, Diane, don't come back.' It's hell on Nelly, she always feels like it's her fault. And Friday I saw how much she's been interfering with me doing my job. I lose that, what have we got? So today I'm gonna file a restraining order and start divorce proceedings.''

''Wow. Well…see you tomorrow, huh?''

''Yes.'' There was something new in his voice, I thought.

Nobody asked about him at the meeting; Bo never said much anyway, and today everybody else in the section wanted to talk. I let them all tell their stories, because I wanted to get everybody on the same page about last week. We all felt good about nailing Art Brown, but the escape of his wife and children kind of took the edge off.

"Not to mention," I said, "that we don't seem to be any closer to knowing who killed the two men in the trash barrel."

"Well, now," Rosie said, "I don't know how much use this will be to you, Jake, but you know I've been talking to Bo's snitches—"

"Please don't tell us you believe anything they have to say," Kevin said.

"Depends. There's this one-kind of like an urban legend that keeps coming up—" Rosie rearranged her notes. "I heard this same yarn three or four times last week, about some Miami drug dealers who got taken to the cleaners in a poker game by some ragtag con man from out of town." Ray made a sound, and she looked up and said, "Hmmm?"

"Nothing. Go ahead," he said.

"He won a huge pot and then disappeared, and they figured out later how he marked the deck, but they couldn't find him. Then the story from the *Times-Courier* got reprinted in the Miami paper." She glanced at Kevin.

"Ain't it fun when a plan comes together?" he said.

"Uh-huh. One of the Miami guys had a former cellmate in Minneapolis who owed him, so he called in his marker and said, 'I'm sending a man to help, a *Cubano* like me who understands how sorry I want this gambler to be.' The deal was, the crooked gambler must be found in downtown Rutherford with thirteen dollars in his mouth, so the story would make the national media again and give the Miami guy bragging rights and a big rep." Rosie smiled around the table. "Big reps are money in the bank to Cuban drug dealers, my guys tell me." Watching Rosie tell the story, I thought of Milo saying, "You guys have all the fun."

"Unfortunately the hit man from Miami was one of those criminals Fidel sent over for a little joke during Mariel. He had been tortured in Fidel's lockup, and it turned him into a nutcase, a sociopath. It happened he met the hit man from the Cities in Rutherford on the night of the magic girl caper in the Chicken Shack. They heard about the big bet being made there, and arrived in time to follow John Morgan. They grabbed him just after he delivered the little girl back to her mother.

"Now, the whacker from the Twins just wanted to kill the mark and get back to his girlfriend, but the Cuban *balsero* said, '*Mira,* now I have some fun.'"

"So he turns out to be Cuban," Ray said, "not Mexican."

"Did I ever say I was perfect?" Rosie pushed her hair around. "They put Morgan in a delivery van and drove to a quiet place, where they broke his legs and arms the way the orders specified, but then the Cuban stripped the gambler almost naked and tied him over a table and began to, uh, have his way with him." Rosie flushed a little and cleared her throat. She said somewhat hurriedly, "My storytellers all agree on this point, that this was a guy who makes noise when he, um, pleasures himself." One of the combs flew out of her hair. Nobody moved or made a sound while she replaced it.

"After a couple of minutes the Minnesota hit man got nervous about so much commotion in a residential neighborhood and said, 'Come on, we gotta get going,' but the Miami guy paid no attention, looked like he could go all night. The Minnesota guy got sick of listening and worrying, so he picked up a tire iron and beat this Cuban's head in. He saw that the mark was dead—everybody thinks he strangled from getting his throat pushed down against the edge of that picnic table—so the local whacker called his boss in Minneapolis and told him he now had two dead guys, and his boss said, 'Here's what you do next.'

"The hit man put the money in Morgan's mouth, put the garbage barrel in the van, and packed both bodies in it. Then he drove to the alley downtown, lowered his ramp, and made the delivery as ordered, only with one extra body. So when the Miami guy got the message that his cheating gambler was dead, he got an extra message along the lines of 'Don't be sending any more jokes up here.'"

There was a small, stunned silence, and then Lou said, "It doesn't sound like the Saran Wrap had anything to do with it."

"Nope. But think how much fun we had finding it," Rosie said, and the two of them enjoyed a hearty laugh.

Finally I asked her, "Any word on why they used Bo Dooley's garbage can?"

Rosie shrugged. "I asked about that and got nothing but blank stares. As far as my snitches know, the Minneapolis guy looked over back fences till he saw a big enough garbage can and took it. I said, 'But Bo's gate was locked,' and the guy I was talking to looked at me like I was this pitifully stupid person and said, 'Rosie, this guy's *connected,* you don't lock him out.'"

Before I went home, I told Rosie's story to the chief. "Every time you come in here, your story gets loonier," he said. "If any of this is true, though, it gets the Dooleys off the hook." I didn't tell him the Dooleys were no longer a couple; Bo might not be able to go through with it, I thought. Frank was in a very good mood; he'd been taking congratulatory phone calls all day about catching

Ernie Brotzman's killer. "What do you think of the story?"

"It works with the facts on the ground," I said.

"Uh-huh. Maybe too well," Frank said.

"Maybe. The spooky thing is, parts of it agree almost exactly with the story Brown told me in jail."

"So?"

"So I'm going to have to change my whole modus operandi," I said, "if it turns out Art Brown sometimes tells the truth."

Frank leaned back in his big swivel chair and laughed. "Hell," he said, "you always have to allow for a few little inconsistencies."

I had lunch with Maxine, later in the week, and told her about Neva Brown's hanging stunt and the way she escaped with her children. "And she still hasn't been found, huh?" Maxine's unmatched eyes met mine across the soup bowls. "You're not exactly sorry, are you?"

"I'm a cop," I said. "It's not my job to be glad or sorry."

"Those children are out there with her, learning how to lie and steal."

"She could have run away and left them," I said. "She risked it all to take them along."

"You think that makes it all right?"

"I think something beats nothing," I said, "usually."

"My Jakey," she said. "More soup?"

A QUINN COLLINS HOLLYWOOD MYSTERY

NANCY BAKER JACOBS

Reporter Quinn Collins thinks she's seen it all—covering the Hollywood beat—until she stumbles onto the body of "baby mogul" producer Shane King, dead in his hot tub.

Quinn, with her snooping skills honed to an art form, can't refuse the plea for help from the boy's father, with whom she once had a torrid affair. She picks up the trail that leads back to a ten-year-old murder and a cover-up by some heavy Hollywood hitters.

Available June 2003 at your favorite retail outlet.

AUSTIN CITY BLUE

A ZOE BARROW MYSTERY

JAN GRAPE

When Austin police officer Zoe Barrow fatally shoots Jesse Garcia during a standoff, Internal Affairs questions her because Garcia is also the guy who put a bullet in Zoe's husband.

Assigned to desk duty, Zoe finds a strange connection to another unofficial case: a friend who thinks his wife has hired someone—a cop—to kill him. Soon Zoe is in the line of fire, fighting to save her badge, her honor and her skin.

Available June 2003 at your favorite retail outlet.

WORLDWIDE LIBRARY ®

WJG460

DEAD AND BREAKFAST

ROBERT NORDAN

A MAVIS LASHLEY MYSTERY

Arriving at her dearest friend's beautiful mountain farm,
Mavis Lashley senses immediately that something
is terribly wrong.

Eileen Hollowell has decided to turn her home into a bed-and-
breakfast. But when the body of a local teenager is found on
the property, suspicion falls on Eileen's mentally impaired
son. Mavis knows poor Claude wouldn't hurt a fly—but
she's beginning to suspect just who might be keeping
secrets that are worth killing to hide.

Available August 2003 at your favorite retail outlet.

WRN465

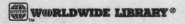